him to the core. Her breathing labored, Charley clung tighter.

The hill leveled off, the ruts not as deep; the wagon ride became less bumpy. Thankful the horses did what was expected of them, Charley breathed a sigh of relief as they reached the bottom of the hill without incident. The steady clomping of the horses hooves evened out as they trotted onto the turnpike.

But sweat was on Emily's brow now, and they had at least another hour before they would arrive in Candor Center. With any luck the doctor wouldn't be out on a call to some hillside farm, taking God-only-knew how long to get back to town. Damned doctors should stay put and not run all over God's creation tracking down the sick. They should keep to one place where they would always be on hand for the sick to come to them.

Almost to Candor village limits, Charley craved a smoke in the worst way. Wanting a cigarette reminded him of the train ride home, which made him think about the pending cut in wages. It was sure to trigger a strike. He was glad he hadn't mentioned anything about the strike to his family. They had enough to worry about without adding to their load. But he'd have to fill Seth in before he left tomorrow night. But not now. Right now Emily needed him.

By the time they arrived at Candor Center, Charley was ready to scream from wanting that smoke. Emily's head bobbed across his chest like Sarah's ragdoll. He lifted her chin only to discover her eyes were closed.

Dear Lord, she'd up and fainted.

Ribbons of Steel

by

Carol Henry

Ribbons of Steel

Cover Art by *Kim Mendoza*

The Wild Rose Press, Inc.
PO Box 708
Adams Basin, NY 14410-0708
Visit us at www.thewildrosepress.com

Publishing History
First Mainstream Edition, 2013
Print ISBN 978-1-61217-958-2
Digital ISBN 978-1-61217-959-9

Published in the United States of America

Dedication

To my husband, Gary—a model train enthusiast, with whom I share all my wonderful adventures.

And to all those who worked those great ribbons of steel, and the families who stood beside them.

Janet ~

all the best ~

Carol

Acknowledgements

Special appreciation to Dennis A. Williams, who taught an Adult University summer writing class at Cornell University. Assignment—take a current event and fictionalize it by saying 'what if'.
That assignment, and my love of history and research, resulted in *Ribbons of Steel*, an assignment I couldn't let go. If not for taking this class, and Dennis' encouragement, I would not have had the confidence to pursue this historic fiction novel.

~

To the Write Now writer's group, thanks so very much for your continued encouragement, friendship, and support—this one's for you.

~

To my early critique partners, Thea McGinnis and Teri Walsh, your continued support and friendship means the world to me.

~

To my editor, Allison Byers, thanks for your support and professionalism while working on this project.

~

To my initial editor, Ally Robertson, thanks for your support and friendship.

~

To the ladies at The Wild Rose Press, thanks for opening your doors to general fiction, giving me the opportunity to finally share Ribbons of Steel…

~

And, to all my family, friends, and fans…
the wait is finally over.

Forward

Philadelphia, Pennsylvania

In 1877, the railroads flowed with America's blood. The nation almost postponed the centennial celebration the year before due to poor economic conditions caused by the war between the North and the South. Families had a hard time making ends meet. The railroads had a stranglehold on the nation.

Charley Carmichael moved his family out of the rundown tenement houses of Philadelphia to his wife's family farm in the pristine hillsides of New York. But Charley isn't a farmer. Railroading is in his blood. And now, the nation's trunk lines threaten to cut wages by another ten percent.

Everyone is talking strike.

Charley's boss demands his loyalty, his co-worker his trust, and his family his love and attention. With his wife's health deteriorating and his family split apart, will the family ties be strong enough to keep the ribbons of steel from pulling them apart?

Prologue

John Donahue looked over his shoulder. Great. No one within earshot. He approached the group of Irishmen who had stopped to take a break.

"Hey, Michael, I hear they're paying fifty cents more a day up the line in Baltimore," Donahue said as he strolled up to the men leaning against the building having a smoke. "Seems to me you guys would want more yourself, seeing as you're working your butts off for nothing in this hell-hole."

"Watch him, Michael," Johann Westmüller spoke up. "He's trying to rile you, that's all. Pay him no never mind. You'd be better not listening to his kind, I tell ya. Charley would have kept us informed."

"He does make sense, Johann. Why should we be slaving away for pittance when those blokes in Baltimore have all the good luck? Fifty cents more a day's nothing to be sniffing at, mind ya. I say we do something about it. *Now!* Why wait on the boss man to try and fix things on his own."

"I agree," said Patrick. "I don't want to be slaving away for nothing, neither. My ma's not well, and we sure could use the extra dough. I say we get this strike underway. Be ready for them big bugs the minute they cut our pay."

"I didn't mean to get you all excited about striking or nothing," John cautioned. "Charles Carmichael was told to keep his mouth shut. The boss would have my ass if he found out I told you what others are getting. Those most affected by the cut should be better informed, is all. You're right." He turned to the other man standing next to Johann. "Seamus, maybe you should think on it, too, before you decide whether or not to go on strike. I won't say nothing to the boss, mind you. You can trust me to keep my mouth shut. I don't rat."

The others nodded.

John turned, hung his head, and walked back to the office. He hid his smile as best he could so as not to give himself away. He'd set the bait, and the stupid fools believed him. It didn't take much to start them fighting amongst themselves, either. Hell, they didn't know enough to check the facts first. They'd head right for that pot of gold in a lightning storm. Fifty cents? *Ha!* The poor souls in Baltimore would love to be getting fifty cents more a day. They were lucky enough to get the ten per cent cut like everyone else and like it. Damn fools.

John couldn't wait to meet with Mr. Rossellini later. A member of the union, the man wanted nothing more than to make Tom Scott suffer the way his family had suffered over the past three years. Mr. Rossellini promised him there'd be something in it for him if he helped stir things up down on the line.

Wait 'til he tells the big union man how he'd blindsided those stupid fools. They might be hard working men, but they weren't any too smart. Mr. Rossellini was sure to give him an extra kickback for his troubles once he had things underway. Cashing in on the strike was a walk down the lane. Talk about a pot of gold. He wasn't sure what Mr. Rossellini's stake in the strike was, but he didn't care so long as he got his cut.

John wiped the grin from his face when he rounded the station and headed back to his office. Climbing the stairs on the left, he set his hat on his desk and knocked on Aderley's office door. Not waiting to be invited to enter, he turned the latch and walked in. Mason Aderley stood over his desk thumbing through a file—the big man looked a bit white around the eyes and mouth.

"John, glad you're here. There's something amiss with the latest shipment from Eckly coal mines. I can't seem to put my hands on the shipping statements. Where the hell are they?"

"Processed and filed already," he answered. "I can get you the books from receiving if you want to see them."

"Good, good. You do that. And, John, I need you here tonight. Scott wants me to institute the ten percent reduction in wages in a few days. I want you to do the paperwork for me this evening. Make sure everything is in order."

"I'm afraid I can't stay tonight, sir. I have other plans." *Damnation.* Mr. Rossellini wasn't going to take kindly to him being late.

"Cancel them!" Aderley boomed.

John jumped back at Aderley's tone. He swallowed hard and knotted his fists to keep his hands from shaking.

"Get those statements and give them a thorough going over. I've put the paperwork on your desk. I want them on *my* desk first thing in the morning. And John, I'm counting on you to keep this quiet."

Aderley took his gold pocket watch from his vest and flicked the lid open to check the time. The man didn't have an inkling of what was going on.

"I have a meeting at the bank in fifteen minutes. I'll be going home from there for the evening."

Aderley placed his gray top hat on his balding head with purpose and strode from the room—and the building.

Dammit. If he hurried, he could see Mr. Rossellini, get back to the office, and still have plenty of time to cover his tracks with the reports he'd padded over the last year. He'd work 'til midnight if he had to in order to make the books look as if they were on the up and up.

John shoved his chair back from behind the wooden desk in a corner of the narrow hallway. A sham of an excuse for an office, seeing as Aderley's office was one of the finest he'd ever seen. It lacked for nothing. He waited to make sure Aderley was gone before he ran from the building. Had Aderley gotten wind of the activity going on down below? If so, then he'd know the rail workers were only interested in one thing—strike.

A strike was sure gonna happen and soon, once the pay cut went into effect. He knew, because he was the one who received the telegram from Camden Junction, just outside Baltimore. Things at the Junction were heating up real good. He had to tell Mr. Rossellini. The man would be delighted.

The Baltimore and Ohio held twenty-seven hundred miles of tracks, and Camden Junction was smack-dab in the center. Trains were switched off to Washington, D.C. or parts out west in the new territory.

The poor fools had suffered a fifty percent cut in wages over the past few years and were now the lowest paid, not counting those working on the New York Central. He'd checked it out. Being Aderley's accountant had its advantages. He snickered. Why, the brakemen on the B&O only made thirty to seventy dollars a month. There sure as hell was gonna be a strike, and not just in Philadelphia. Pittsburgh was hot, too. Damn hot, according to the union boss.

Strike? It was closer than the old geezer's pair of breaches. And the entire countryside was behind those wanting it. He didn't make much money either, but if he continued to play his cards right and keep Mr. Rossellini happy, he'd be rolling in dough and long gone before things really heated up.

Chapter One

Charley stepped away from the tracks as the six-o-five rattled down the steel rails to a screeching stop in front of the station platform. Steam screamed from around the iron wheels, and a sooty puff of smoke streamed into the air from the smokestack.

Right on schedule.

He looked up in time to see John Donahue coming toward him at a dead run. Mason's skinny secretary never moved any faster than he had to. Matter-of-fact, he didn't think the sneaky rat could get out of the way of an on-coming locomotive fast enough to save his own hide. He didn't trust the man. And he didn't understand why Aderley kept him on his payroll.

"The boss man wants to see you right away," John Donahue gasped, drawing up next to him. "Best not keep him waiting. He doesn't seem in the best of spirits today."

The man wheezed, clutched his chest, and then started coughing. Charley ignored the weasel. He had a feeling deep in his gut whatever Mason Aderley was about to say couldn't be good. *Shit.* He didn't need this on top of everything else.

Not today.

Further down the track the men unloaded coal. The mining town of Eckly produced anthracite round the clock. Not only did it keep their trains running, it kept the need for them to run profitable. Wagons lined up waiting, and men scurried to do their jobs.

They looked like a pack of mad dogs let out of their kennels for the first time in weeks.

Scott had added a passenger coach to the line this past year, and people milled about down below waiting for those aboard to disembark.

Such chaos. Such chaos.

Charley shook his head and stepped back from the hot rails as a second train screeched to a stop alongside the first.

"Hey, Seamus," he called to one of the workers. "I'm going up to the office. Take over for me, will ya? I'll be back as soon as I can." He sidestepped Donahue and headed toward Aderley's office. His work boots crunched into the gravel in the well-worn path which led to the station. The sun had been up for hours, and the heat had taken a toll on everyone's nerves. The men were riled already over the talk of another wage cut.

They were talking strike.

Charley arrived at the large, three-story brick building, bounded up the cement steps two at a time, and entered the darkened foyer. He welcomed the coolness as he climbed the mahogany staircase to the left. Aderley's office door stood open. He hesitated as the boss man slid his timepiece back in his vest pocket and reached for one of his Havana cigars, then raised the long brown smoke to his nose, sniffed at it with undisguised pleasure, clipped the end of it, and clamped it between his teeth. He leaned across his desk, took a match from a small box, struck the miniature wooden stick against the box, and lit the cigar. He drew in and let the embers simmer and glow a bright red.

The man's bushy eyebrows were drawn in tight, and his short stocky body slouched over his polished desk, a sure indication he wasn't happy. Charley hated to disturb the man, but then, Aderley had summoned *him*.

He rapped on the doorframe to get Aderley's attention. Aderley jumped at the loud sound, turned, and looked his way. A pretense of a smile didn't quite match the man's stern blue eyes.

"Come in, come in," Aderley called, swinging his arm in the air, motioning him inside.

"Donahue says you wanted to see me about something important," Charley said, entering the room.

"Yes. Yes. Have a seat. You haven't been up to steam this past week. What's going on? It's not like you to be so distracted. The talk of a strike has me a bit concerned, I can tell you. What are those jackasses thinking? Just what do they want?"

Charley didn't know where to start. But he had to be honest.

"To get paid for a day's work," he said. "They've heard about the cut in pay."

Aderley jumped from his chair, paced the floor, and then settled next to the window. He stood with his hands behind his back staring out in silence. Charley wondered, not for the first time, if Aderley made it a habit to stand there all day making sure everyone did his job.

What did his boss have to worry about? The man lived in a mansion on the other side of town. What did he know about the little guys, working ten to twelve hours a day busting their asses along the rails? The firemen who stoked the fires or shoveled the coal? The engineers had to keep their eyes open as they sped along forty miles an hour over tracks where people and cows didn't seem able to stay off. Aderley's two young boys attended the best boarding schools, and his wife had daily help. At least she wasn't sick like Emily.

Dear Lord. Emily had been sick with fever the last few times he'd been able to make it home. There hadn't been anything he could do to relieve her pain. Especially when he had to be in Philadelphia overseeing men who couldn't make ends meet.

Charley didn't care how impressed the nation was with the strides the railroads had made over the last couple of decades. He didn't care that only eight years ago in Promontory, Utah, the golden spike had been hammered into the ground. He didn't give a damn that not only did the tracks unite the East with the West by rail, or that a telegraph connected them as well.

But Emily cared.

Mail was delivered faster now that the rails cut across the vast countryside. Keeping in touch with her cousin, Marybelle, was more convenient. Emily lived for the occasional letter from her cousin. And Charley loved to see the happiness shining in her eyes whenever she received those letters.

What was a man to do? He wanted to be there for his wife. If not for the trouble ahead on the railroad, he would be. But he needed the pay, just like everyone else. If the big bugs cut their pay, and the workers called a strike, he didn't know how they would all survive.

"I asked you a question, damn it," Aderley spat, bringing Charley out of his contemplations. "What the hell is going on?"

"There's talk. That's all I know right now. Nothing definite yet. The men know Tom Scott was in Chicago last month to meet with the other railroad owners. They know the two of you have been talking and are considering a ten percent cut."

"I don't like this. What are they up to?"

"I'm not sure. Something about a walkout, but nothing definite. If they get hit with the ten percent cut, they'll strike for sure. They need the money. And they're not happy with the present working conditions. Too many of them are getting hurt. Don't forget that last week Schmidt died when he was caught between the cars and cut in half."

"They need to be more careful."

Charley had heard it all before. True, many had been killed on the job, or were hurt and unable to work. And when they didn't work, they didn't get paid. Families whose husbands and fathers were killed had no income and had a hard time making ends meet. Many of them were starving, even with their current wages.

"Damn it, Charles, you know as well as I do the bargaining unit isn't worth the price of hen's teeth. This time it isn't going to make any difference. The agreement in Chicago was unanimous—from coast to coast. I have no control over their decisions."

"But Scott does."

Aderley ignored him.

"Have those fools already forgotten about the strike three years ago? The mayhem created by their actions? All the major trunk lines were disrupted for weeks. What a horrible mess that was. We can't let that happen this time." Aderley puffed on his cigar, the smoke curling up around his head.

"I don't think they care. They don't have much left to lose."

The strike three years ago might have created a mess for the trunk lines, but the workers had made their point.

"They tore up sections of the rails and cut the telegraph wires," Aderley continued as if Charley didn't know. "They even removed the pins from the freight cars and destroyed water towers." Aderley ran his hands through his receding hair, and then clenched them at his sides. "It didn't help that the citizens and police sympathized with the strikers."

"It's bound to happen again," Charley said.

"Big trouble, Charles. Real big. I need to know where you stand. I need to know, *now!*" Aderley barked. "All the major trunk lines agreed to this cut, and I have to follow through. Tell your men that as of today we'll be double-heading the freight cars."

"They aren't going to like it. As for announcing a cut, the repercussions will be devastating. The merchants, the mills, the coal mines, not to mention other smaller industries depend on products transported by rail. If the men strike, the rails don't run, and the businesses will create a ruckus."

Charley was caught between a rock and a very hard place with no give in between. The best place for him right now was on Mason Aderley's and Thomas Scott's side. He needed to do all the ass-kissing he could do to keep his job. But he didn't want to leave his men to flounder on their own.

"I need the work. Just like the others. You know I'll work 'til I can't work no more. Strike or no strike. I have a family to support. Just like everyone else down below."

Charley moved to stand next to Aderley, the two looking at the men working in the yard. The Boss Man had him over a barrel. Charley knew it. Aderley knew it; had counted on it.

Charley had to keep things from exploding.

"I promise you, Charles, you'll be rewarded for your trust and loyalty to the company once this fiasco is over."

Aderley combed his large shaking hand over his face, and then heaved a deep sigh.

"How long do you think we have before it blows?" Aderley asked, defeated. "A month? Two?" He turned and looked Charley square in the eyes.

The man was scared. Charley read it in the slump of his shoulders, the white at the corners of his pinched lips. Again, as much as he wanted to, he couldn't lie. The situation was too dire.

"It's been simmering ever since Chicago," Charley said. "They're just waiting for the axe to fall. If you make the announcement today, could be tomorrow."

"If we have to call in the militia, we will," Aderley said. "Scott and the others are determined to call in every favor they have owing them, and then some. I want you to go back down below. Pacify the engineers and trainmen as best you can. You're able to talk to them better than anyone. Convince them not to strike."

"If you can hold off for a couple of days, I'll see what I can do."

"Watch your back, Charles. Someone's been riling up the men. I don't know who, but if I catch him, I'll wring his neck in front of the whole lot of them."

Charley'd been thinking the same thing. Someone had them worked up, talking strike. John Donahue came to mind. He didn't trust the man any farther than he could spit, and he'd never won a spitting contest. The weasel rubbed him the wrong way.

"Do you think Donahue is behind it?" Charley asked. Not a betting man, he'd lay odds he was right. "I've seen him down there a few times."

"I'd bet my best race horse he's not the one."

"Still, I wouldn't rule him out, seeing as he handles all your business. He knows what's going on."

"I think you're wrong, but I'll keep it in mind." Aderley rubbed his eyes with the palm of his hands and sighed. "I want you to know I'll stand beside Scott to fight, every railroad spike by every railroad spike along the way if I have to. I want you to promise me you'll be right beside me."

"I'll be there." Charley didn't hesitate, nor did he flinch at his own words. Words that laid heavy in his gut.

"I have another matter I want to discuss with you. A private matter," Aderley said, his voice low, his eyes focused on his wide, uncluttered desk. "Have a seat."

Mason Aderley was a private person. He never shared family news with him or any of the other men. This had to be something serious.

Aderley sat at his desk and then stretched forward toward his humidor. He ran his hand over the smooth, deep, rich, polished tiger-maple box. He drew in on his cigar, blowing another puff of smoke into the office. Charlie wished he could afford to buy just one of those expensive stogies.

"It's an unusual piece, isn't it?" Aderley stroked

the unique box. "It belonged to a relative on my father's side of the family. They were coal miners."

Charley stared at the hand-carved box with interwoven circles in the center of the lid and a large, handsome diamond inset in the center of the middle ring. He always admired it whenever he was in Aderley's office.

"The diamond represents coal," he continued. "The circles, the family bond of coalminers. My father died of lung disease when I was thirteen. As the oldest of five sons, my mother passed the humidor on to me. I vowed never to work the mines. I keep this close by as a reminder that I can do better."

And, like Tom Scott, president of the Pennsylvania Trunk Line, Aderley was a self-educated man who had earned the respect of the other railroad magnates. He'd climbed the ranks of the rails on his own steam.

As Scott's manager, Aderley was well aware the trainmen down below were unhappy. That wasn't anything private. Charley wondered where Aderley was going with his story, what it had to do with the strike.

"Sorry to burden you with this, Charles, but you might be able to help." Aderley choked up.

The man's change in direction was hard to follow. Confused, Charley sat in silence waiting for him to speak.

After a loud meditative exhale, the man continued. "My wife has received kidnapping threats. Someone is threatening to abduct my two boys."

"Kidnapping? Have you called in the law?"

No wonder the man looked so haggard. Something like that would worry any man. God forbid someone try to take one of his children; he'd kill the son-of-a-bitch himself. His kids might be a handful and rub him the wrong way sometimes, but they were his. No way would he stand by and let someone hurt them.

Aderley didn't need this on top of the pending strike. With everyone's pockets empty these days, Charley figured anyone could be the culprit, someone trying to survive. But to use kidnapping as a means to get money, well, this was serious business. Someone had to be desperate, or crazy. But then again, Aderley had the money to pay a ransom, no matter how much they asked.

"Yes. But we've been advised to stay quiet for now. I'm only telling you because the authorities think you might hear something from the men down below."

"Nothing so far. But I'll keep my eyes peeled."

"My wife has a sister who lives out west. I'm going to send my family to stay with her until things here blow over. With any luck, they'll be long gone before this strike hits. You're lucky, Charles, your family is in New York. Away from this turmoil."

"They're away from the danger of the strike, but my wife hasn't been well." Charley figured if Aderley could share his family problems, then his boss needed to know he had problems of his own. "If this strike is just around the bend, then I want a few days to go home to check on Emily. Make sure things are in order."

"I don't know, Charles. I'll try to hold off on making this announcement for a couple more days, no more. I need you here without any distractions. Let's hope we can put down this strike before things get started."

Charley didn't think it possible, but he didn't say so. If Aderley allowed him to go home to check on

Emily, make sure she was doing all right, he'd be able to come back and concentrate on the strike.

"Get things worked out down below before you go. And take the next train out. You've got two days. And then I want you back here to put a stop to this nonsense."

Chapter Two

The train from Philadelphia to Owego, New York, was a beehive with many of the men already worked-up over the talk of strike. And word everywhere was a strike was imminent. Charley listened as they ranted on and on about the pending cut in wages.

"I tell ya, Danny, those damn owners dun our pay ten percent like they threaten, there's gonna be hell to pay."

"Can't believe everything ya hear, Hennessey. They can't squeeze another cent outta us. They're already bleeding us dry as is."

"That won't stop them. You mark my words. From what I'm hearing down at the tracks, this one's gonna travel right on out west."

"Then we'll strike. Just like three years ago."

"Don't mean it's gonna work this time, you two. Word I hear is they aren't concerned whether we strike or not. They can hold out longer than we can, that's for sure. Best be careful 'bout spreading rumors. Wait for the facts before you get us all hanging out to dry."

Charley kept to himself as he listened to their annoying chatter. Normally, he used this time traveling from work to relax and wipe away the strains of the job before he arrived home to his family. But this evening the noise droned on and on in rhythm with the turning of the locomotive wheels. Charley's nerves twisted him into knots.

Strike. Strike. Strike.

A person had to be crazy to work the hours with the conditions he and the men did. They were tired and had little to show for it at the end of the day. Luckier than most, being higher up the ladder of command as Aderley's right-hand man meant he got more pay. Still, it was a meager wage, and the compensation didn't even begin to make up the difference. What they all needed were higher wages, halfway decent benefits, and one hell-of-a-lot more respect.

The voices on the train grew loud and angry. The man named Hennessy stood waving his hands at the other workers, trying to win their support.

"Strike now before they cut our hard-earned wages. We can't afford less pay. I say we work together to set those big bugs straight. Let them know they can't shove us around. Are ya with me?"

"Hell, yes, we're with you."

"They're not gonna cut *my* pay. I can't feed my family now."

"Let them call out the militia. We'll band together and face them, hit for hit."

"Strike."

"Strike."

"Strike."

The entire rail car chanted. Charley wanted to stand up and chant with them. Maybe it was time to get something started for the men who did all the dirty work, month after month, with no time to rest so they could have a life of their own with their families.

Maybe he would join them this time.

But he'd already given Mason Aderley his word.

And he always kept his word.

By the time the train arrived in Owego, the clouds had rolled in, and the rain had begun in earnest. The rowdy bunch hadn't stopped chanting for a strike, and Charley's head throbbed in unison with their one word cry. As soon as the train stopped, Charley rushed from the confines of the car and dashed between the rails to board the smaller train headed for Candor. He found an empty seat and settled in, relieved at the quiet despite the constant ringing in his ears. He took a cigarette from his pocket, checked his dented silver pocket-watch, then leaned back against the wooden bench with a sigh and lit his smoke. He inhaled; the nicotine circulated throughout his insides soothed his weary nerves.

Thank God the train departed on time. And, thank God the others weren't traveling to Candor.

The Delaware, Lackawanna, and Western was a small rail running through the countryside with several stops between the Susquehanna River and Cayuga Lake. Candor was one of the major stops along the way. Charley was always able to relax on this last leg of his journey home, but tonight the clickity-clack, clickity-clack of the metal wheels on steel rails droned in his ears like a million tiny buzzing insects. His nerves were about shot to hell. Knowing Tom Scott had a mind to cut wages didn't help none.

Strike. Strike. Strike.

Charley threw the cigarette on the already littered hardwood floor and stomped the glowing ember out with the heel of his well-worn work boot. He leaned his head back on the edge of the seat to rest. His head bounced back and forth against the wooden seat as the train rattled over the rough rail ties. He gave in and sat up. He looked around. Several families huddled together in the sofa-like seats facing each other. In one seat, two boys had their noses pressed against the soot-covered windows, the bill of their hats tapping the window with the sway of the train. Three demure young girls sat next to their mother dressed in the latest finery from their pointed, laced-up shoes peeking out from under their long frothy dresses to their stylish hats. When was the last time Emily had a new dress? Or a hat? And Catherine? What simple frock did she wear to school these days?

By the time Charley arrived in Candor, he had worked himself up over the inevitability of there being a strike. Being away from his family for days at a time didn't improve his disposition none, either. God forgive him, he would have the devil's own time putting up with any one of his six children's shenanigans. But he needed to check on Emily. If the strike broke, make that 'when' the strike broke, he wouldn't be able to get back home anytime soon.

What a life. What a rut.

Being born and raised in Philadelphia where trains and coal mines were the mainstay of every family, every member of his family had swallowed trains at every meal, breathed coal and steam with every breath. Charley figured God had given him the opportunity to get his family out of the rat-infested, dirty slums of the city and move them to the country where they could breathe some sweet smelling fresh air and not have to live in the awful beggar conditions the trunk lines had created over the past three years.

The train companies owned everything. The

general stores, the dry goods stores, the filthy overcrowded tenements houses.

They owned everyone.

Didn't these owners see what they were doing to the country? If they'd lower the rent on the tenement shacks the workers called homes, they wouldn't have to scrape up enough money for food. As it was, the railroad took back just about every cent they gave their workers in monthly wages.

Charley looked out the window into the fading light already obscured by the heavy clouds and fog. Still, he could see the outline of the countryside. He'd never seen anything so beautiful as the rolling fields passing by as the train hugged the low hillsides alongside the quick flowing creek on his way home. Behind tonight's blanket of rain, fields of green stretched for miles. Trees. Trees everywhere. The smell of coal and oil didn't exist. The heat or stench of sweaty workers no longer filled his nostrils and upset his stomach. He couldn't wait to get off the train and take a real deep breath; rain or no rain. Just to inhale the sweet fresh air was always worth the long ride home.

The train whistle blew two long, one short, and one long blast as they approached the intersection just before pulling into the Candor depot. One last long blast filled the air. Old Henry up ahead signaled their arrival with his light. First he'd swung the lantern up and down in a slowing motion, then to and fro in front of him, telling the conductor to break. The minute Henry motioned the train to stop, it lurched forward, metal slid on metal, and the engine screeched to a stop.

The hissing of steam exasperated into silence.

Charley took a moment to let the others disembark.

He knew in his heart, where it counted, that the railroad was a hardship for him and his family. But it was still his life. It was in his blood.

He stepped onto the depot platform and into the pouring rain. He was drenched within seconds. He vowed, strike or no strike, if he had anything to do with it, his own family's bloodline of working the rails would end here. It had to. He wanted better for his sons. His family. His Emily.

The torrential downpour and the ensuing mist made visibility difficult. Somewhere in all this mess was his eldest son, Seth. At least he'd better be.

"Pa. Over here," Seth called.

Like a miracle from above, the mist parted and Seth materialized, walking toward him from the other end of the wooden platform, his footsteps muffled. Rain poured off his son's hat like the mighty Niagara over the falls.

As Seth drew near, Charley spotted his six-year-old son, Robert, running double time to keep up with Seth's pace. The tarp wrapped around his thin frame hung down to the kid's ankles. Robert's shoes were already soaked through. The kid should be home keeping warm and dry with the others. Seth had no business dragging him out on a night like this. No business at all. He had enough to worry about with Emily being ill; he didn't need Robert catching his death in this weather.

Charley's rain gear did little in the way of keeping him dry. He drew the coat tighter around his chest as his heavy boots clomped against the hollow plank floorboards.

"Hello, Pa," Seth said through the spill of the rain as they drew near. "Before you get your dander up, Ma said Robert should come along 'cause she's not feeling well."

"Your sister could've taken care of him," Charley said, tired to the bone. "Your sister needs to get her nose out of those books long enough to help out around the place. Why your mother lets her spend so much time daydreaming over them is beyond me."

"She's taking care of baby Sarah so Ma can rest. Michael and Timothy are doing evening chores. Here, let me take your satchel. I packed some hides to cover your gear to keep things from getting drenched on the way home. The horses are just over here."

Seth disappeared around the corner of the station with his bag. Not for the first time was Charley thankful Seth was old enough to care for things on the farm while he worked the rails in Pennsylvania. Having Seth in charge of the family while he was away gave him the much-needed peace of mind to deal with his everyday problems.

Charley leaned over and tucked Robert's cap low over his forehead.

"Howdy, kid. You being good for Ma?"

Robert looked up and nodded; his mouth hung open, the hat shadowed his raised eyebrows and wide eyes. What Charley wouldn't give to be able to spend more time with his family. Already Seth was a grown man, and he hadn't had a chance to get to know him. Robert would be all grown up and moving on, too. Not to mention the others.

Damn trains.

Charley sighed and turned toward the wagon. He should be thankful Mason Aderley had given him this time to put things in order here at home.

Still...

"Come on, kid; let's get home and out of this rain before we get good and soaked. Don't want you to catch a cough. Ma don't need any more worries than she's got already."

Charley lifted Robert into his arms and carried him to the wagon. He placed him in the center of the buckboard, then climbed up beside him. Seth jumped aboard and took up the reins. He led the horses out of the station yard and into the dark night, made even bleaker by the heavy downpour.

Despite his foul mood, Charley appreciated the way his son handled the reins. For a kid of eighteen going on nineteen, Seth had shouldered the responsibility of the family and the running of the farm without complaint. The kid was better at farming and handling horses then he'd ever be.

"You need to find yourself a wife, son."

"I'm doing fine, Pa. No need to rush."

"When was the last time you got off the farm? Got to town and mingled with the town folks?"

"I manage on occasion. Gotta get to town and buy supplies."

"But have you got yourself a woman?"

"I'm working on it, Pa."

"Good. Good. You're good at farming, but you need to find yourself a wife. Someone who will make a good farmer's wife."

Seth didn't answer. Instead, he called "gee" to the horses as they turned onto the north route out of town.

"You need someone like your ma. Someone strong, dependable. Someone to give you children, raise a good family. Help out on the farm."

Again, Seth didn't answer but remained focused on the horses. Charley turned up the collar on his coat to keep the rain from running down his back. He opened his coat and drew Robert's thin frame next to him. The boy snuggled into the warmth of his body and nodded off.

They drove deeper into the dark night. Seth knew what he was about, and even the horses didn't need much prompting. Seth yelled "gee" again, yanked on the reins, and in one fluid motion, horses and wagon veered right. The span of horses whinnied in unison as they left the main route and headed up the hill to the farm. The hill grew steeper, making it harder for the wagon to slosh through the rain-gutted, tree-lined road. The horses had their job cut out for them. Charley kept his mouth shut as Seth managed the pair all the way to the top.

Seth had done a fine job when he insisted on purchasing these two. Hell, his family had done good about many things, being stuck way up in the hills by themselves. They survived fine without him. He wanted nothing more than to spend time helping his family, but he couldn't do a damn thing about it.

Not yet, anyway.

Seth maneuvered the wagon to the front of the small, plank-board house. The kerosene lantern in the kitchen cast a yellow glow from the miniature window. Charley's insides warmed. He was home. This was his refuge; Emily waiting for him. The door opened wide despite the rain, and there she stood.

With open arms.

"Emily," he breathed.

In seconds Charley was out of the wagon, onto the

front steps, and in her arms. Seth, Robert, everyone, and everything else evaporated into the night along with the rain and the worries of the railroad.

"Charles," she whispered. He took her into his arms, nuzzled her neck. She was hot to the touch with fever.

"You should be in bed, not standing out here in the damp night air, Em."

But by God, holding her was heaven, and he was pleased she had met him at the door. From the first day they were married, she'd never missed standing in the doorway, greeting him with outstretched arms whenever he came home. And he had the whole weekend to soak in this warmth. This woman made his miserable life worthwhile. If anyone or anything could take away his worries and carry him through the coming days ahead, it was his Emily.

Emily made life worth living.

Charley picked her up and carried her inside, out of the storm, and into the shelter of the sweet fragrance of yeast bread rising on the back of the stove, and the sun-kissed bedding in their small bedroom down the hall. Concerns of trains and the threat of a strike no longer existed.

He was home.

Chapter Three

The spot where Emily had lain next to him during the night was empty. Charley rolled over and breathed in her sweet, womanly scent that lingered on the bedding. Mingled with the fragrance of her favorite lemon verbena soap and the fresh smell of sheets that had flapped in the clean country breeze on a warm sunny day was all so seductive.

While he worked the rails alongside grease and grime and the odor of soiled, worn bodies all day, he craved this intoxicating woman.

Emily.

Her image made Charley smile. Emily was nobody's fool. She had the guts to stand up to him. And he loved her all the more for it.

He'd met Emily when she had come to Philadelphia to visit her cousin, Marybelle, who had been about to embark on an overland trip with her new husband, William Landon. They were headed to the California goldmines to make their fortune. Charley had been there when Emily had disembarked from the train at Union Station. He couldn't take his eyes off her and had fallen in love at first sight.

But now, Emily was real sick. Still, she hadn't let her illness get in the way of their lovemaking last night. He'd just wanted to hold her. But she wouldn't listen, and their usual heated passion had taken over. Her loving arms had circled his body as she'd snuggled close after their bout of passion. He'd tugged her into the protection of his embrace and leaned his cheek on top of her head, then tucked her into his shoulder. He'd placed a tender kiss on her forehead and sighed in contentment. They had both fallen asleep, exhausted in each other's arms.

She shouldn't even be out of bed now. She should be the one sleeping in, not him.

"Damned trains," he mumbled as he slid from the bed, bumping his knees against the wall. "Damned walls."

He rubbed his knees, stretched, then put on the clean pair of trousers and crisp ironed shirt Emily had lain out for him. They smelled of country sunshine. He held the collar to his face and drank in the freshness.

A far cry from oil, coal, and smoke.

In the half-light of day, he dressed quickly in the cramped room and was reminded of the hardships Emily endured. Their room was only big enough for a bed, a set of drawers, and a commode. But during the night, with just the two of them, the tight space didn't matter. In the light of day, it reminded him of the cramped quarters of the tenements in Philadelphia.

He'd only transferred her from one cramped quarter to another.

At least here she had the expanse of the outdoors, he reasoned, not the mobs of families living on top of each other.

Charley opened the bedroom door and made his way to the kitchen, buttoning his shirtsleeves along the way. Emily stepped in from the outdoors, the screen door banging shut behind her.

"You shouldn't have gone out this morning. You've a fever." He took her in his arms, rubbing her back. "Your fever is getting worse. You should have called on the doctor by now."

"One of the horses was acting up. Seth needed a gentle hand. Don't worry so, Charles. I'll be fine."

Emily laid her cheek on his chest and leaned into him. He tightened his hold. She was weaker this morning. He put his hands on her shoulders and set her away from him so he could look down into her eyes. They were dull and filled with pain.

"You aren't fine. You had a fever last time I was home. You have a fever now. Why haven't you called for the doctor, woman? I must have been crazy to think you'd be better off here in the country to manage all on your own after your mother passed on."

"I have Catherine and the boys, Charles. We're doing fine."

Emily tried to hide her pain with a smile, but he was wise to her discomfort. She'd never recovered her strength after she'd given birth to baby Sarah nine months ago.

"Don't lie to me, Em," he grumbled over her head. "I have eyes. I can see. You've been getting sicker and sicker. You need to take care of yourself. The kids need a mother."

"Charles, don't yell." Emily raised her face, her eyes pleading, her voice smooth, but weak. "You'll wake Sarah. She didn't sleep well last night. She needs her rest."

"I'm not yelling, damn it. And you need *your* rest, too."

"Shhhh."

"Don't shush me. You were more than likely up with our babe all night, weren't you? You should have woken me up, Em. I would have helped out."

"Now hush. Go outside and breathe the fresh air. I've got to help Catherine with breakfast. The boys will be here in a minute."

"You need to go to bed. *Now.* Catherine can do breakfast."

"Morning, Pa," Catherine called from the other side of the kitchen, a tentative smile on her face. She slid a pan of biscuits in the oven. "Breakfast will be ready soon."

"Your ma's gonna need a tray in bed this morning. Make sure she gets fed before the boys sit down to eat," he ordered.

"Yes, Pa."

Charley picked Emily up and headed toward their bedroom.

"Charles. Put me down," she protested.

"You're going nowhere but bed."

Emily gave in and laid her head on his shoulder. He could feel her weakness and cussed himself for last night. He should have been more gentle. He laid her on the bed, kissed her forehead, and then drew the old quilt her grandmother had made for their wedding up around her shoulders.

"I'll get you a cup of cold water from the well. You're burning up." He stood over her and pointed his finger at her as if she were a child. "And don't get up 'til I tell you. Understand?"

Charley didn't wait for Emily's reply. Instead, he headed to the barn to find the boys.

Foolish woman. Didn't she know being near her

took the edge off? Didn't she know he worried about her? Right after breakfast he would take her into town to see old Doc Wooster. Kicking and screaming if he had to.

Stubborn woman.

****

The torrential rains had ceased during the night, but the ground was still soaked. A fair breeze blew across the hilltop. Charley breathed in the heavy scent of damp hay spilling out into the early morning mist. He walked to the barn and caught the stench of animal scents— even that was far headier then the coal and grease from the rails. The barn was big enough to hold the extra milk cows Seth had accumulated since he'd taken over the running of the farm from Emily's family.

Emily's father had been killed when a hay wagon rolled over and crushed him underneath. Her mother had taken ill shortly after, and died. Emily said it was from a broken heart. Charley hadn't taken to that nonsense at the time, but if anything happened to Emily, he could very well imagine he would die of a broken heart, too.

Charley walked through the open barn doors. Seth sat on a three-legged stool milking one of the goats.

"How's those tin-eaters, boy?" Charley asked.

"Got five cents a pound this week on the cheese. Mrs. Johnson says it's a delicacy, and people will pay more if they can get it."

"That so? Then guess you'd better keep supplying it."

Those goats sure could smell up a place. Worse than a cow any day. But goat cheese was a good sale at the Ithaca markets according to Seth, and the income helped out with the expenses on the farm.

"What about the main dairy?"

"Holding steady. No complaints."

Seth kept milking the brown speckled goat. The kid could milk a goat as well as he did a cow, plow the fields, and handle a team of horses. A reliable kid, he deserved better. He deserved his own family.

"Where's Timothy and Robert? Ma needs fresh water from the well to help cool her fever."

"Gathering eggs. The hens have been laying real good lately."

Charley circled the side of the barn just as Robert and Timothy rounded the corner.

"Timothy, give those eggs to Robert, and fetch a jug of fresh water from the well for your mother. She's down with fever."

"Yes, Pa." They both bobbed in unison and did as they were told.

Charley stood a moment before going back inside the barn where he surveyed the clean interior. Yes sir, some woman was surely missing out on not latching onto Seth Carmichael.

"I see you built a corral for the horses on the back side of the barn," Charley said. He scanned the rest of the interior of the mid-size building to see what else Seth had accomplished.

"I have one for the goats with an overhang on the south side of the barn, too. Put the pigs next to them in a separate pen so we don't have to chase them all over the farm. Keeps the smell away from the house when the wind blows up here on the hill."

"What about those chickens?"

"Mostly run loose for now. Come fall, I plan to

build them a separate coop so they don't freeze to death."

"Catherine was in the kitchen making breakfast when I left the house. As soon as we finish eating, I want you to get the wagon ready. I aim to take your ma to visit Doc Wooster. So best hurry up with the milking and get washed up."

"Yes, sir."

The sky remained overcast from the night before, but the sun filtered through the spotty holes in the clouds. He took his time walking back to the farmhouse. He hoped the rain would hold off 'til he got Emily to town. The old reprobate better be in; he was the only doctor for miles.

After breakfast, Charley met Seth out front.

"The buckboard's ready," Seth said. "I'll drive you in."

Charley wanted to argue with Seth, but the boy could handle the reins better. He rationalized he could take better care of Emily if he didn't have to control the team at the same time. He strode back inside to get her.

He met Catherine in the kitchen.

"I don't know when we'll be back, so you're to take care of things while we're gone. Seth is going with me, so make sure the boys get the rest of the chores done."

Catherine nodded. Her lips clamped shut, then twitched to the side. Hell, maybe she'd been a bigger help to Emily than he'd figured. "Right," he mumbled. He proceeded to the back of the house to get Emily.

She was bent over Sarah's cradle, tucking a hand-stitched blanket around the sleeping baby with such loving hands; he almost didn't want to disturb her. She looked up at him with flushed, feverish eyes and smiled. He caught the fragrance of her lemon soap. And sunshine.

"This isn't necessary. I'll be okay with a few days of bed rest."

"Don't argue with me. Seth has the horses ready." He wrapped a quilt around her shoulders, lifted her into his arms, and carried her down the hall and out to the waiting wagon.

"I'm too heavy. Put me down. I can walk."

"You're light as a feather." He lifted her up onto the seat, then jumped up and settled in beside her.

Seth yanked the wooden brake away from the wagon wheel, then hopped aboard. He took the reins, gave them a jerk with his wrist, and the horses gingerly stepped forward.

Emily's face was even more drawn and pale than when he'd put her to bed a short while ago. He wrapped his arm around her and hugged her tight. Couldn't nothing happen to Emily. He didn't want to think about his life without her.

Instead, he concentrated on how Seth would manage the horses down from the rain-gutted hillside without ending up at the bottom of the cliff in a heap. The narrow road barely passed for an excuse of a road. But it was the only way off the hill. Even though Seth drove the team slowly, the jarring had an effect on Emily.

"You're a brave woman, Em, but a foolish one to try to hide your pain. We've been through too much over the years for you to start keeping things to yourself. You should've told me you were getting worse."

He rubbed his calloused hand over her arm. The thinness of her bones through the quilt shook him to the core. Her breathing labored, Charley clung tighter.

The hill leveled off, the ruts not as deep; the wagon ride became less bumpy. Thankful the horses did what was expected of them, Charley breathed a sigh of relief as they reached the bottom of the hill without incident. The steady clomping of the horses' hooves evened out as they trotted onto the turnpike.

But sweat was on Emily's brow now, and they had at least another hour before they would arrive in Candor Center. With any luck the doctor wouldn't be out on a call to some hillside farm, taking God-only-knew how long to get back to town. Damned doctors should stay put and not run all over God's creation tracking down the sick. They should keep to one place where they would always be on hand for the sick to come to them.

Almost to Candor village limits, Charley craved a smoke in the worst way. Wanting a cigarette reminded him of the train ride home, which made him think about the pending cut in wages. It was sure to trigger a strike. He was glad he hadn't mentioned anything about the strike to his family. They had enough to worry about without adding to their load. But he'd have to fill Seth in before he left tomorrow night. But not now. Right now Emily needed him.

By the time they arrived at Candor Center, Charley was ready to scream from wanting that smoke. Emily's head bobbed across his chest like Sarah's ragdoll. He lifted her chin only to discover her eyes were closed.

Dear Lord, she'd up and fainted.

"Get this wagon moving, son. Your ma's passed out."

He laid her head in his lap to make her more comfortable.

Seth yanked on the reins, the crack of the whip echoing across the valley. The team bolted forward and picked up speed. Charley smelled the dampness in the air. The sun had disappeared behind a heavy blanket of clouds, and a heavy mist covered them as they turned onto Main Street. By the time Seth led the horses to the hitching post in front of Doc Wooster's, the mist had turned into a steady downpour.

Charley jumped from the wagon and slid Emily across the bench into his arms. He was up on the boardwalk under a protective awning within seconds, pounding on Doc Wooster's door.

"Open the door," he barked.

Seth was by his side and opened the door, not bothering to wait for someone else to open it from the other side. The dimly lit interior smelled of disinfectant.

"Doc? You in there?" Charley called out.

A short, dark-haired, middle-aged woman with bright green eyes ran from the other room, wiping her hands on a long white no-nonsense apron. An odor of vanilla drifted in around her.

"What do we have here?" She inspected the bundle in Charley's arms.

"My wife is with fever. She passed out on the way here. Where's the Doc?"

"Follow me." The woman indicated a stark, spacious, clean room to the left. A pristine bed was made up in one corner. A kerosene lantern sat on a nightstand, and a chamber pot hugged the wall.

The woman hovered over Emily as soon as Charley laid her down. "If you'll kindly wait outside, I'll take over from here."

"You ain't the doc," Charley said. "Where the hell is he?"

"With another patient in another room. He'll be here soon. Please wait outside," she said, her hands affixed to wide hips. "The sooner you leave, the sooner I can ready your wife to be seen by the doctor."

Charley could tell the bossy woman wouldn't take no for an answer. He nodded, then joined Seth in the sitting room. Emily's health was more important than his standing in the way.

Charley paced the floor in front of Seth, who had taken a seat.

"Sit down, Pa. Your walking the floorboards ain't gonna fetch the doctor here any sooner."

"What's takin' him so long?"

"At least he's in there with Ma, now. We'll know something soon enough."

Doc Wooster finally emerged from behind closed doors and strode toward the sitting room. Charley jumped up so fast from the hard chair that it teetered back and forth before settling in place.

"What's wrong with her?"

"I'm afraid your wife is suffering from consumption. She needs to be placed in a sanitarium."

Charley's heart sank. "We can't afford a sanitarium."

"She needs total rest. Someone to look after her. Do you have someone to care for her at home?"

Charley cast his gaze to the floor, shaking his head. A knot formed in his stomach. Charley looked at Seth, then back at the doctor and shook his head.

"No."

"I thought not. I can make arrangements at a sanitarium upstate. Payment there will be minimal."

"Do you think she'd be able to handle a train ride?" Seth stepped forward.

"What the hell, boy," Charley bellowed. "Of course she can't. She didn't even make it here without passing out. I know what you're thinking son, but going out to Marybelle's is out of the question."

"Actually," Doc Wooster interrupted. "I can give her a dram or two of opium, some Dover's powder, to help make her more comfortable on the train. Exactly what did you have in mind?"

The doctor looked at Seth as if he were the one in charge. Bothered by the doc's assumption, Charley eyed his son, then filled the doctor in on what Seth had in mind.

"Emily's cousin lives out west. She's been inviting her to visit for some time. If you think she's up to traveling so far under her current condition, I can send a telegram to her cousin. See if she'd be willing to look after Emily for a while."

"The air out there might do her some good. But the fact of the matter is, her lungs are giving out. You should make the arrangements as soon as possible. I've given your wife something to make her sleep for a few hours. Mrs. Wooster will look after her while you send a telegram and make the arrangements."

Charley shot out of the door and headed straight for the train depot's telegraph office across the street. He hoped Marybelle would send a favorable reply.

And soon.

Chapter Four

Marybelle's warm reply was a welcomed relief. He should send Emily to her for complete rest to recuperate as soon as they could make arrangements. He could go back to Philadelphia and concentrate on the strike knowing Emily would be in good hands.

A second telegram had arrived; Aderley sent word that a hundred Pennsylvania Longshoremen working on the New York docks would walk out if the wage cut was initiated, and come hell or high water, Charley'd better hurry back to Philadelphia. The telegram implied he'd be spending more time than he wanted at the yards keeping the workers from rioting.

"I hate to leave all of you like this. But if I don't get back to Philadelphia, I'll be out of a job. See your mother doesn't get out of bed 'til it's time to get on the train. I'll meet her when she transfers in Philadelphia; see she makes her connection out west. By damn, Marybelle best be waiting for her at the other end."

"We'll see she's taken care of, Pa," Seth promised. "Catherine will wash and pack her clothes this afternoon. We'll get her to the station on time, day after tomorrow."

"What about the baby?"

"I'll take good care of Sarah," Catherine said. "Seth can handle the boys."

Charley shook his head. Not much else he could

do.

With things settled, he nodded to his family and headed inside to say goodbye to Emily.

"Seth, get the rig ready. I'll only be a minute."

He hated to leave Emily so soon, but he took heart seeing Seth and Catherine take charge without a fuss.

****

After waiting and watching and wondering when things would erupt at the tracks the week before, sensing how riled up everyone was, Charley hoped he could resolve the situation before things got out of hand.

He hoped he wasn't wishing in a bucket instead of a well.

Damn trains. Everyone considered they were going to revolutionize the country, and all they'd done so far was create a lower class dependent on the few crumbs thrown their way by the wealthy owners. He felt sorry for them.

Hell, he was sorry for himself.

His nerves were shot to hell and so far gone, he was ready to explode. He worried about the men at the yard, he worried about straddling the line between the workers and management, and now he was worried about Emily. If it weren't for Aderley nailing down his loyalty to the railroad, he'd be home with Emily right now. She wouldn't have to be going so far away from him.

And her family.

The train wheels squealed on the iron tracks, the hiss of steam mingled with the blast of the horn, and the train jerked to a stop. The smell of the rails filled his nostrils as others got off the train and rushed past him to the platform in front of the station. He took his time, more relaxed than he'd anticipated. He was in his element. He couldn't help it; it was in his blood. But it was one hell-of-a-way to live.

Right away he could see something was wrong.

"Hey, Michael, where are the men? Why are these rail cars lined up on the holding tracks?"

Charley didn't wait for an answer. He picked up his satchel and made a bee-line to the station office. He had to find out from Aderley what was going on. Had the man not waited 'til he got back, as promised?

He rounded the corner and started toward Aderley's office only to have Donahue step in front of him, closing off entry to the building.

"Where do you think you're going, Carmichael?" John Donahue sneered. He folded his arms in front of his wheezing chest, his long, skinny legs planted inches apart.

Huh, as if that would stop him from entering the building. The rat had a smirk on his face itching to be knocked off. Charley was ready to oblige him.

"You can't go up there just yet," Donahue said, the dare evident in his beady, little eyes. "There's a meeting going on. Aderley has his hands full with some of the fellas." He braced himself into a more solid stance. "They don't want their wages cut. In case you haven't heard, it's already been settled. It's gonna happen, and I don't intend to stand by. Those big bugs don't care if we all starve to death."

"I'm surprised you're still here." Charley stood his ground. The only way to handle this good-for-nothing rat was to sweet-talk him out of his own thinking. Charley could see by the look in the man's eyes that it would be a waste of time.

"I suspected you were the instigator all along. You've been spending a lot of time at the yard talking to the men. You're getting a pretty penny for your job, you fool. Your job's secure. Why make life more miserable for the others."

"Yeah, well I don't earn as much as you think. But that's gonna change real soon."

Charley didn't see how Donahue would be bringing in more than he got already. "It's more than you'll be making elsewhere. Now, step aside and let me pass. I'll see for myself what's going on up there. Stop the bedlam you've created before someone gets hurt."

Charley stepped around Donahue, but Donahue again blocked his access to the entrance.

"I can't let you do that," he said. "You might just as well join us, or pack up and go home. I'm getting better wages just keeping the strikers riled up."

Charley didn't doubt him one bit. The weasely-eyed fool was raking in the dough from somewhere. Knotting his hands into fists at his sides, Charley wanted to take a pop-swing at the guy.

"Get out of my way. I'm going through."

Donahue swung at him.

The punch landed to the side of his right eye taking him by surprise and knocking him to the ground. Tears pooled, blocking his vision. His face stung, but it was nothing compared to the instant headache that left him stunned when his head connected with the concrete steps.

Charley took a steadying breath then bounded back up, fists raised, and stood face to face with the tall, skinny, seething Irishman. Charley's dark hair hung over his left eye; he blew it out of the way, not letting his guard down. He'd have one hell-of-a-shiner come morning.

But right now he had a job to do.

"I'm going up those stairs if I have to take you down first. Now, get the hell out of my way, or I'll kill you where you stand."

Donahue smiled, planted his feet securely in front of Charley, and swung his fisted hands to his hips. "Be my guest if you think you're stupid enough."

Charley didn't want to fight him. He sidestepped around him, looked back to see Donahue's hand slip inside his pocket.

The damn fool had a knife.

Charley swung around, doubled up his fist, and hit Donahue broadside. With a single punch, the man fell backward with a thud, then lay still, his eyes staring up toward heaven. Charley hoped he was praying for forgiveness.

Charley turned away, then bounded up the steps without a backward glance. May God help him; he didn't care if he'd killed the agitator.

Engineers and trainmen alike littered the hallway at the top of the stairs. Charley elbowed his way through but was shoved aside.

"Let me through. Let me talk to them," he demanded.

"You think you can do any good? You can't."

"Too late. Go back to New York, Carmichael. Go milk your cows. We don't want you here."

"Yeah, you're nothing but a turncoat, Carmichael. You're on their side."

"Go on, get outta here."

"I can help," he reasoned, but the din drowned out his words. No one paid him any attention. How the hell could he reason with a gang of angry men?

"If you strike now, you won't work," Charley raised his voice. "No work, no pay. How are you going to feed your families with no pay?"

His cries fell on deaf ears. Didn't they know what little they earned was better than nothing? Things had deteriorated faster than he or Aderley had anticipated.

What a God-awful mess.

Charley leaned against the stairwell and rested his throbbing head against the wall. He dragged his fingers through his thick, damp hair. It was hotter than hell in here, and the tempers and temperature were rising.

He looked to his left and spotted his friend, Seamus, standing against the wall on the opposite side of the hallway. Head bowed, Seamus looked to be studying his worn out work boots.

"What's going on, Seamus?" Charley called over the bedlam.

Men tried to pack themselves into Aderley's office. Seamus' head shot up.

Charley waited until his friend's blank eyes cleared and focused. "What's going on here?"

Seamus stepped away from the wall and wound his way through the tight crowd toward the top of the stairs.

"We're protesting the cut, we are." He stopped in front of Charley. "And rightly so. By all that's holy, we can't live on the little we get. How can we face our wives? What do we tell our children? I'm telling you, if we don't do something now, if we don't band together, we'll be rotting in our houses, dying of starvation. That is if we don't get thrown out for not paying rent."

"It's not just here." Michael appeared at Seamus' side. "The vote was unanimous. All the trunk lines are cutting back on wages. And for what? Just so they can line their pretty pockets, I ask ya? To fill their already full pockets while ours are empty and getting emptier?"

"Are you sure a strike is the best way to go?" Charley asked. "Donahue instigated this, didn't he? I knew he wasn't to be trusted. He's the one who's been at the tracks talking all of you into striking, hasn't he? He just tried to stop me from coming up here and talking sense into you."

"Listen, Charley, a trainmen's union has been organized in Allegheny City. A union for all railroad workers. If we can't talk sense into management, we start to strike on June twenty-seventh, and they'll join us. Robert Ammon, freight brakeman on the Pittsburgh, Fort Wayne & Chicago's line is going to be chief organizer."

"You're talking, what, three-, five-hundred trainmen? Are other trunk lines involved, Seamus?"

"Pittsburgh-Allegheny City have locals organized on the B&O line from Pittsburgh all the way to Baltimore; the Fort Wayne line from Pittsburgh to Chicago. The Northern Central, the Atlantic & Great Western, and even the Erie lines up into New York. I hear the entire Pennsy line is going, too. For sure Pittsburgh will be the hot spot."

"That covers more than two-thousand miles of rails." Charley shook his head.

"You've got to take sides, Charley. Figure out if you're sticking with the bosses, Aderley and Scott, in there, or the workers out here. From the looks of things, there's going to be a strike. Those two big bugs in there ain't gonna back down for nothing."

Charley slumped down on the top step. He rested his elbows on his knees and dropped his head in his hands. "What an awful mess," he mumbled. "What a damned awful mess."

He reached for a cigarette from his breast pocket, but they weren't there. He patted his pants pockets, but they were empty as well. Those gathered in the hallway headed for the stairs. He stood and inched his way into the corner to let them pass.

"I'll see you later." Seamus handed him a smoke.

He watched as Michael joined the others. They filed down the stairs and left the building, Seamus right behind them. Charley shook his head, lit the cigarette, and sat back down.

An eerie quiet hung in the air.

Charley finished his smoke, then made his way to Aderley's office. The boss man sat behind his desk looking dazed. His face was drained, pinched, and defeated. He lowered his head in his hands—drops of sweat dripped between his fingers

Or were they tears?

Scott was no longer in the room.

Charley dragged his feet as he walked into his manager's office. The silence was as heavy as a train car full of coal. He had no idea what Mason Aderley had in mind. But one thing was for sure, he was going to find out. Charley approached the desk and sat in the chair across from Aderley.

"I can't go back on my word, Charles." A deep sigh escaped the harried manager. "Scott agreed to this cut along with everyone else. I stand behind him. But,

I'm afraid. I'm afraid for all those dirty slobs down there. They have no idea what's to come if they strike. There will be bloodshed before this is over, I tell you. Maybe even yours and mine. I don't know. But what I do know..." Aderley peered into Charley's eyes, a determined, almost threatening stare. He shook his fist in the air, then jabbed his finger at Charley. "...I can count on you to be by my side. Help pacify the men."

Charley sat riveted to his chair. He wasn't given a chance in hell of refusing.

And that rankled. He sympathized with the workers—he didn't want a cut in pay, either.

For the second time in days, Aderley questioned his loyalty. No. He demanded it.

Charley hesitated, trying to think how best to respond. He was caught between a rock and the damnedest hard place he'd ever been in. And he'd sure been in a few.

"I *can* count on you can't I, Charles?" Aderley slapped his large, firm hand down on the desk.

Charley jumped. There it was. The question he didn't want to answer.

"I need you to talk to them, to help mediate, and to explain to them exactly what's going to happen and why, if they go on strike. I want you to keep me informed as to what they're saying, what they're doing, what they're planning. I need you to report to me as soon as you learn anything. *Everything.*"

The man's eyebrows rose to his thinning hairline, and his eyes bulged to near popping. "I expect you to be here for the company. I *need* you here."

Once again the decision had been made for him. Come hell or high water or bloodshed, which was surely on the way, Charley was on the company's side. He'd stay and try to make it a bit easier for the men.

Did that make him the turncoat the men had called him?

"I've made the necessary arrangements with my family, so I'm here for the duration," Charley said, defeated. May God forgive him, he wanted to walk out on Aderley right now. He wanted to side with the workers—where his heart said he should be.

Where Emily would say he should be, too.

****

Donahue was nowhere to be seen when Charley walked out of the building. The weasel was no doubt on his way to report to the leader of the Mollies.

The Mollies had increased in strength and power along with the population in the coal mining areas over the past ten years. They were a rugged bunch originating from the Ancient Order of Hibernians and had come to work the coal fields of Pennsylvania. The Mollies controlled the Order. As far as Charley could tell, their main reason for banding together was to shoot up agents of the Irish landlords, especially in the Schuylkill and Carbon areas. The secret organization of these buckshots was no real secret. If there was violence involved, the Molly McGuire's were involved.

Charley didn't believe all the rubbish about the Mollies having been cowered into non-existence. Donahue was a Molly sure as Charley had any breath left in him.

A bitter taste swirled in his mouth.

He headed for the Blue Bottle Pub where the men congregated at the end of the work day to let off steam before they went home to their families.

Charley walked in and gave Mac a holler. Michael Mackenzie was a tall, burly man with raven hair waxed and parted in the middle. He wore his mustache greased into rounded handlebars within an inch of touching his ears. He resembled an Italian rather than an Irishman, which made him the butt-end of many jokes on a regular basis.

Mac held up a tankard in greeting as Charley wormed his way through the tight group of angry, boisterous men. Mac's large black eyes rolled in chagrin at the frenzied atmosphere. He glanced around the room then nodded for Charley to proceed to the bar.

"Trouble's a'brew'en, Charles. Everyone's all a'buzz."

Mac's white bib apron stretched taut but still didn't cover his large middle. The apron showed signs of use, either from Mac wiping his wet hands or from splatters of ale.

Charley rubbed his forehead where Donahue had hit him. Hopefully, a pint of ale would ease the pain. If nothing else, it would help him sleep better tonight.

The pub was loud, smoky, and crowded. It was a small place where men didn't worry about sitting on doily-covered furniture or walking on waxed and polished floors. A place where they could wash away their cares and concerns after working the hot, steamy, oily rails. A place to ponder the strike and whether they would have a job at the end of the day. Today, they discussed the meeting which had just taken place.

The odor of coal, engine grease, beer, and tobacco filled the air. In the corner, two rotund, burly Irishmen covered in dust and grease argued with a German, both accents so heavy it was hard to understand what they were saying. They bumped shoulders, just short of knocking each other over. The room was asses-to-elbows full, preventing the men from falling to the floor; otherwise, it would have been a free-for-all. As it was, the three men turned back to guzzling beer as if they'd been involved in nothing more than telling a funny joke.

Charley turned away.

The strike was no joke.

Charley squinted, searching for Seamus who stood with his arms wrapped around a large pitcher of ale, his head bent over with long strands of reddish-blonde hair hanging over his half empty glass. Charley edged his way through the crowd, slid up next to him, and ordered another pint. He clasped his hand on the small Irishman's shoulder, startling him.

"Let's find someplace to sit and talk, Seamus. Those men fighting over there don't need their corner anymore."

Seamus nodded and followed Charley. They made their way to the corner where they dragged small wooden chairs from under a rough table splattered with beer from the scuffle of the previous occupants, who were working their way out the door and into the street.

"So, Charley. Whose side ya on?" Seamus didn't look at him.

Charley figured his friend already knew. "I haven't a choice. Aderley made the decision for me. I've got to tell you, though, I don't like it."

"I see ya got a shiner. How'd that come about?"

"Donahue gave me one hell-of-a-wallop. Knocked me down." He put his hand to the side of his head where a small lump had formed. "It's Donahue we need to fight against. Aderley may be the one going along with this cut in pay, but it's people like Donahue that keep things agitated. They're the ones who rile up all the workers with half-truths."

Charley took a long swallow of his beer, then swiped his shirt sleeve across his mouth with a loud sigh.

"They do make sense, Charley. I got to say, if we don't fight for our rights and better pay, our families are gonna starve to death before the year is out."

Seamus offered Charley a cigarette, even though the man couldn't afford them, let alone afford food to feed his family. As bad as he wanted a smoke, Charley refused.

"I know, Seamus. I know. My sympathies are with you, but my loyalties are with Aderley. The way I figure it, if I can work both sides maybe things won't be so bad."

"You're only fooling yourself, ya are. There's no middle ground here, I'm sorry to say. You're gonna have to choose."

Seamus stroked a dry match along the table twice before the tip ignited and he was able to light his cigarette. His hands shook. He drew in a deep breath, then exhaled when the tobacco caught hold. Charley waited until he had Seamus' attention again. His friend dipped his forefinger in his beer then pinched the end of the lit match 'til the small flame extinguished.

"Choosing isn't an easy thing to do," Charley said. "If I can get someone on your side to keep me posted, someone who I can funnel information to in order to make sure everyone hears the truth, not half lies like Donahue's been spewing, we just might be able to stop things from going all to hell."

"Good luck, to ya, friend. Once they find out you're siding with Aderley, there ain't no one gonna even want to talk to ya." Seamus looked around the room. "'Specially if this strike happens on the twenty-seventh like everyone's been saying."

The smoke from Seamus' cigarette hung in the air around Charley's head, then mingled with the rest of the blue smoke in the room.

Seamus was right. None of them had wanted to have anything to do with him outside Aderley's office just a bit ago. It didn't bode well.

"I know, Seamus. I know. Listen, friend, you're the person I'm talking about." Charley drew closer to Seamus so his friend could hear without others listening. "You're the one who can keep me informed. You're a good fella; the men listen to you. I need your help."

God help him, he sounded like Mason Aderley. But Seamus *was* a good man and was well respected.

"I ain't no informant. If the boys ever found out, they'd lynch me. I can't do it. If I did, Maggie's life would be in danger."

"Maggie and Madeline can move to the country with Seth and the children. Emily's real sick. She's going out west to be with her cousin Marybelle. There is plenty of room at the homestead. And your wife will be doing me a favor. Catherine could use some help around the place. At least for the summer. Just until this mess is taken care of."

"You've put me in a situation, ya have. I don't think my life is going to be worth a damn if word gets out." Seamus shook his head, looked down at his beer, then back up at Charley.

"I'll see what the Missus says and let you know."

"There isn't time." Charley met Seamus' gaze. "Get them out on the next train tomorrow. You can always pack up their things later. Say they're to visit family. By the time they come back the strike will be over, and no one will be the wiser."

"I won't put her on a train. She don't much like riding the rails, ya know." He shook his head again, then drank from his tankard. "This strike is gonna be worse than you or me could ever imagine."

"The stage coach runs up the Montrose Turnpike into Owego. They can switch coaches there and take one into Candor. No matter what you decide, the best thing you can do for your family right now is to get them out of Philadelphia."

Chapter Five

The wooded hillside behind the depot and the rolling hills opposite the valley cocooned the sleepy village of Candor. The echo of the loud clanging of metal on metal as the coal cars were being uncoupled and the screeching and hissing of iron wheels on iron tracks as the cars were transferred onto the side tracks announced the day had begun.

Shopkeepers threw open their doors and closed them based on the coming and going of the train. And already this morning, the 7:45 had arrived from Ithaca, having made stops at Slaterville and Smith Valley, with coal, cattle, sheep, produce, and passengers who planned to shop, open shop, conduct business, or visit friends and relatives for the day.

A hushed chaos filled the early morning as fog lifted from the thick forested countryside. People milled around in slow motion. Emily was glad of Seth's help down from the wagon. The powder Doc Wooster had given her had helped keep the fever down yesterday, and the small dose of opium helped her sleep most of the night. This morning, however, her brain was a bit addled and lethargic.

Charley had made the necessary arrangements for her travels to the California Territory before he'd left for Philadelphia. She hadn't had time to contemplate how the decision would affect her family, but this morning her mind had settled on the situation. How would they survive without her? She was their mother. What if they got hurt? Who would tend to them? Love them? Cuddle them? They needed her.

She needed them.

The air was still chilled from the cool morning hours. The sun drew moisture from the earth. Emily tugged her white crocheted shawl around her shoulders to ward off the slight breeze tossing the morning air around. Walking the platform like a mother hen with her brood of six following behind, she wished she had the strength to gather them under her wings and whisk them off to Marybelle's right along with her on the train.

She held back tears. *No use upsetting the children anymore than they were already.*

As one, they entered the station.

"Wait right here, Ma." Seth pointed to an empty bench in the middle of the room. "I'll get your ticket." He waited until she was seated, then turned to Catherine.

"You make sure she's okay while I stand in line."

"You don't have to be so bossy, Seth Carmichael. I know how to take care of people." Catherine hitched baby Sarah up on her hip.

Emily observed the interaction between her two oldest children. She had raised them to be responsible. Thank God for them, otherwise there was no way on God's green earth she would ever have consented to leave them behind. Her only saving grace was she'd recuperate faster at Marybelle's so she could come back home to be with her family.

The station filled with passengers coming and

going, but the background chatter and shuffling of feet was just that. Emily only had eyes and ears for her family. She would miss baby Sarah's first steps, her first words, her baby antics. Her youngest boys were at the age where they almost grew right before her eyes. And Catherine needed to study for her teaching exams.

When would she see them again?

Emily's eyes misted. She held back the tears threatening to overflow and looked up at her youngest. Catherine cooed to her darling baby, Sarah. She should be the one doing the cooing. She should be the one holding Sarah, cuddling her and loving her. Would Sarah forget she was her mother, not Catherine?

Tears pooled in the corner of her eyes.

The boys sat still beside her, a sure sign they had something on their minds. Although well behaved for the most part, boys their age weren't known for sitting still and being quiet. She would miss their antics as well. Would they be a big help to Seth? Would they listen well to Catherine? Would they turn out to be outlaws without her steady hand?

Emily rubbed her temples and hung her head. Her shawl slipped, and she wrapped it around her middle, then clasped her hands in the lap of her gray gingham dress. She hoped the children didn't notice her distress and the tears she had a hard time holding back.

"What did they do to upset Ma?" Seth asked Catherine when he returned with her ticket. "You were supposed to keep an eye on them."

"Nothing. I swear, Seth, you're like an old mother hen."

"Children, please. No one has done anything. We're all a little tense this morning, is all." Emily couldn't help smile at the mother hen reference. "I'm okay. Honest, you don't have to worry about me. Once I get aboard I'll be fine. I'll take the powder Doc Wooster gave me and get some rest."

As if on cue the conductor bellowed "all aboard" over the clanging of the new cars being coupled together. The engine churned to life as side-car doors were slammed shut and passengers rushed about to say their final goodbyes to loved ones.

Emily gathered her own six children to her side. Timothy, fourteen, hung back, but she stepped around Michael, eight, and led him with shaking hands into the fold. "I will miss you all," she said, her voice just as shaky as her hands. After only one day of bed rest, she was still weak. She hadn't counted on saying goodbye to her children being this hard. Thankfully, Seth stood beside her so she could lean on him, otherwise her quivering legs would give out, and she'd fall over. She couldn't let her children see how frail she was. They didn't need the worry.

Emily turned to Catherine and baby Sarah. Catherine was a responsible young lady and would do a fine job taking care of everything while she was away—as would Seth. Between the two of them, they had already shouldered the majority of the responsibilities of the family the past few months. Nothing would change. Except she wouldn't be there to help.

"Take good care of them, Catherine. I want them in fine shape when I return. You're their momma for now." Emily turned to the boys, dabbing her eyes with an already soaked hanky. "I'll see you all in a couple of months. Be good for Seth and Catherine," she said to

Michael and Robert who were now clinging to her in tears, her own tears flowing unchecked.

Reluctant to go, she took Sarah from Catherine and cradled her to her bosom and nuzzled her one last time.

The train whistle shrilled. No time for a second embrace. Catherine took Sarah, and Seth untangled the two boys from her legs, then handed her the small grip she'd borrowed from their nearest neighbor, Lizzy Hayland. She'd packed a change of clothes and sleepwear, plus the necessary toiletries needed during the week-long journey. The rest of her belongings were already aboard in the baggage compartment.

"Take care of everything for me, Seth. I'll wire you as soon as I arrive at Marybelle's."

"I will, Ma, just don't you worry. We'll be fine. You take care of yourself."

"I'll still worry, son."

The rest of her words were drowned out as the whistle sounded two long blasts, and steam from the engine covered the entire area, competing with the heavy fog rising over the mountainside. Emily lifted her long skirt and stepped up onto the cold metal stairs with the help of the conductor and entered the coach filled with an assortment of passengers. She made her way along the rose-patterned aisle runner toward her seat. Overhead, the lamps suspended from the center of the ceiling following the length of the car emitted a faint scent of kerosene. The narrow cushioned seats, although straight back, were colorful and inviting.

Emily found her place next to the window, and with a sigh of relief from the exhaustion of saying goodbye, she settled in her seat for the short trip to Owego. She leaned closer to the window and looked out in search of her children. She spotted them and waved, then placed her hand against the glass and let tears stream down her face. She blew them a kiss as they stood in a tight row on the wooden platform watching the train as it chugged down the tracks. When she could see them no longer, she turned, found a dry hanky in her bag, and dabbed her eyes dry.

Would she ever see her children again?

If she were as sick as Doctor Wooster said, there didn't seem to be much hope; consumption was not to be taken lightly. The image of those who had suffered from the disease had her close to breaking down in front of her brave family. She could only pray they had made the right decision by sending her out to her cousin Marybelle's to recuperate.

Doctor Wooster had insisted a warmer, dryer climate with fresh air and ample bed rest to regain her health was just the ticket. He'd told her to drink fresh cream with a spoonful of brandy. She hoped Marybelle had a cow or two. For the fever, he'd recommended Sassafras tea, which her cousin said she always kept on hand.

"You need some time to mend, my dear," he'd said. "You need rest. Nothing more strenuous than a nice afternoon walk. And absolutely no work."

Marybelle would make sure she followed doctor's instructions. That was Marybelle. One of the kindest women she'd ever met.

The doctor had insisted she carry the packet of opium as a sedative should she need a pain reliever on the train ride. As much as she was tempted to succumb to taking a small dram now, this part of the trip was a short one. She needed to keep her wits about her when she transferred to the various connections. She had two more train transfers before she arrived at her final destination. Perhaps if she sat quietly and relaxed, her headache would go away. She patted the packets of medicine in her dress pocket. They were there if need be.

Emily settled back and closed her eyes. When she opened them, the train was pulling into the Catatonk station. The stop lasted half an hour; long enough to switch cars and pick up a few more passengers.

Transferring in Owego happened without a hitch, and Emily enjoyed the familiar sights of the homes along the great Susquehanna River as the locomotive passed over the curved bridge. Farmers were tilling their fields, and boats were carrying lumber down river. A late spring with the ice not melting until early May and relentless rains until mid-June made the river deep enough for lumber barges and ferries to sail the wide waterway.

The ride to Philadelphia to pick up the train west was uneventful. When they arrived at Union Station, the undercurrents of the pending strike were heavy.

Emily stepped down from the train. Courtesy was not much in evidence, and a sense of haste prevailed as people jostled each other to make their connections or meet loved ones. Relieved when she spotted Charles waving his hand high in the air, Emily sighed. Within seconds she was in his arms, her small grip dropped to the wooden platform, forgotten.

"God, Em, it's good to see you. I've been so worried. You look ready to fall over. Did you take any of the medicine the old reprobate prescribed?"

"Not yet. I didn't want to fall asleep and miss my

connections."

"If only you didn't have to leave. I hate having to send you so far away from the children."

"At least I'll be with family. Cousin Marybelle will take good care of me. I will worry about the children though. It was so hard leaving them behind. Please try to go home once in a while to look in on things."

"Seamus' wife, Maggie, and her daughter, Madeline, are going to stay at the farm. Catherine will have plenty of help." He let her lean into him, then picked up her grip, and together they walked along the platform.

"Oh, Charles, that's wonderful. But I'll still worry some. And I'll miss them all. Especially my baby, Sarah."

"Ah, Em. This is so unfair. If not for this strike I'd take you there myself. If I'd been home with you more and taken care of you, this would never have happened."

"It's not your fault I'm ill, Charles. Don't keep blaming yourself. Besides, right now your place is here with the railroad."

"*No.* You and the children need me now."

"I'll be fine, Charles. You'll see."

"Come with me, Em. You need to sit down 'til this place clears a bit. I want to introduce you to Mrs. Aderley. She'll be traveling with you. She and her boys are headed to San Francisco to spend the summer with her sister."

"How wonderful for them," Emily said. If only *her* children could have accompanied her, the journey would be ideal. "Mrs. Aderley must be thrilled to have her children with her."

"Don't do this to yourself, Em. I know you'll be missing the children, but Seth and Catherine will take good care of them. Don't you worry yourself none. I mean it, Em. You have to think of yourself and get better. Now sit here while I find Mason and his family. I'll be right back."

Emily wished she could spend more time with Charles before she had to board the train again. As he disappeared from sight, she glanced around. Union Station was huge compared to the tiny depot in Candor. Well-dressed people in fine, ruffled day dresses milled about. They made her homespun traveling dress appear shabby. Why, the selection of colors alone flitting about the cavernous room would put a rainbow to shame. But in her present state, she closed her eyes to dispel the colorful chaos. When she opened them again, Charles was standing in front of her.

"I'm sorry, dear. I couldn't locate them. Mason assured me you would be sitting with his wife on the train. I'm afraid you'll have to introduce yourself when you board."

"Not to worry, Charles. I'll manage. Come. Sit beside me." She patted the empty spot next to her. As soon as Charles sat, she snuggled closer, laying her head in the crook of his shoulder. With a deep sigh, she closed her eyes.

"I will miss you, Charles. I will miss the children."

"I know, Em." He patted her back and slid his hand down her arm. "It's a damn shame you have to go so far away from them. And me."

"Watch your language, Charles. There are too many people around. I don't want them to think badly of you."

"I don't care what they think, Em."

Emily smiled and forgave him his transgression. After all, she didn't want to waste time arguing over a cuss word.

"I'll write as soon as I arrive at Marybelle's. I promise."

"I'll be waiting for your letter. With any luck, the strike will be put down right fast, and I'll be able to get away and come get you."

The shrill whistle sounded, startling both of them, cutting their goodbye short. They clung together for a brief but heart-wrenching embrace before Charles helped her to the waiting train where he bypassed the conductor and lifted her off her feet and up into the coach. He placed her grip in her hands and kissed her soundly in front of everyone. Emily didn't mind in the least. She would miss his kisses.

"I'd hoped we would have had more time together, Em. Mason Aderley's wife is a fine woman. She'll look out for you. I love you, Em."

"I love you too, Charles. You be careful as well. I'll see you soon." Tears ran down her hot cheeks. She retrieved her already tear-stained white hanky from her pocket and dabbed at her eyes. She should have packed a dozen, instead of just the two.

"Send a telegram as soon as you get there, Em. I don't want to wait for a letter. I'll worry the whole time until I hear from you. Promise?"

"I promise."

Emily stepped into the car. She turned to wave to Charles, but he was lost in the sea of waving hands through her watery eyes. With a soft sob, she turned back around and looked for her assigned seat. As she did, the train lunged forward, the jerking motion tossing her sideways into the shoulder of a burly man dressed all in black.

"I'm so sorry." Emily stepped back as best she could. The man tipped his hat and let her pass.

The lanterns bobbed back and forth overhead, and the sharp, grinding sound of the train rolling out of the station filled the car. Emily's head pounded, her eyes blurred from the tears still streaming down her face, and her legs threatened to give out. She made her way down the aisle in search of her seat.

"My dear, let me help you." A tall, thin lady stood to assist her; her flowered bonnet slightly askew. "I'm Mrs. Aderley. Marian Aderley, and these are my two sons, Jason and Jonathan. I've saved you the seat next to the window."

"Ma'am," Emily sighed, thankful, and fell into the cushioned seat just as her legs gave out. "I'm pleased to meet you."

Chapter Six

Seth readied the team to the wagon loaded down with silver cans full of the morning's milk. The fields whispered to him as the breeze ruffled the fresh crop of buckwheat on the acres beyond the barn. It swished back and forth like waves on a rolling sea. Even the corn was shooting up through the cool earth and doing well. He expected to get a good yield come fall. He'd have to hire the Hayland boys over on Eastman Hill to give him and his brothers a hand when the tassels turned a golden brown.

He loved to hear the wind blow though the rows of corn close to the house as the long slender leaves brushed up against each other as if they had secrets to share. If the weather held out, they would have plenty of silage for the winter months.

Seth yelled to Catherine as he jumped up on the buckboard and clicked the reins, setting the horses in motion.

"I'll be back about noon," he called. "Make sure the boys get their chores done. We've got fencing and crops to check after lunch."

He didn't wait for a reply. The horses clip-clopped along the bumpy dirt road as his sister stood in the kitchen door and waved him off.

The weight of the milk in the heavy cans kept the wheels of the wagon on the rutted tracks. He descended the steep section of the trail along the tree-lined hillside. The horses had the devil's own time keeping the wagon from careening over the edge. Seth yanked on the wooden-handled brake, giving just enough pressure against the wheels to keep them from spinning out of control. At the bottom, he released it. The horses relaxed into a steady pace once they turned onto the valley road along the flats.

Adding on to the goat herd this past year had been a smart decision. The milk production had increased, providing a good quantity which enabled him to supply the eastern markets all the way into New York City. Even though he headed into Candor Center, more than another hour's ride, it was better to unload his milk at the station in Smith Valley where it would be put on the ice cars so it wouldn't spoil.

Thankfully, the trains were still running. Not sure how much longer they would continue to run because of the pending strike, he could only hope this batch would make it to market.

"Hi'ya, young man," Amos Grant called as Seth maneuvered his wagon to the platform to unload in front of the station. The man's smile forced his weather-worn cheeks up against his eyes and made it look as if he was squinting. His silver-gray hair was slicked back. The wide, red suspenders did little to hold up his britches around his plump middle. But Amos Grant was a decent man who would lend a hand in a pinch.

"Ya think'en maybe this shipment is going to make it all the way to the big city? I hear all the main lines are starting to have trouble. Hear they're shutting down."

"I hope it gets through. According to my pa, he's trying hard to keep his men from going out." Seth jumped out of the wagon to help Amos unload the cans. His boots hit the wide pine floorboards with a thud.

"Can't say as I envy him his job," Amos replied, going right to work, hauling out the first can without so much as a grunt. "Now that's a hard one to deal with for sure. There ain't no stopping a great many men once they make their mind up against something."

"You're probably right. I wish my pa would give up the rails. He's been talking about leaving them behind for as long as I can remember, but it don't do no good. He just keeps at it."

"Must be hard with your ma laid up now. I hear she's left town to visit a relative out in the California Territory. I don't know as if I'd chance going out there; it's Injun territory, son. A woman all alone won't be able to defend herself none. No siree. Don't know if I'd let my Millie run off on her own, and she's not sick like your ma."

Seth didn't want to think about the dangers. He'd understood the West to have calmed down some since the treaties with the different tribes were in place. Travel was said to be much safer by train than when Marybelle had gone overland in a covered wagon several years ago.

"She's not alone. Pa's boss' wife and boys are traveling with her."

Seth handed the billing papers to Amos after the milk was unloaded. The two of them entered the depot office together. Once the station master's signature and stamp were affixed, Seth shook Amos' hand.

"Thanks for the help, Amos. I'll see you again

tomorrow morning."

Amos called to him before he got out the door.

"I hear old Clancy on the other side of the hill had to shoot his dog clean dead. Rabies. They're suspecting the dang dog got in a fight with a fox. Better watch things up there on your mountain, son. Ain't nice when someone gets bit by rabies."

"Thanks, Amos. I'll be sure to tell Catherine and the boys to be on the lookout. I'll pick up more ammunition for the rifles so they'll be ready."

Seth climbed back up on the wagon and gripped the reins, ready to leave. He prayed the train got through in time. He needed those accounts to help get them through the coming winter months in case his father ended up out of work. Once the strike hit, they'd have a hard time making ends meet without his father's pay. He was in charge and had to make sure the family didn't starve.

"How's Miss Catherine doing?" Amos stopped him before he got under motion. "She gonna be able to manage on her own with her ma gone?"

Seth liked talking to Amos, but this morning the man was in too talkative a mood.

"Catherine's doing just fine," Seth assured him. "She's a good shot, too, even though she's more of a bookworm. Target practices with Timothy and Michael on occasion."

She might be doing well now, but with their mother out west, they wouldn't have the canned goods their ma usually put up come harvest. Catherine wouldn't have the time to do all the work by herself.

"She still aiming to become one of them fancy school-marms?"

"Yep. Planning on taking her exams this summer if all goes well."

With Catherine trying to manage baby Sarah and the house, Seth didn't know when she would have time to study for exams. He'd have the boys help with the vegetable garden. Perhaps they could sell some of the extra produce at the markets in Candor.

He'd talk to Catherine to see what she thought.

"Well, you give her our best. If'en she needs anything, you have her give my missus a holler."

"Thanks. I will."

Amos' wife often visited his mother in the afternoons. Perhaps she would consider helping Catherine instead of sitting at the kitchen table sipping tea the entire time she visited.

Seth waved to Amos, turned the wagon around, and headed out.

After miles of traveling, Seth turned his team onto Mill Street along the Catatonk Creek next to Locey's mill, then down Main Street. Doc Wooster staggered down his front steps. The man was getting on in years. Or he was addicted to his own vials of snake oil. Still, he was the only doctor around for miles.

Seth's team clopped along on the dry roadway kicking up dust. He slowed the pair so dirt wouldn't blow against the people walking along the street.

"How's your mother, young man?" Doc Wooster called out. "She get off okay?"

The doctor was a short, squatty old man. Dressed in a black topcoat and a large black hat added a dash of stature and respect to his position, as did his black, bushy eyebrows and long beard speckled with white. Seth wasn't fooled for a minute. He nodded and waved, then drove on, making sure the horses didn't draw too close to the boardwalks where other horses were secured.

Homes at this end of town housed the more wealthy founding fathers and leaders of the community. Seth wasn't envious of the big, statuesque homes, some with pillars, some more modest but still large and imposing. Large maple trees lined both sides of the wide dirt road. Seth waved to the residents who were out and about. He turned and headed toward Weston's hay barn next to the tracks.

Dillard Moore arrived as Seth rounded the bend. He skirted around Dillard's rig and positioned his own team next to the loading platform.

"Hey, Seth, how's it going? Didn't see you at the agriculture meeting the other day. Things okay up on the hill?"

"Been busy with family, so couldn't make the meeting. But the farming end of things is going good. Just took three more cans of goat's milk to the station heading to Ithaca and New York City. I appreciate the advice you gave me about the herd."

Seth jumped down from the wagon, sauntered over to Dillard, and shook hands. For a young man, Dillard had a firm grip and a likable smile. His red hair matched his freckle-dotted face. Raised on his family's farm, he had been a big help to Seth over the past two years.

"Glad to be of assistance. How's Catherine? She get her nose out of those school books yet?"

"Doesn't have a choice now, what with Ma gone out west."

Dillard had a crush a mile wide on his sister, but he

knew Catherine wasn't interested in Dillard, or any other man right now for that matter. How many times had he heard her say that nothing was going to stand in her way of becoming a teacher? Except now she might have to put those dreams on hold to take care of the family.

"A darn shame." Dillard shook his head as if he were concerned Catherine didn't want any part of farming. Seth figured Dillard's hopes just jumped a notch, and the kid would appear at their doorstep with some lame excuse before long. He wanted to tell Dillard he didn't have a chance in hell, but the young man would find out soon enough.

Dillard followed him up the steps to the mill.

"Hi, ya, boys. How 'bout that strike. A whopper, huh?" Stanley Frost grinned, a sack of feed slung over his shoulder. "Best get your milk and feed on the next train while you can. No telling how long before they stop these trains dead on their tracks."

"Sure hope we aren't affected," Dillard said.

Seth had to agree. He vowed he'd never work the rails. *Never.*

"The other day I was talking to Buck Tanner who works the rails in Hoboken. He says the number of men getting killed from train accidents was hard to be believed. He told me the wages were already so low half the families were dying from hunger."

What could Seth say? Accidents were almost as common these days as marking a sow's ear before the town set down an ordinance to keep them from running loose in the neighbors' yards.

"I hear tell some poor soul was crushed coupling the rail cars together," Dillard said, shaking his head.

"Buck told me 'bout a fella who lost his legs when the train wheels caught him off-guard and knocked him to the tracks. Train rolled over him before he could get out of the way. He almost got left for dead and might just as well have died. They say he couldn't work no more. His missus is having a hard time trying to scrape enough money to keep them fed. For certain the trunk line ain't handing out any benefits or recompense." Stanley hefted his sack to the other shoulder. "Gotta get Mr. Strang's wagon loaded, boys, or I'd stand and chat a bit longer. Go on in and give my son your order. I'll be right back."

Yes sir, moving to the country had been the best thing Pa could have done for them. At least in the country they could farm, hunt, and grow food to put on the table. No need to starve here.

Dillard opened the door for Seth. They headed for the counter where Stanley's son Harold was writing in his ledger. He was a pimple-faced kid who was good with numbers and keeping the mill organized after school and during summer. He was the town's intellect, but not much common sense. Seth figured he'd be off to one of those highfalutin colleges or universities somewhere, but the family needed him at home to help with finances. Too bad, because Harold would probably make more money elsewhere.

"You two here for the usual?" Harold smiled up at them.

"Sure am," Dillard said.

Seth nodded.

Harold wrote in his ledger and walked toward the back of the building and out the door without a word.

"He don't talk much, does he?" Seth turned to

Dillard who was propped up against the counter.

"Nope. Quiet kid. Surprised they let him work here at all."

"His uncle owns the place. Amos was telling me Randall Weston and Stanley Frost are half-brothers. Randall's father died in a haying accident when Randall was six. His mother remarried old Stanley Frost."

Before they could expound further on the Weston and Frost connection, Harold returned. His father followed closely behind.

"Got your order sitting outside for you, gentlemen. I'll help load in a minute."

Seth signed his receipt, then headed outside with a quick goodbye to everyone. He loaded the wagon in record time and was ready to visit Anna Louise Mitchell.

Miss Mitchell's father was president of the Candor National Bank. They lived in the big two-story turreted Victorian home on the outskirts of the village, just around the corner from the bank. Miss Anna Louise Mitchell was a lovely girl, very proper, and Seth had had a hard time catching her eye. He'd seen her a couple of times at the dry goods store in Candor when he had stopped by to place his mother's orders when they'd first come to town. Anna Louise had been there with her mother. Mrs. Mitchell was a very becoming woman, and Seth figured Anna Louise's looks were going to be as good as her mother's in later years. He considered he had picked well.

The first time they had struck up a friendship was during last year's Fourth of July's Old Home Day Celebration. Everyone from miles around attended the big picnic at McCarty's Field across from the

Mitchell's home. Anna Louise had told him Mr. McCarty had given the site to the village as an athletic field for the town's ball players and a place to hold special events.

The event had been a day to remember, too. The train carried people in to attend the celebration from the surrounding areas, and the Federated Church next to the bank held a ham dinner. Anna Louise served everyone at the tables. He rallied the nerve to ask her to accompany him to the fireworks later that evening, and she had consented once she learned his entire family would be in attendance. Just being with her that day was like magic.

And it had nothing to do with the star-filled evening sky or the exploding fireworks display. Anna Louise glowed like an angel in the moonlight. He hoped having known her for a full year would open her eyes to his feelings.

Seth made a quick stop at McCarty and Payne's general store on the corner of Mill and Spencer Street to drop off Catherine's list for Miss Hyatt to fill while he stepped next door to the tonsorial. He wanted to look his best when he proposed to Miss Anna Louise Mitchell.

Seth felt like a million bucks when he finally knocked on the Mitchell's front door half an hour later. Their housekeeper, Macey Woodlow, greeted him at the door wearing a long black dress and a white apron with her springy black hair tied back with a red and black bandana. Macey was middle-aged and stout. She and her husband had earned their freedom from a southern plantation some years back, before many of the slaves were given their freedom. Many had funneled through the area coming from Montrose in Pennsylvania to various towns and villages throughout New York on their way to Canada where their southern masters had no jurisdiction over them.

Macey and her husband, Wilson, had long ago stopped carrying their cards. In fact, they were so well liked in Candor they were given jobs and had stayed on. Wilson was a blacksmith over at Brown's Livery. Seth had taken his horses there for shoeing a couple of times.

"I'll tell Miss Mitchell you've come, sir. Please, have a seat in the parlor."

He had just sat when the entrance way was filled with the presence of Anna Louise. Good Lord, her light blonde hair and blue eyes were unmistakably heavenly. Dressed in a sky-blue frock, her black shoes peeked out from under her skirt's folds as she walked toward him. Seth stood to meet her; his heart raced wildly. He took her hands, his eyes raised to meet hers. He swallowed.

"You look very lovely today, Anna Louise."

"Thank you, Seth. It's a surprise to see you. Come, let's sit by the window, and you can tell me why you've come."

She sauntered toward the wide bay overlooking the backyard. The alcove seat cushions were inviting. His smile deepened and his confidence rose as he contemplated sitting next to Anna Louise.

But she directed him instead to the two twin high-back cushioned chairs. A small mahogany coffee table was centered between them. Seth waited for her to be seated before he sat. He looked across at Anna Louise. She just couldn't get any lovelier.

No man should be so lucky.

"I will get to the point," Seth said. "I don't know

any other way to say this. I've come to declare my love for you, Anna Louise. I've come to ask for your hand in marriage. There. I've said it. I know this is sudden, so I'll give you some thinking time. Please don't take too long. You see, come September, Catherine will be leaving the farm to start her studies at the Academy. I need to have everything worked out by then. She shouldn't be missing out on her education. She's dreamed of being a teacher for years now, and this is her only opportunity."

Seth wrung his hands in anticipation of Anna Louise's answer. She was being awfully quiet. She nibbled her lips and brushed her hands down the front of her dress, then fluffed the folds out and around her ankles. Her sparkling eyes grew rounder, and the rouge on her cheeks rosier, just like those China dolls he'd seen in the novelty shops in Philadelphia. Lord, she was more than lovely; she was beautiful.

Seth rubbed his palms down the side of his pant legs to wipe the moisture from his shaking, sweaty hands. He didn't understand why she was being so hesitant. After all, he'd made her a fair offer. And he did love her as much as any man could love a beautiful lady.

Anna Louise stood, then stepped behind her chair where she rested her slim, smooth, delicate hands. She stood tall, her chin rose. She took a deep breath.

"I too have a dream, Seth. Just like Catherine. Should I give up my dream so Catherine can seek hers?"

Seth had no idea Anna Louise was interested in teaching. She was involved in many community organizations, but they'd never talked about teaching.

What could he say?

"I'm not willing to become a farmer's wife, Seth. I don't want to slop hogs, milk cattle, and throw seed to the hens. I can cook, but I'm not ready to have children of my own, let alone raise someone else's."

Seth jumped to his feet and stepped forward only to run his shin into the hard table blocking his way. "You don't love me as I love you?" He couldn't believe her. He was sure she reciprocated his feelings.

"I do like you Seth. Very much. Please believe me. I'd give up almost anything but this. I have to think of my future. I'm not ready to make the kind of commitment you seek, or to a way of life you want your wife to succumb. I'm not ready to live in the wilderness and give birth to one child after another. Why, the world is full of so much imbibing radicals already. Until we've rid this town of such dredges of society, I prefer not to have any children. And I want to be able to teach my own children to be better educated about such things. There is so much I want to learn and do. Taking care of a ready-made family would be detrimental to my own dreams. You just have to look at your mother's health to understand what I'm talking about."

Stunned was too mild a word. He loved Anna Louise, and he wanted to see her loveliness every single day for the rest of his life. He wanted to be able to hold her and kiss her and know she was his and would always be near.

Seth circled the table and took a step closer to Anna Louise. Her delicate fingers played with a dainty, white-lace hanky. She had misunderstood him. She must have.

"I don't drink, Anna Louise. And drink isn't what

sent my mother away. My father never drank when he was at home. I might not get to church every Sunday, after all I have a farm to tend. I think the good Lord would forgive me."

Seth took another step closer to Anna Louise. Anna Louise took a step backwards.

"Oh, Seth. I know you're a good man. I just want more for myself."

How could he convince her he loved her and didn't want to lose her? Didn't she know she was made for him?

"It's that women's group, isn't it? That…that… Women's Christian Temperance Union," Seth sputtered. "Those unions are breaking up the continent. Good Lord, men are fighting at work over unions, and women are fighting in homes because of them. What's to become of our nation?"

Seth was surprised when Anna Louise took his hands. They were soft and warm and made his hands feel huge.

"I'm sorry, Seth. I really am."

Her eyes implored him to understand. Her touch had his heart racing. The doorbell pealed long and loud. They jumped apart. Anna Louise's touch disappeared, leaving a cold hard lump in Seth's throat.

She'd withdrawn right before his eyes.

The door opened, and Mr. Linsky stood there, as if he'd been expected and was on time.

Mr. Linsky, a tall, prominent Polish immigrant, had made it big in the Catatonk area in lumbering. He was in his late twenties and worth a fortune. And obviously the man was sweet on Anna Louise, if the glare in his eyes at seeing the two of them together was anything to go by. Anna Louise turned a bright pink.

Was Anna Louise smitten with Mr. Linsky?

Seth drew Anna Louise into his arms and covered her lips with his in a kiss he hoped left nothing to chance. The deep, passionate kiss took Seth by surprise.

He set Anna Louise aside and walked past Mr. Linsky, almost knocking the burly man over on his way to the front door.

He climbed into his wagon and clicked the horses into motion, urging them toward home. His smile broadened. At least he had given Anna Louise something to think about.

Not to mention Mr. Linsky.

Chapter Seven

"The engineers refuse to sign a no-strike pledge. Scott wants to halt all westbound freights, and it's my job to put his plan into motion," Aderley told Charley. "Between the two of us, we have no choice but to follow Scott's directive."

Thankfully, the longshoremen at the New York harbor had returned to work. The strike scheduled for June twenty-seventh had been canceled, and the newly formed trainmen's union was in trouble. Still, dissention existed in the ranks.

Charley stood next to Aderley at the open window overlooking the entire rail yard, and several blocks of homes and businesses. The rumbling from the crowd down below was like a droning fan, masking the angry words filling the air. Even the loud clatter of the telegraph keys coming from Donahue's desk in the hallway office didn't hide the cries of outrage rising in anguish.

Charley lowered his head, heavy hearted, and turned to sit in the chair on the other side of Aderley's desk. Aderley sat in his massive leather chair, thumbs looped inside his vest pockets, his gold pocket-watch dangling loose. He drew in a hearty puff on his cigar, then exhaled a spiral of smoke toward the ceiling. The man looked exhausted, and the strike wasn't even in full swing.

"Pittsburgh's a workingman's town, Charles. They're blaming the trunk lines for their hard luck. Hell, with seventy-three glass factories alone, not to mention all the mills and oil refineries and coal mines in the area, those stern-wheelers are towing coal barges along the Allegheny and the Monongahela to the shores, daily. What do they have to complain about? Coal is still rolling in. They ought to be able to run their own operations regardless of the trains running or not."

"Pittsburgh is a noisy place for sure," Charley agreed. "You should be there when the gears, rollers, flywheels, steam hammers, and blast furnaces are in full bore. Smoke and steam billowing into the air." Charley shook his head. "There's constant noise with everything in motion. I'm glad to be well away from there, I can tell ya."

"Yes, those mill men are a burly, hardworking lot, and they know the success of winning a strike. They won't be easily taken down or stopped this time."

"Still, there won't be enough fuel coming in to operate their mills nor their homes for very long, if the trains don't run. Their allegiance is with the railroad workers," Charley reminded him.

"I hear the Pittsburgh division ordered all through freights to be run as double-headers on July sixteenth."

"As superintendent of the Pittsburgh division, Pitcairn has the final say. Just like Scott does here," Charley said. He puffed on his thin, half-smoked cigarette; the tip burned red, then a dark, charred tinge appeared.

"Double-heading two engines cuts labor costs and saves time," Aderley said as if Charley didn't know.

"It may be good for the engineers and firemen,"

Charley replied. "You need the same number of men to keep things going. The conductors and brakemen are the ones who lose their jobs."

Charley wasn't lost on the numbers. He wasn't Aderley's right-hand man for nothing. The ones left would have more work to do. They would have to tend to twice as many cars, which would make their job more dangerous with longer hours, not to mention less pay. More accidents were bound to happen when the workers were overtired.

"Hell, Charles, everyone understood the Trainmen's Union was dead. Even Pitcairn didn't expect this strike. It's sad, I tell you. Real sad. Damn if they haven't already called for our own militia to troop on over there and take care of business in Pittsburgh." Aderley paused, in deep thought. He leaned over the desk and pointed his finger at Charley. "I want you to go there right away. Find out what you can. If we can figure out what caused all the problems there, maybe we can stop things before they get out of hand here."

Charley took a moment to think about what Aderley was asking. He was right. Pittsburgh was ready to blow. If he didn't report back, he'd lose his own job. He took a puff on his cigarette and tamped the ashes against the large, black onyx ashtray on Aderley's desk. A half dozen smoke stubs lined the dish, a sure sign nerves were fraught with worry over the strike.

"I've been told the union has a number of Pinkerton agents as members," Charley mentioned. He'd been surprised the Pinkerton's would side with the strikers instead of the militia.

"Yeah. Hard to believe." Aderley shook his head. "Yet, the strike started on the Baltimore, and Ohio didn't stop the tramps from pouring into Pittsburgh in sympathy for the workers, too. They're out there now just drifting like sewer rats waiting for something to happen. I hear gangs of vagrants are wandering the streets anticipating the calm will erupt into pandemonium. Let me tell you, Charles, from what I hear, they'll be here before long, just to stir things up." He took another deep drag on his cigar and exhaled.

Aderley was right. Charley lit another cigarette, and the two of them paused to reflect on the possibilities of what was to come in Pittsburgh and how it would affect their situation in Philadelphia.

"Sam Muscle's president of the Pittsburgh division of the Trainmen's Union. Wasn't he aware of the build up?" Charley broke the silence. "What about Robert Ammon?"

"That's the sad part, I tell you. Everything was supposed to be under control. Hell, Muscle left town to take a job in the oil regions someplace. Even Pitcairn took his family to the Jersey seashore for a vacation. Who wanders off on vacation during a time of crisis, I ask you?" Aderley shook his head. "Well, Pittsburgh is in deep debt. They can't even borrow money from the state. They're all out of funds. Half the police force got fired due to lack of money to pay them. How can you control a strike with only eight men left on the force? People are flocking into town like locusts. The sooner you get over there and report back to me, the better. We don't want any tramps coming here and causing trouble."

"I'll see what I can do. Like you said, we don't have the mills and factories Pittsburgh does. One good thing in our favor right now."

"I've made the arrangements. You can leave by stagecoach this afternoon."

Charley wasn't surprised Aderley assumed he'd go without a fuss. Truth be told, if he could learn anything to help them here in Philadelphia, it would be worth the trip.

****

Charley arrived in Pittsburgh the following day to silent mills and closed businesses and factories. Only a small crowd of men blocked the crossing of an outgoing freight when he approached the rail yard. He headed for the hotel next to the station, had a bit of lunch, and then worked his way down to the yards. He'd just crossed the tracks when someone shouted into the stillness of the day.

"I'll turn that switch."

"We might as well die right here," someone else yelled out, only to be grabbed around the neck and held captive by an officer, and then dragged down the street.

Charley turned his head just in time to see another man get his eye blackened with a billy-club. Charley hung back; he didn't need to be involved and dragged off as well. Good Lord, the man hadn't done anything to deserve such a fate. He simply hadn't been fast enough in his escape.

The street was packed. The crowd gathered in size, voices raised. To the right, a small group of young boys began throwing stones. No one stopped them. Tension simmered all around Charley as he leaned up against the nearest building. It wouldn't take much for the powder keg of emotions to explode.

The blue-coats stormed the area and made short order of the unruly. Including the boys who threw stones. As more and more agitated people gathered, however, the police backed off.

Charley couldn't let the same thing happen in Philadelphia.

By late afternoon the crowd had grown to over two hundred. Men, women, and children, mere onlookers waiting to see what would transpire, lined the streets. Before long there were many more sympathizers than actual strikers.

Charley headed back to the hotel, an audible sigh escaping his tense lips.

He washed up, ate, and then returned to his room. He opened the window. The cool night air blew in and cleared out the staleness of the day. He unbuttoned his shirt and shrugged out of it, folding and placing it at the foot of the bed. A slight breeze blew across his bare chest, cool but refreshing. He stretched out on top of the covers and shut his eyes against the mayhem outside his window.

****

Charley woke to the sound of gunshots zinging into the evening sky. He rubbed his eyes and levered himself up against the headboard, then walked to the window. All was quiet. No sound of guns being fired. Had he been dreaming?

He lay back on the bed, but the sheet, hot and sweaty, clung to him. He sifted, rolled over on his side, punched at the pillow, and scrunched it up underneath his neck. The night air drifted in through the open window, cooler this time, but soothing against his exhausted and feverish body. He rolled over and settled in, hoping the dream wouldn't return.

Two pistol shots rang out in the still of the night.

Charley jumped from the bed and ran to the window, his head still fuzzy from sleep. More gunshots rang out. Screams rent the air. *Good, God!* He wasn't dreaming.

He slipped his shirt on over his head, stepped into his shoes, and raced out the door buttoning his shirt as he ran. He met a handful of men in the hotel lobby all rushing out of the building. Together they headed toward Liberty Street.

Crowds filling the street hampered Charley's progress. The people jostled him about, almost knocking him over twice. Eventually, he wound his way through the commotion to reach the front of the crowd. Had anyone been shot? No one appeared to be wounded. *Yet.*

The county sheriff stood atop a pile of lumber stacked to the side of the tracks, yelling at the rumbling, angry crowd in vain. The officer fired into the air to get the people's attention. A foolish mistake, in Charley's estimation. Any number of skittish strikers or sympathizers could have started shooting back if they had guns and a mind to. Thankfully, most of them didn't carry weapons.

"Take a walk, Coleman," someone called out above the yelling voices.

"We don't want no trouble from you," someone else shouted.

Others joined in. The sheriff climbed down from the make-shift platform and walked away, leaving an angry crowd ranting and raving.

The crowd refused to disperse and grew in numbers. Charley worked his way to the opposite side of the street and stood on a bench where he could watch without getting caught up in the mêlée.

When the sun rose over the mountains several hours later, not a single train ran. Engines were fired up, and rail crews were ready to go. The mob controlled the switches. They climbed aboard the trains, riding them back and forth between the stations at Twenty-Eighth Street and Torrens Station. Not a single passenger train was allowed to leave.

"Can ya believe it, chap. They've taken a loaded cattle car to the edge of town and let the dang livestock loose." The man on Charley's left laughed and slapped the sides of his legs in mirth. "That'll teach'em, it will."

Once again, Sheriff Coleman stood in the middle of the crowd trying to get them to disperse. Cries of 'Bread or Blood' roared over the sheriff's pleading.

"All you women take your children and go home," Coleman urged. "Get out of harm's way. Go home. We don't want anyone to get hurt. The militia's on their way. Go home."

"We won't be leaving our men to fight alone," several women yelled back. "We have nothing more to lose."

Unsuccessful at pleading with the masses to disperse, the chief left, defeated. When the militia arrived, he'd be back with the back-up necessary to help confront the situation.

Back in his room, Charlie stood at the hotel window. Thousands of people milled about, many of them looting and trashing storefronts. They lit fires in the middle of the street. Rioters threw goods from the stores they either didn't need or couldn't carry into the middle of the flames. Men who worked the rails, as well as women and children, walked in and out of the open storefronts grabbing whatever they could carry.

God Almighty, these people were just as needy here as they were back in Philadelphia.

How had things become so desperate?

Charley shook his head at the chaos an hour later, waiting for the militia to arrive. When the troops crested the horizon, they marched into town with bayonets raised. Charley cringed as they rushed straight into the crowd without impunity. A shot rang out, followed by more shots and shouts. Charley recoiled at the piercing, blood curdling screams. He closed his eyes, but the people's cries of pain penetrated his senses. More yelling, screaming, and now crying followed. Good Lord, he couldn't take much more.

Charley opened his watery eyes in time to see a man's big burly body go down. Then another. Two children were being shoved to the cobbled street, blood pooling from the sides of their faces. A mother's scream filled the air like banshees blowing down the lane. Charley shut his eyes at the mournful sound, but the vision, vivid and horrifying remained; the mother bent over her bloodied child. He sent up a silent thanks his family was nowhere near any of this chaotic bloodbath.

The crowd gathered like a million ants on a mission and forced the militia into the roundhouse despite their lack of weapons. There had to be fifty to seventy-five of them pushing the troops back. A flame shot up as several rail cars were engulfed by fire. Before he could catch his breath, the depot burst into flames. Yelling and screaming and cries of torment tore at his heart. He couldn't take another moment of the chaos and loss of life happening right before his eyes.

Aderley was right. Pittsburgh's mill town was

filled with a burly lot of men, young and old alike. Men and women and children. And despite the consequences, they stood up for what they believed in. The entire town, along with those who had come to support the workers and fight the militia, grew in numbers.

He needed to get back to Philadelphia and report to Aderley. A strike in Philadelphia was inevitable. Aderley was going to need all the reinforcements he could get as soon as he could get them.

How the hell were they going to stop the madness? How were they going to deal with the trouble coming their way? How in God's name were they going to keep the bloodshed from taking its toll in Philadelphia?

Charley hopped the next stagecoach back to Philadelphia hoping he would arrive before this bloodshed in Pittsburg beat him there.

****

The train curved into the countryside and chugged past dense forests. Emily wanted nothing more than to lay her head back and sleep. The steady motion of the train, however noisy, soothed her mind. Even the Aderley boys, usually squirming in their seats, had quieted. Marian Aderley's head bobbed back and forth with the motion of the train as it swayed westward toward Marshall, Michigan.

Emily's stomach grew queasy. She dozed uncomfortably.

"Mrs. Carmichael. Emily."

Emily woke to Marian Aderley's hand gently shaking her arm.

"I'm sorry, dear," Marian said. "We're nearing Detroit. It's our last connection. The conductor says we'll pick up the Chicago and Northwestern Line after we eat. We'll be able to get out and stretch our legs and walk around a bit."

Emily's head buzzed with the lack of sleep. Half an hour later, the train stopped at the depot. Emily stretched before following the others outside into the bright, hot sunshine. After the initial hustle and bustle, things settled down, and the passengers were ushered into a small dining hall for a noonday meal.

"That's Mrs. Young sitting at the far table with the baby." Marian leaned across their table and whispered to Emily.

Emily glanced across the room to find a young mother holding a tiny bundle in protective arms, a broad smile shining lovingly down at her child. The mother's face looked pale, her light brown hair brushed back into a knot on the top of her head. Her maroon frock with lace around the neckline was simple.

"When did they board?" Emily asked.

"Oh, my dear, they've been with us since Philadelphia. The baby has been such a dear," Marian said. "She must be a very loving mother to manage her child so well."

"I've not heard a peep out of the child. Are you sure they've been traveling with us?"

"Oh, yes, poor dear. I conversed with her while you slept the other day. She confided in me. Said her husband was killed in some kind of accident. Farming, I believe she said."

"She looks a bit frail."

"Yes. So tragic. Leaving the poor woman without a means of support. And with a child, too, poor thing."

"What of her family?"

"Said she has none to speak of, poor, poor dear. A child herself."

Emily looked over at the young mother. Her eyes settled on the small bundle. If only her Sarah were with her now so she could cuddle her. Eyes bright and blurry, Emily lowered her head to hide the tears threatening to spill onto her cheeks. But she needn't have bothered hiding them. Marian tried to settle a dispute between her boys who had grown tired of remaining still for so long only to have to sit at a table and mind their manners. She couldn't imagine her own boys sitting still for so long, either.

By the time Marian had her sons under control, Emily had wiped the tears away with unsteady fingertips. The urge to go to Mrs. Young and ask to hold the baby was almost vital.

In an effort to take her mind off her family, Emily looked around at the other passengers as they filed into the dining hall. She found it difficult to concentrate and had all she could do to lift the fork to her mouth to eat the food in front of her.

Lord, she was more than ready for this journey to end.

After the lunch, Emily stayed behind to enjoy a cup of tea while Marian ushered her boys outside so they could run off their pent-up energy before boarding the train. The dining hall emptied of many of the passengers. Emily smiled as two elderly women approached. They had boarded the train at the last stop and sat several seats behind her, across the aisle. The ladies were as different as day and night. Possibly in their late fifties, they had a vitality Emily envied.

"Hello, dearie, I'm Pansy Weaver and this is my

sister Violet. I hope you don't mind if we sit and have tea with you." Pansy set her cup and saucer down and pulled a chair out at the same time. "It's such a shame about our Mrs. Young losing her husband at such an early age. Why, what gumption she has traveling alone to such a God-forsaken place as the West."

"Now Violet, it's not God-forsaken else we wouldn't be traveling it ourselves, now would we? Pay her no never mind." She waved her hand at her sister, then sipped her tea. "Why, we enjoy an adventure just as much as the next person. Ain't that right?"

"So, Mrs. Carmichael, what's your story? Everyone has a story." Pansy bit into a pastry that looked as if it'd been in her bag for days.

"Pansy," Violet gushed. "You should not be so rude. Now Mrs. Carmichael, pay her no mind. You don't have to answer if you don't have a mind to."

Emily's insides warmed at the exchange between the two women. "I don't mind," she told them. "There isn't much to tell. I'm on my way to stay with my cousin in the northern California Territory. I've been ill and need the rest from my family."

"Tell us about your family, then, dearie," Pansy encouraged. "It must be hard to leave them behind."

Emily took a deep breath. The sisters had no idea how unbearable it had been to step on the train in Candor with her children in tears, waving goodbye and not knowing if she'd ever see them again. With a heavy heart, she shared her family with the two inquisitive sisters.

Before long the train whistle blew and the conductor called 'all aboard.' Once everyone was on the train and settled, the locomotive jerked forward, slowly at first, then worked up steam and a steady, rocking pace. They crossed the steam-powered drawbridge over the mile-wide Mississippi and the pleasant and prosperous lands of Iowa. Emily's head drooped and nodded uncomfortably with the motion of the train. When the conductor stopped by to chat with the Aderley boys, she managed to sit up so as not to appear rude.

"This here's Council Bluffs, a real bustling city," the conductor told Jonathan and Jason. The man had kept the boys busy with tales about each of the locations they passed through to help keep them occupied. "Lewis and Clark held council with the Indians here not so long ago, ya know."

Jonathan's and Jason's eyes shot up at the mention of Indians.

"Will we see an Indian?" Jason asked. "Will they shoot at us with their bow and arrows? I've never seen a real Indian before."

"Now boys," Marian admonished. "Of course we won't be seeing any Indians. I told you we have nothing to worry about on this trip. Indians have been civilized for some time. They don't attack people, do they, sir?" She looked to the conductor for confirmation.

Emily hoped Marian was right. They still had a ways to go without having to worry about an Indian attack.

The two boys became subdued once again, and she welcomed the quiet as the afternoon disappeared. She rested her head against the window and shut her eyes. Her arms and legs were as limp and as heavy as bed sheets on wash day thanks to the medicine she had taken back in Detroit.

"My dear," Marian nudged her in a soft, caring voice. "Why don't you find your berth and have a good rest? The sleeping car on this train isn't too far back; you can settle in for the night. Let me call the conductor."

"Thank you, Marian, I appreciate your concern."

****

By the time they got to the endless flats of Nebraska and Wyoming the next day, Emily was past caring what the outside vistas held in store. Others on the train became restless, too. Mrs. Aderley and her children were in conversation, and even she looked annoyed.

Having had enough of the confinement of the sitting car, Emily stood, gathered her gingham skirt with one hand, and using the other, balanced herself against the rocking of the train on her way to the observation car. Careful so as not to trip down the carpeted aisle, she made her way toward the back of the coach, not an easy feat with the swaying of the train.

The older gentleman with a long gray beard and mustache she'd learned was a Mr. O'Leary, sat hunched against the window, his hat down over his eyes at a comical angle. As Emily passed him, she clutched the back of his seat for support. Just then the man snorted, and her hand flew to her bosom. Lord, was she ever going to survive this trip?

She hadn't paid much attention to the other passengers, but she took the time now to observe a few of them. This man's hat had ridden even farther down over his face, and his snoring was making the cap flap up and down. Catching her balance, she once more made her way to the observation car. This time her eyes settled on Mrs. Young who was trying to pacify her infant, now crying loud enough to wake the dead. So much for a contented baby. Head bent, the young mother nuzzled the infant, cooing in a vain attempt to quiet her child. Emily resisted the urge to comfort the babe herself.

The narrow passage between cars rocked back and forth over the couplings of the train as it clacked along the tracks, making walking between the cars dangerous. Emily looked straight ahead and made her way over the length between the cars. The breeze from the open car tugged at her hair. She brushed at the errant tendrils as they sprang loose from under her bonnet. She took in a deep, steadying breath and sank into one of the observation seats where she was afforded an unobstructed view of the Wasatch Rocky Range.

"We're just north of Salt Lake City," Marian said from behind her. "Just look at those snow-capped mountains. Aren't they majestic? I hope you don't mind my joining you. I decided I needed some fresh air."

Emily rested her arms alongside the open window and leaned her chin on them for support. The sight was wondrous. Although the majestic mountain tops were covered in snow, the desert they passed through bloomed in a rainbow of colors. Instead of seeing herds of bison she'd anticipated, prairie dogs popped in and out of holes and frolicked everywhere. And the weather had changed. No longer cool or damp, the dry, warm air relaxed her. The desert, despite the delicate, wispy flowers, looked as if it hadn't seen rain in months.

Emily breathed in the fresh scents; warm and filling the senses, a welcome change from the stuffy, odorous passenger car. The smell of the kerosene lanterns had become nauseating over the past several days. Would she ever get the odor out of her clothes? They were sure to reek for months.

The Aderley boys had followed their mother, as well, and were leaning over the side of the car, counting the prairie dogs. Up ahead, Emily spotted a huge wooden trestle in the bend of the tracks. They would soon be going over the bridge. A frightening-looking contraption, the trestle resembled corn stalks and bean poles in late harvest. Was it safe? Sturdy enough to carry the long, heavy, iron locomotive as it thundered along the tracks? Why, there had to be at least a mile long drop off to the canyon floor on either side.

Jason and Jonathan spotted the canyon and jumped up and down as they pointed with glee. Their words and laughter were drowned out over the roar of the train as it sped along the rails.

Emily stood, ready to go back inside, then turned to let Marian know of her intentions.

"Marian, I... *Marian!*" Emily exclaimed. The woman frowned, her cheeks pale despite the two bright spots of rouge on her smooth cheeks. "What is it, Marian? What's wrong?" The worry in her travel companion's eyes didn't hide the sparkle of blue, a perfect match to her bright flowered hat and the fine organdy dress of sky blue. The hem billowed in the breeze. But something was wrong.

"We're stopping," Marian said. "We can't get over the trestle. Look." She pointed. "There's something in the way."

The boys gave a hoot, then jumped up and down. "Now we can get off the train. We can explore," the older of the two yelled, a wide smile taking up most of his face, his long blond bangs clinging to his forehead. He had the same blue eyes as his mother's, only his eyes sparkled with merriment in the bright afternoon sunshine. Not distress.

"Do you think we'll see Indians?" the youngest asked, his excitement obvious.

Emily scanned the area. A large object blocked the rails. The train slowed to a crawl. But nothing in the vastness indicated imminent danger. Seth had told her Billy the Kid and the James Brothers were still on the loose. She wondered if they still robbed trains. Were they responsible for the blocked bridge? Stories had grown rampant back east as the rails out west carried goods and money to banks. The tabloids had reported many times both had not made it past the Rockies.

Mrs. Aderley laid a hand on Emily's shoulder. "Now, don't you worry, Mrs. Carmichael. I'm sure everything will be fine. The engineers know what to do in such cases."

Emily prayed Marian Aderley was right.

Chapter Eight

Seamus' wife, Maggie, and her twelve-year-old daughter, Madeline, journeyed overnight on the stagecoach traveling through the Montrose Turnpike. Seth greeted them when they arrived, having spotted them with ease, seeing as they were the only mother and daughter alighting from the stage. Mrs. Flanagan wore a yellow frock with a matching bonnet. Madeline, a shorter version of her mother, was dressed the same, only without the hat—a riot of fiery red locks. And from their looks, they both appeared as if they'd seen better days. The young girl wasn't holding up any better than her mother.

After introductions, Seth gathered the Flanagan's cases and loaded them and their travel trunk onto the wagon.

"I've arranged tea at the Spinning Wheel just down the street," Seth informed Seamus' wife. "It's not far, but you'll want to ride on over. You look licked after your long journey."

"If ya don't mind, I'd like to walk a bit after being cooped up in this contraption." Mrs. Flanagan waved his concern away.

"If you're sure, Ma'am," Seth said. "I can take your daughter with me, if you like."

"No need. Just be pointing us in the right direction."

"You cross the street right here, then walk straight up the boardwalk to the left until you come to the Spinning Wheel. There's a sign on the front of the building. You can't miss it. I'll lead the horses and wagon around so you won't have to walk all the way back to the station."

Seth had the wagon and horses hitched to the post outside the Spinning Wheel before the Flanagan's arrived. He waited for them as they walked down the street, then helped the Missus up the front steps.

The Spinning Wheel, a cozy tea-room and small hotel, catered to wintertime boarders from neighboring farms and students attending the academy. In the summer months, residents found the inn a relaxing place to eat. He figured Mrs. Flanagan and her daughter might like a bite and a chance to relax in refined surroundings before they traveled to the farm. His two charges appeared fragile and pale after their long and tiring trip. Why, Mrs. Flanagan's daughter's head had been just a-bobbing up and down as her mother towed her down the street to the tearoom.

Seth opened the door and let the ladies precede him inside. When he entered, he spotted Anna Louise Mitchell first thing. She sat on the far side of the room opposite the door with none other than Mr. Linsky.

Seth's heart dropped to his feet.

Anna Louise, hearing the tinkle of the bell over the door, looked at him. Her mouth dropped open, then shut immediately. Her face turned crimson, but she didn't look away. She hadn't expected to see him either.

Seth smiled, gave a curt nod, lowered his eyes, and continued to see his new charges to a table; as far away from Anna Louise and Mr. Linsky as he could manage.

The establishment wasn't very roomy, so he didn't get far.

Despite his consternation at being in the same room, Seth covered his displeasure as best he could so as not to alarm the Flanagan's.

Their waitress, Amanda Huff, rushed to their table and handed them a small hand-printed menu.

"How are you, Seth?" Her sparkling personality was lost on him today. "Is Catherine studying hard for her exams?"

"Not since Ma left. She hasn't had time," Seth said.

"I'm here now to help the family," Mrs. Flanagan cut in. "She'll have plenty of time. I'll see to it; don't you be fretting none."

"Amanda, this here is Mrs. Seamus Flanagan and her daughter, Madeline, from Philadelphia. They're going to be staying at the farm for the summer."

"Please. Ya can be calling me Maggie, dear." She turned to Seth with a smile, then back to Amanda. "Like I said, I'll be making sure Seth's sister has plenty of time to study. What about you? Are you preparing for them, too?"

"I have a job right here. Me and Jed Huckle are just about engaged." Her smile broadened.

"Tell Jed I said hi," Seth said. He didn't know much about Jed other than the boy was a hard worker at the flour mill. Seth wouldn't be surprised if he didn't become manager one of these days.

"So, what can I get for you today? Are you interested in a meal, or one of our special berry pies and tea?"

"Just tea and maybe a biscuit for me and my daughter, thank you."

"Seth?"

"I'll have the pie."

After they had given their order, Seth couldn't help himself but glance over at Anna Louise. Yep. She watched him; their gazes met. He caught the glow of her cheeks a moment before she lowered her eyes and turned back around. Seth seethed as Mr. Linsky leaned across the table and took hold of Anna Louise's gloved hands, then looked at him. Seth gritted his teeth. The burly man's tactics worked. Anna Louise's attention was once again drawn back to the wealthy lumberman.

"She's such an adorable girl," Maggie said.

"Yes, she is," Seth agreed. Mrs. Flanagan was talking about Amanda, but Seth meant Anna Louise.

Seth's chest ached. For the first time ever, he discovered loneliness in a room full of people. Anna Louise should belong to him, not that old duffer who sat across the table from her.

Seth didn't consider himself mean spirited, but right now he would enjoy punching Mr. Linsky in the nose. He so badly wanted to talk sense into Anna Louise. Mr. Linsky wasn't the man for her. No sir!

He was the man for Anna Louise. Seth. No one else.

He just had to figure out how to convince Anna Louise.

"I'm sorry to be putting you to so much trouble, my dear boy. Your pa said as how you would be able to set things up for us. We won't be much bother, Madeline and me. For certain we want to be a big help to the family, if we may. I can be helping Catherine with the housework and cooking. Madeline is real good with the young'uns."

He hadn't heard much of what she had said, his mind on Anna Louise. Catching the last few words, Seth hoped he hadn't missed anything important.

"That's right kind of you. Please, don't worry. Get settled in and rest for a day or two and then we'll talk," Seth told her. "I'm sure Catherine will be more than happy for your help around the house. Pa said the strike was heating up something fierce."

Seth's change in topic upset Mrs. Flanagan. He was sorry, but he needed to know what was going on. If there were going to be a nation-wide strike, he would have to find another means of transporting his milk and goods. He had picked up more business recently, and if the trains stopped running, he would lose money, not to mention time and effort.

The family would be able to survive the winter if they were careful. But he couldn't stop fretting. Why, just worrying about Catherine's schooling, the farm, his mother out west, and the strike in Philadelphia, and now Anna Louise...

Seth ran his hands through his hair that had been tossed by the breeze while driving across town. Maybe he should be the one put in an institution—not his mother. If Anna Louise had accepted his offer of marriage, all of his problems would be taken care of.

Didn't she realize how much he needed her? Loved her?

"...so we had to leave as soon as possible without making a fuss," Mrs. Flanagan said. "I'm looking forward to spending time in the country with these delightful rolling hills like the green fields of my Ireland. Seamus assured me and Madeline we'd love the New York countryside so much we wouldn't be wanting to go back home to our small tenement flat in Philadelphia."

Once again Seth hadn't listened to a word Seamus' wife had said. They had been served tea and pie, and he hadn't even been aware. The Flanagans had done a fair job cleaning their plates. He had to stop thinking about Anna Louise or his whole life wasn't going to be worth a tinker's damn.

Seth cleaned his plate and wiped his mouth and hands on the dainty cloth napkin. "We should be leaving, Ma'am. By the time we hit the turnoff to head up the hill to the homestead, the darkness will have settled in. The first mile up is kinda bumpy, but then it gets better. There are extra blankets for you to sit on to cushion the bumps."

Not able to leave the Spinning Wheel without taking one last look at Anna Louise, Seth turned only to find her facing in the opposite direction. He shook his head, shut the door behind them, and walked down the two steps to the boardwalk. He heaved a deep sigh, then led Seamus' family across the street to the waiting wagon. There was a hole the size of a cannon ball in his chest where his heart should be. Farming might be his calling, but love, on the other hand, didn't seem to be his destiny.

Seth settled Mrs. Flanagan and her daughter in the wagon and jumped up beside them. With no room in the back for Madeline to rest because of their large trunks, the young girl sat between her mother and Seth. Before long, she was fast asleep with her head resting across her mother's knees.

Thankful for Mrs. Flanagan's silence, Seth's mind was filled with Anna Louise, who sat in a tearoom with another man.

The kiss they had shared the other day proved she had feelings for him. Didn't it? She had responded to his advances. Didn't she? Maybe she was upset with him because of the way he proposed. And if truth be told, he had botched it good. He guessed he shouldn't have started out by telling her all about his problems at home. About Catherine wanting to come into town to become a teacher. About his needing a wife to help out at the farm. Telling her he loved her would have been enough. The rest would have taken care of itself. He was certain of it.

Next time he was in town he'd stop by and make sure Mr. Linsky wasn't around, or likely to show up. Then he'd declare himself to Anna Louise properly. He'd explain Mrs. Flanagan was on hand, now, and Anna Louise wouldn't have the responsibilities of the children or have to do any of the farm chores if she didn't have a mind to.

All she had to do was be his wife.

That settled, Seth concentrated on making the turn up the rutted road to the farm. Madeline moaned, lifted her head to get comfortable, and then settled back down in her mother's lap. Driving the rig up the hill to the homestead always gave Seth a sense of belonging. He had to admit he loved working the farm. Even though his father didn't like farm life as such, deep down where it counted, farming was a better way of life than working the rails.

Seth thanked God every night before he shut his eyes he wouldn't have to work the rails alongside his father, as many young men were forced to do just to make ends meet. He had clean fresh air every day, plenty of food on the table, and the freedom to wander their eighty acres of fine producing soil and pasture land. So far, everything was paying for itself.

The kerosene lamp in the kitchen sent a golden glow through the window as Seth drew up to the front of the house. Catherine was kneading dough on the kitchen table when they walked in. The smell of warm yeast filled the room.

Anna Louise should be the one standing in the kitchen kneading dough. Anna Louise should be the one waiting for *him*.

Seth didn't have much time to dwell on his problems. He helped Mrs. Flanagan and her daughter into the house.

"Catherine, this here is Mrs. Maggie Flanagan and her daughter Madeline. Is their room ready? They're right tuckered out after their long travels."

"I don't mean to be no trouble," Mrs. Flanagan told Catherine. "Any place to lay my head for the night will do. We can work everything out tomorrow. My Madeline is a wee bit tired, though, so I would appreciate a place for her to be settling in for the night."

"No trouble," Catherine said, wiping her hands on her ruffled apron. Her hair was pulled back in a long single braid, and damp tendrils hung around her flushed, tired face. "I've arranged our parents' room for the two of you. It's ready now. There's fresh water from the well on the stand, and a chamber pot in the far corner. I'll have Seth go and get your travel bag. We can sort out the rest of the baggage tomorrow."

Without another word, Seth hefted the travel bags from the wagon, carried them inside, and laid them at the foot of the bed.

"Good night, Ma'am." He tipped his hat and left them to it.

Seth returned outside to tend to the horses and wagon, then led them to the barn. Before going in for the night, he checked on the other animals, making sure his brothers had settled them properly.

His feet dragged and scuffed at the dry path between the barn and the house. Truth be told, he wasn't about to get much sleep tonight even though he was tuckered out. Just thinking about Anna Louise was sure to keep him awake. He was going to have to find a good reason to get back into town soon so he could get her alone, and set things straight.

****

After a near sleepless night, Seth woke to the smell of fresh perked coffee and flapjacks cooking on the wood stove. He threw on his barn clothes and headed for the kitchen only to find Mrs. Flanagan standing at the stove fixing breakfast.

"Well, now, Seth. Good morning to ya. Be sitting yerself down and helping yerself to some of my special griddlecakes. 'Tis a special recipe I saved from the old country, and if I do say so, they always disappear before I'm done making them. Would you be liking some coffee with those?"

"They smell real good." Seth sat, and Mrs. Flanagan placed a large plate of cakes in front of him. He cut into them with his fork and shoved a heaping helping into his mouth. They were as tasty as they smelled. He was half done with his plateful before he offered his appreciation.

"It's kind of you to go to so much trouble. Are you always up so early? Everyone around here sleeps in 'til

I get back from the barn."

"Well now, I figured as how you shouldn't be going to the barn on an empty stomach. Give Catherine a rest for a change, as well. She looked mighty tired last night after making bread. And the wee one woke up a few times. A girl like Catherine shouldn't have to be worrying about young'uns at her age. I can see I arrived at just the right time to help. Now finish your coffee and be off with ya. The chores are waiting, I'm sure."

So much for the quiet Mrs. Flanagan. The woman didn't give a person a chance to say a word. Her cooking, however, made up for her non-stop chatter.

****

Charley arrived in Philadelphia as the sun set. He was ready to tell Aderley what had happened in Pittsburgh but discovered much of the news had already broken in Philadelphia. The telegraph spread news quickly these days.

"What a blood bath," Aderley shouted when Charley knocked on his door. "Damn it, Charles, we can't let that happen here. Get the men together, and we'll see what we can do. Get down there and talk to them. Calm them down. Find out what's going on. I don't want a shooting mess on our hands."

Charley left the station office at a run. Tired or not, he had to talk to the men. They'd be congregating at the Blue Bottle at the end of the block.

Charley didn't trust Donahue. He had spotted the dirty weasel talking to the fellas down behind the roundhouse on several occasions. He'd also caught him talking to Seamus a couple of times, but Seamus wasn't falling for the man's claptrap.

The Blue Bottle was crowded and hazy blue from

cigarette and cigar smoke. The name of the tavern was an apt description. He found Seamus leaning against the bar. Charley sidled up to him and offered him a cigarette. Seamus' hands shook as he reached for the smoke.

"What's going on, Seamus?"

"I hear it's bad in Pittsburgh. What if the miners from Shawnee come here to do battle and stir up trouble? We'd have a massacre on our hands, too, we would. They like to stick their noses in where it does no good."

"Listen, Seamus. This isn't the only line having trouble. It's bad in Ohio, too. Hell, it's all around us. Up in Cincinnati, in Erie, in Buffalo, and even in Baltimore. Heaven help us, it's all over the place. I just finished talking with Aderley. What a mess. Pittsburgh was a blood bath. I've seen it myself. Just got back an hour ago. We have to keep things here under control. The militia didn't fare too well in Pittsburgh, and it's going to be hard for them to show their faces here. But they'll come. They'll be looking to prove themselves, they will. We better be mighty careful what we stir up. We don't want our women and children killed like they were in Pittsburgh."

Charley puffed on his cigarette, his eyes watering just thinking about the child having been beaten and bloodied. The picture was still vividly etched in his mind.

"I understand Secretary of War McCrary is going to represent Aderley and Scott. For God's sake, General Dodge and Tom Scott have McCrary in their pockets." Charley combed his hand through his hair. He looked at Seamus. "I tell you they have powerful people on the books. We can't win this one with such men of power."

"If we don't fight back, Charley, we give them the power. We have to unite. The entire population of Philadelphia is behind us. You saw the way they supported us the other day."

"You didn't see what I did in Pittsburgh. Women and children bleeding all over the streets. The looting and disregard for each other."

Seamus looked at Charley and shook his head.

"They might just as well be murdered in the streets for all the good it'll do them without a means of pay."

Charlie blinked at Seamus' words. Had it come to this? Donahue had muddied the waters this time. But if he was honest with himself, he'd admit Seamus was right. He didn't know what more he could say except to warn everyone about what was headed their way. They needed to be better prepared for the consequences of their actions.

"Why don't you go on home, Seamus. I want to talk to a couple other men before I take you up on your offer to stay at your place. They have to know what I saw. Maybe then they'll see reason and at least keep their women and children at home where they'll be safe."

Seamus tamped his cigarette out on the plank-board floor already littered with a wealth of cigarette butts. It was a wonder the place didn't go up in flames from the number of cigarettes half-stomped out by a booted foot, embers still glowing.

****

Charley left the tavern and everyone to their own disgruntled contemplations much later. He hadn't gotten anyone to listen. For once the Irish, Hungarians,

Poles, and Scots were getting along; all agreeing to strike.

He walked the three blocks to Seamus' house, the kerosene street lanterns casting a yellow, hazy glow along the dark plank board walkway on the side of the dirt street. The leaves on the trees shadowed his steps, and an uncomfortable feeling had him looking over his shoulder. Nothing jumped out at him on his way to Seamus' tenement. He let out a sigh of relief and walked up the five steps to the front door, a small home attached to a row of homes along the street. They were narrow, two story, drab, townhouses. Charley had no trouble recognizing company issue. He and his family had lived in one for far too long. Each house was the same inside. A narrow hallway led back into a small living room area with a kitchen off to the side. A fruit cellar in the stone-walled basement along with a tiny area with a bathtub and a commode off to one corner. The second floor housed two bedrooms. At least they had windows in each room to let in air during the hot summer days. In the small, narrow yard, there was just enough room for a garden and a clothes line. They were lucky they had running water.

Charley knocked on the door. No answer. He wasn't surprised. Seamus had no doubt already gone to bed. He let himself in, but before he could take a single step, his foot struck an object on the floor. He swung the door wider, letting the light from the street lantern in so he could see what was blocking his entrance.

Lord. God. Almighty.

Seamus lay sprawled on his side. Blood trickled down the side of his face—his swollen eyes already turning an ugly shade of purple. This was no simple fall. Seamus had been beaten and left for dead.

Charley bent down and put his fingers to Seamus' neck. The man was just about breathing, his heartbeat weak. But at least he was alive.

"Holy, Mary, Mother of God, Seamus. You poor soul. Who did this to you?" He nudged his friend, hoping for a response, but Seamus was beyond speaking.

Careful not to hurt him further, he rolled Seamus over onto his back. Seamus grunted, then fell silent. Charley kicked the front door shut and locked it, then checked his friend's breathing again. He ran his fingers over the prone body to check for broken bones; there were none. Charley sighed, took a deep breath, and slid his hands under Seamus' armpits and dragged him into the living room. Seamus wasn't a big man, but he was dead weight. Charley drew in another deep breath, hefted him over his shoulder, and then laid him on the settee.

Seamus grunted once again as his body sank into the soft, plump cushions.

Dear Lord, don't let there be any internal injuries.

Charley ran to the kitchen, pumped water from the dry sink into a pan, and grabbed a wash cloth and towel to take back to the sitting room. He washed the blood away from his friend's face and discovered a large cut above Seamus' right eye and one on his chin. Both continued to ooze. Charley figured Seamus' nose was broken, so he took his thumb and forefinger on either side in an effort to realign it while Seamus was still unconscious. Seamus' eyes flew open, then shut on another gasping moan. The man's body went limp.

Charley cleaned Seamus as best he could while his

friend was out cold, then covered the battered man with the quilt he found thrown over the edge of the sofa. When he bent to retrieve the soiled water and rag, a hand shot out and grasped his wrist. The water sloshed over the side of the basin.

"What happened?" Seamus demanded. "Why do I feel like I've been hit by one of them damn trains?"

Seamus started to sit up, but Charley placed a hand on his chest and coaxed him back down against the cushions with his free hand while he set the bowl back on the floor.

"Hold up friend. Take it easy," he said. "What happened here? Looks like someone did a once-over on you, twice. Did you see who did this?"

Seamus sat back and took a couple of deep breaths before answering.

"No. But for sure there was more than one. At first I figured they thought I was you, but they told me to tell you if you didn't side with them, you'd be next."

"I'm sorry, Seamus." Charley rubbed his hand over his face. "I never meant this to happen to you. Donahue is more than likely still upset with me over our scuffle the other day."

"I can't imagine what would have happened had Maggie and Madeline still been here. Likely beaten them as well, they would. I'm thankful I let you talk me into sending them north to be with your family. They grabbed me from behind just as I entered the house. They were inside waiting. Someone hauled my hands behind my back, and the other did the dirty work. I didn't see much after the first punch."

"Looks like they messed up the house just for fun." Charley looked around at the chaos all around them.

Sofa cushions were scattered on the floor. Newspapers lay in a heap on the end table. Coffee cups, dinner plates, and beer bottles were everywhere.

"Nawh," Seamus drawled, a lopsided grin on his beaten face. "T'was me made the mess, I'm embarrassed to say. I'm in and out so much I don't keep up like my Maggie does. A bit of a slob, I am. My head throbs like hell." Seamus rubbed the palm of his hand over a lump on his temple and lay back against the arm rest and the crocheted doily.

"You were lucky they didn't kill you. How's your nose?"

Seamus winced. "A bit bruised and tender. I don't think it's broken."

"I straightened it while you were out cold."

"I don't recall a thing, thank the Lord. You know, Charley, you'd better be more careful yourself. If they can sneak up on me, they'll have no trouble coming after you, too. If they suspect you're staying here tonight, we might both be lying on the floor."

"You're right. Although I expect they won't be back. I'll secure things just in case the bums decide to finish the job. You stay right here. I'll fix us some coffee and something to eat in a minute."

Charley didn't dally. He checked all the doors and windows, then prepared a simple meal of fried potatoes and coffee. Seamus' store of food was as low as everyone else's in the city. With Maggie gone, there was no fresh baked bread in the house, either.

Charley placed the fried potatoes in front of Seamus, who had propped himself up against the cushions. Charley then dished himself up a plateful and sat in the overstuffed chair next to the settee and joined his friend. The two ate in silence.

Finished eating, Charley cleaned up the kitchen and then the two of them prepared to settle down for the night. It didn't take Seamus long to fall fast asleep right where Charley had laid him.

Charley did another quick check around the house. Seamus was snoring loud enough to bring the house down when Charley returned to make sure he was okay for the night. He then climbed the stairs and found a small tidy bedroom. He lay on top of the quilt he was sure Seamus' wife had stitched. It reminded him of the one on his and Emily's bed in Candor.

Sleep was impossible. He tossed and turned and lay awake contemplating the recent events in Philadelphia and Candor. Was this nightmare ever going to end?

Would they all survive?

And at what cost?

Chapter Nine

The shrill blast of the train whistle filled the empty desert. The forlorn sound reverberated against the wall of the distant mountains and hung in the air.

Emily, Marian, and her boys leaned around the corner of the observation car to see what was happening up ahead. The monstrous black engine had stopped. The cow-catcher landing within arm's length of three wooden ties stacked on top of each other across the tracks in front of the trestle.

The Aderley boys were the first to jump off the train before their mother could stop them, their excitement evident at a new adventure. Their confinement of the past few days found them running faster than mustangs on an open range. But before they could go too far, the conductor's loud bellow stopped them in their tracks.

"Whoa, there, laddies. You ain't thinking 'bout crossing this here bridge are ya? There's a hole in it as big as a Chinaman's laundry pot. We don't want ya to be slipping down through it. It's a long ways to the bottom, it is."

Jonathan and Jason looked from the conductor to the bridge and back again, their curiosity piqued. Emily could tell the boys wanted to walk right up to the gaping hole halfway across the trestle.

A white-gloved porter stepped forward and helped

Marian down the steep iron steps to the hot desert floor where she proceeded to scold her sons.

Emily waited her turn for assistance down off the railcar. Behind her, Elizabeth Young, with her sound asleep baby in tow, was next. The snoring passenger, Mr. O'Leary, followed. He wore his chesterfield with a velvety black collar a bit wrinkled and out of place in the heat of the afternoon. He rubbed his eyes, squinting in the blinding sunlight overhead, and yawned. He nodded to Emily, then wandered a ways from the steel rails and hissing train. The porter helped the sisters, Pansy and Violet Weaver down next. They straightened their hats and smoothed their skirts when they stepped away from the train onto the dry earth, their thick-heeled shoes digging into the coarse, sandy soil.

Others climbed down, fanning themselves against the arid desert heat. Emily's gingham dress clung to her legs, her skin damp from perspiring. She ruffled the hem hoping for a bit of air to cool her body. But her skirts flapped back against her legs, making it difficult to find relief.

The train gave a final burst of steam. A billow of sooty smoke rose quickly, then drifted back down. The silence was heaven. No loud clicking of the train wheels, or loud steam hissing from the monster locomotive. Emily soaked up the silence and made her way toward the edge of the steep ravine, being mindful not to get too close. She could see the trestle in the bend up ahead. Nothing looked amiss at this angle. She looked down into the ravine to her left. The great gushing river far below churned and twisted as it made its way along its well-worn path.

Emily longed for a cool drink of water. Even a cup

of Sassafras tea would go a long way to help reduce her fever, which had spiked with the heat. She dabbed at the moisture on her forehead. The hot sun baked down on them with no relief in sight. Emily wiped her brow and sighed. She stretched her back and momentarily wondered what it would feel like to submerge her weary body in the flowing river down below to relieve her aches and pains. She took a step closer.

The conductor shouted to the crowd. "Stay close to the train. Do not wander too far away. We'll telegram ahead for assistance."

She froze. His loud voice drew her back.

How long would they have to wait for help to arrive way out here in the middle of nowhere?

"You expect us to simply sit down and wait for help to come from the other side of Weber Canyon?" one of the passengers called out.

"Why not turn around and go back to the last town?" Mr. O'Leary asked.

"Impossible," the conductor said. "We have no means of turning this locomotive around. Besides, the coal supply is too low, and there isn't a water tower close by to get enough steam going."

"There's plenty of water down below," another passenger spoke up, pointing down at the flowing river.

"Won't do us any good, sir. Like I said, the coal supply is low, and we can't get turned around."

Mumbles from the crowd ensued. Emily crossed to Marian's side as Jonathan and Jason made a mad dash toward the edge of the ravine. But before their mother could stop them, Mr. O'Leary called out to them.

"Boys, you don't want to be getting too close. You go over the edge, and there's no telling how we're going to rescue you."

"Thank you, kind sir, for keeping the boys in line," Marian said. "You surely saved them from a bad fall."

"I won't fall," the younger boy boldly said. He turned to defy Mr. O'Leary's claim, never looking at his mother. "'Sides, I'm strong, and I can climb back up by myself."

"That may be," Mr. O'Leary said, hands on his cane, his hat tipped back on his head, "But your mother here isn't going to appreciate the fact you aren't minding your manners in this difficult situation."

"Mr. O'Leary's right," Marian scolded. "Both of you come back over here in the shade this instant." Marian took her daredevil son by the collar and frog-marched him toward the train where she could keep an eye on them. "Come sit here in what little shade we have. It's altogether too hot to be working up a sweat with your misbehaving."

Emily hadn't paid much attention, but Marian was right. The only shade visible was next to the train, the sun having dipped over the other side of the big, black, lifeless locomotive. People stretched along the rails hugging what little shade they could find. Still, it wasn't sufficient to cool their heated bodies.

An hour later, there was still no word on what was to become of them. The boys grew restless, and several of the passengers wandered away from the train.

"When the night cools, the cars will cool down as well and we can go back inside," the conductor said. "You'll all be able to get some rest in the sleeping cars."

"Do you think this has anything to do with the strike back east?" Emily sighed.

"I bet bandits are gonna come and rob the train," Jonathan announced, matter-of-factly. "I bet they are."

"Are not," Jason taunted his brother. "I bet it'll be Injuns. This is Injun country."

"Bandits. Injuns don't rob trains."

"Do too."

"Do not."

"Boys. Please. We're not going to be robbed. By bandits or Indians."

Emily hoped Marian was right. She looked over at Elizabeth Young to see how she was fairing with the little one. But like others, they had climbed back on board to find a more comfortable seat despite the extreme heat.

As the afternoon wore on, the heat from the desert sun baked down on the stranded passengers and crew. The inside of the train was hotter than a wood stove. Those who had gone inside were forced out by the extreme temperatures. They came out wiping at their temples and necks, their hair damp, their clothes and bodies limp. They joined the trainmen who still lined the rails using the shadow of the railcars for shade. Some found shelter next to a large cactus growing next to the bridge. Emily hoped they didn't get pricked by the long quills sticking out of the odd-looking plant.

Two men climbed up from the ravine with buckets of water. Going from person to person, women and children first, they dipped into the cold water and distributed it. Emily drank from the tin cup. She let the cool liquid slide slowly down her throat before she drained the rest of the sweetness to help quench her parched mouth.

The men made several trips up and down the ravine

until everyone had been given sufficient water.

Unfortunately, the drink revived the Aderley boys, and they grew even more restless and wandered off. Emily, no longer able to just sit by and watch the young mother try to soothe her whimpering baby, wandered over and introduced herself.

"I'm Emily Carmichael. I have children and a young baby back home in New York. You look to be worn out. Why don't you let me hold your baby while you get a bit of rest?"

"I'm Elizabeth Young. Thanks for your offer, Mrs. Carmichael, but I'm fine."

"My dear, you won't do your child any good if you pass out. Let me help."

The young mother's face changed from concern to resignation.

"If you're sure you don't mind, I am feeling a bit fatigued."

Emily took the baby from Elizabeth. The darling baby girl reminded her of little Sarah. She had the same hair coloring. Tufts of dark black stuck up and curled at the very ends. Large dark brown eyes, just like Sarah's, gazed up at Emily. Her smooth, pink complexion was identical to her own sweet baby's. Emily's heart ached. She nuzzled the baby, placed a gentle kiss on her forehead, and rocked her in her arms. The baby quieted. Emily spread the hand-crocheted blanket on the ground and gently laid the baby down in her own shadow. Still too hot, the child whimpered, her arms and legs kicking in protest. Emily removed unnecessary pieces of clothing from the baby with infinite care. She soaked her handkerchief in the cool water the men furnished from the river. She sponged the baby down to cool her off. The baby finally relaxed and lay limp, exhausted from the heat. Only then did Emily proceed to cool her own brow.

Tears trickled from the corner of Emily's eyes. She blinked them back, but they rolled down her dust covered cheeks. She rinsed the hanky out and wiped her own face and neck again to remove some of the dust. She sighed and sat back, making sure the baby lay within the cover of her shadow. She hadn't wanted to leave her children. Mrs. Aderley might be having a hard time of it with her two boys on this trip, but she was fortunate to have them near. Her boys would have enjoyed the adventure. Just like Jason and Jonathan. And, Mrs. Young. Oh, to have Sarah in her arms again. She missed them so much.

A rumble shook the ground. Small pebbles in the desert sand jumped up and down. A hush fell over the stranded group as the sound of thundering hooves drew in from every direction. Alert, everyone stood, circling together to peer in between the stranded cars to see what the ruckus was all about.

In the far distance, a cloud of dust met the clear blue skies. For what seemed like miles, a screen of brown obliterated the cause of the sand storm. Emily grabbed the baby from the blanket and held her close to her bosom. Mrs. Young, frantic, ran toward Emily, yelling, her arms outstretched.

"My baby. My baby. Give me my baby."

Emily handed the baby to Elizabeth who clutched her baby and ran up into the train.

Others ran for the safety of the train as well. Emily, too transfixed to do anything, stood by and stared in awe at what looked like a sandstorm blowing across the plains. A shrill, piercing scream filled the air as Marian Aderley called for her boys.

"Jonathan. Jason. Where are you? *Jonathan! Jason!* Come here. Quick. Get inside the train."

But there was no answer. Marian called again, her voice strained. Emily sympathized with the alarmed mother and ran to her side.

"Help," Marian screamed. "I can't find my boys. My boys are missing. I can't find my boys."

Emily couldn't see them either. They had been exploring and had, more likely than not, wandered to the other side of the observation car.

"Around the back side," Emily yelled, and motioned with her hand. "Check round the back."

No time for modesty, both women lifted their skirts high, simultaneously, mindless of the show of their stockings. There was no telling what was headed their way.

Marian was already around the back of the train just as Emily approached the glistening, hot rails.

"Buffalo. A dang herd of buffalo coming our way," a man shouted.

"Get back inside the train," the conductor yelled to those still standing, gaping at the bizarre scene in front of them. He blew his whistle to get their attention. Everyone milling about rushed toward the train.

Emily screamed to Marian to get back inside, but the herd of shaggy buffalo's hooves hitting the desert floor grew louder the closer they approached.

The boys were nowhere to be seen.

Marian disappeared in the brown haze obliterating everything including the train. The dry, gritty sand flew everywhere for miles. Emily covered her eyes to keep the sharp, prickling, stinging sand out, but the tiny granules clung to her hair and penetrated right through her clothing into her skin. Dust blew up her nose, making breathing difficult. She covered her face with her hands and bowed her head, turning away.

The thundering noise grew loud, closer. Emily turned her back, but not before she got a mouthful of the gritty, earthy, salty desert. Tumbleweed blew up against her back and almost knocked her over. She leaned into the train and hung on to the side rail for support.

The buffalo kept coming. On and on they thundered past as the passengers stared from inside the train through the dusty windows. The train swayed with the vibration of the herd and the wind their stampeding created. Emily didn't know what had become of Marian Aderley and her boys. But right now, she had to think of her own safety. She let go of the rails and dove underneath the train. She inched her way over the track to the opposite side. Her dust-ridden skirt slid up around her waist, and her once white cotton petticoat caught on the rails and tore. She couldn't see the entrance to the train; the sand storm was so thick. A welcomed hand grabbed hers, lifting her up into the coach as if she were nothing more than a flimsy rag doll. Her legs scraped against the iron steps. Her stockings tore.

A pair of strong arms held her steady as she was ushered toward the center of the car just as someone yelled, *"Indians! Heaven help us! Indians!"*

An empty seat appeared. Emily sank down with a sigh. She rested her head against the windowpane and shut her eyes tight. Her strength spent, she wanted nothing more than to sleep for a long time. Indians, or no Indians, buffalo, or no buffalo, she wanted to be anywhere but in the middle of the desert, in the middle of a wild Indian hunt where buffalo were being hunted. And slaughtered.

She wanted to be anywhere but stranded on a train going nowhere.

She was weak, shaky; she wished she were back home. The vision of those Indians riding like the wind across the desert floor and slaughtering buffalo, one after the other, remained no matter how tight she shut her eyes. She opened them, her curiosity getting the better of her. They were full of sand. The large dark-skinned, bare-chested Indians carrying guns and bows and arrows were a sight she could have lived without seeing again. Such carnage. They yelled and screamed in a strange tongue. The thudding of the horses and buffalo continued in a deadly chase.

Emily sagged against the seat and gave in to the fatigue. Men lined up along the windows, squeezing their faces against the dirty panes in an effort to see what was happening. Women crouched along the opposite side of the aisle, covering their faces in fright.

The sandstorm settled. Indians tended to the dead buffalo as if the train and passengers didn't exist. Buffalo lay slaughtered on the dusty, desert floor. Indians stood over the large beasts, concentrating on their kill. Several of them rode their great white and chocolate colored pintos at a canter now the killing was over. Chests puffed up in pride, the Indians pranced around the outside of the killing area as if to keep hungry wild beasts at bay. They sat bareback, their own backs ram-rod straight.

Emily couldn't take her eyes off them.

The desert sand soaked up the blood as the animals were cut and gutted. More Indians rode in with long logs tied with ropes and wrapped in canvas behind their horses. Their kill was hoisted onto a litter and carted away. They were an intense lot, and before long, they had slaughtered, gutted, and taken almost every scrap of the beasts.

Emily didn't realize she held her breath until she released a long, deep sigh, and sat back, exhausted.

"We're lucky," the bearded Mr. O'Leary said. "Those Injuns are too busy gutting their kill to come after us. I suspect, depending on how far away their village is, they'll be back to get what they can from us. Most likely during the night."

Emily shivered. Did Mr. O'Leary know what he was talking about? She was afraid to find out.

"Don't let them fool ya," a gentleman on her left said to the tall conductor who was walking down the aisle to check on everyone. "They'll be back, they will. They'll be waiting 'til after dark and come to find what they can aboard. They know we have supplies. Could be they're the ones who put that big hole in the trestle so's we couldn't cross."

Emily took heart when the conductor spoke up.

"We'll be one step ahead of them, sir. We've telegraphed ahead and told the authorities at Silver Springs we're in a bit of a fix and need reinforcements tonight. We won't be waiting for no measly "grasshopper" to be pumped up and down by hand to come tomorrow to take a few of us at a time. We'll cross the ravine tonight and make our way to the town up ahead."

The conductor informed them the Sioux might be after supplies from the train, but they hadn't hurt passengers in a long while. However, they all needed to be diligent and not tempt fate.

"Take only what's necessary," he said. "Just what you can carry. We'll stow your items under the trestle until we can come back and fetch it later and hope the Sioux don't find it first."

The conductor stopped at Emily's seat and looked down with concern. "Well, Mrs. Carmichael, how you doing, Ma'am? You were a might bit luckier than Mrs. Aderley and her two young'ens."

Emily eyes shot opened wide. "What of Marian Aderley? Did she find her boys? What do you mean they weren't lucky? They're not dead are they?" Emily's heart raced. She drew her hanky tight in her hands.

"The Missus found the one and lay atop him to keep him from getting trampled. She's bruised up a bit. Her left leg is broken, and she has a few broken ribs, no doubt. The leg had to be splint. The older boy's feeling mighty sorry for himself. He has a broken leg as well. Feels guilty, he does. The younger one wasn't so lucky. He got kicked in the head. Not sure if he's going to be okay."

"Where is Mrs. Aderley? Can I see her?" Emily's head buzzed. She wasn't sure her legs could hold her, but she wanted to see how badly Marian was hurt.

Oh, dear Lord. What if her children had traveled with her? For the first time, she was glad they were home, safe. Her stomach lurched, and a hot, searing flush rose and heated her face. She gripped the seat ahead of her and took a couple of deep breaths.

"She's up at the head of the car," the conductor said, sounding as if he were far away. "We'll have a devil's own time getting her and the boys down the ravine and over the river. The men are in the process of making a sturdy hoist and raft to help everyone cross. Hope you're feeling up to it, too, Miss, 'cause we have to get going real soon."

The conductor made his way throughout the car telling everyone to shut the shades and start preparing for the crossing. They might not be bothered by the Indians at the moment, but they would surely be back sometime during the night or early morning to scavenge for anything of value on the train.

Emily ignored the rest of the conductor's words as he wandered throughout the coach. Her own worries forgotten, Emily lifted her sand-soaked, tar-smeared petticoats and walked to the front of the car where Marian Aderley sat huddled in a corner with her oldest son, Jonathan. They sat with their broken legs propped up on a board that rested across the aisle on to the opposite seat. Marian's arm was wrapped and tucked next to her ribs, which were also bandaged. Her beautiful day dress was covered with dirt, now ground into the delicate fabric. For sure it would never wash out. On closer inspection, washing wouldn't help; the dress was torn, the left sleeve missing. Her son's face was bruised, ashen, and tear-streaked. A far cry from the laughing, playful fellow who had been jumping up and down a few hours ago with his brother. Now sad and distraught, the boy hung his head in pain.

Jason lay on the floor unconscious, a folded blanket under his head. His body was swollen and distorted from being trampled. Emily looked away. She agreed with the conductor. Jason wasn't going to survive the night. Her heart ached for Marian Aderley. She sent up a silent pray to help them all through this horrendous evening and get them to safety. And soon.

"Are they going to shoot us like they do horses because we broke our legs?" Jonathan cried, a low whimpering, agonizing plea from such a small child. "I saw Doc Hadley shoot Dad's horse last year after it tumbled down a hillside and broke two legs. The buckboard rolled on top of the horse. Pa said if I ever broke my leg, he'd shoot me." He hung his head, his hands shaking.

"They don't shoot people when they break a leg," Emily reassured him. "Your father was just concerned you take care not to do so. Already your leg has been put in a splint, just like your mother's, until you can get proper attention in San Francisco. In the meantime, just try not to worry. Has anyone given either of you something for the pain?"

Marian shook her head, tears flowing down her ashen cheeks.

"I have some Dover's powder in my bag. I'll be right back."

Emily rushed back to her seat in search of her carry bag. She rifled through it until she found the packet. The Aderley's needed it more than she did at the moment. If nothing else, it would make the crossing less painful for them.

The engineers and trainmen prepared a wooden platform constructed with the timber from the broken trestle. Using twine and rope they found in the baggage car, they wove it around the lumber to create a good-sized hoist. As the evening shadows fell, the descent got underway. They tested the winch by loading food, blankets, and other necessary items onto the platform, swung it out over the edge of the ravine, then slowly hoisted it into the canyon below. Once they were sure it would hold the weight, they began conveying the Aderleys and more elderly passengers into the gully.

"Careful of your leg now, Mrs. Aderley. Lay still so's we can lift ya onto the platform. 'Tis safe to be sure," Mr. O'Leary cautioned. "Once ya settle, the men will help load the boys."

Emily stood to the side as Mr. O'Leary helped the trainmen maneuver Marian onto the platform. She put her arms around Jonathan to comfort him while his limp and lifeless brother was carefully placed next to her. Only then did Emily let go and allow the men to swing the boy's broken leg onto the wooden platform so he could be with his family. The Dover's powder she'd given them had helped to ease their pain, but no way did it alleviate their mental agony.

Elizabeth Young and her infant were next. She clung to her baby and stepped onto the platform, then sat down in the center of the make-shift contraption.

"Mrs. Carmichael, I think you're next."

The two Weaver sisters stood huddled nearby, deep in worried conversation.

"Let the sisters go with Mrs. Young. I can wait."

"That's right kind of ya, Ma'am. Ladies," he called to the elderly sisters. "'Tis time to be getting aboard."

Pansy and Violet rushed forward. Violet stopped in front of Emily.

"Thank you, my dear. Pansy is in a snit, and it'd be best if we get her on the other side so she don't fret about those Indians."

"You're more than welcome. We'll all be down in no time."

The women climbed aboard, sat close to Elizabeth Young, and gripped each other as the hoist was lifted and swung over the edge. They disappeared over the side and down into the ravine.

Those waiting their turn lent a helping-hand to others in need. When the family with two young ladies was taken care of, Emily allowed Mr. O'Leary to help her onto the lift. Once settled in the center, she clung to the ropes for support and closed her eyes tight as the apparatus swung out over the jagged rocks and down into the ravine far below.

As she neared the ravine floor, she heard others as they cried out in pain. Too anxious to get down below, many had refused to wait for the lift. They started down on their own. One man lost his footing and slid over sharp jagged rocks, landing on his back. Stone and gravel gave way. Emily cringed, and at the same time breathed in the dirt and dust from the rock slides. Two other men ignored the man's dilemma and started down over the side as well. The men slid to the bottom and landed with a heavy thud as they hit the hard basin floor, unhurt. The fear of staying behind in the event the Indians returned was far greater than a bruise or two, or even a broken bone like the Aderley's. She didn't blame any of them for not wanting to spend the night in the train not knowing what might happen come dawn.

The lift settled on the edge of the flowing river. Emily paused until her legs could support her shaking body. She sent up a silent prayer of thanks she'd landed safety on solid ground. After a steadying breath, she searched out the Aderleys and Elizabeth Young.

The others gathered next to the rushing current of the river. They stood in expectation as several men traversed the rapids in search of the shallowest spot in which to cross; away from the quick, churning rapids. Water rose above the knees of three of the men and up to the waist on the others. The men finally gained control, raised their arms in success, and gave a hearty cheer. It echoed across the ravine as others joined in the celebration.

Belongings were rafted across first in an attempt to make sure the passage would be safe to transport everyone across. At one point the raft tipped precariously.

"Dear Lord, they're going to fall into the drink. Look," someone yelled from the shore.

Two hefty men ran toward the river's edge, mindless of their clothes, and rushed to help. The current held them back, but with effort they finally caught hold of the small raft. One of the men climbed up on the raft for extra weight, while the other grabbed the cable and helped the men steady the raft in the water before jumping up onto the small flat structure to maintain better control. In the meantime, several more ventured forward to assist but were met with the heavy rapids. They were dragged under, bobbed up and down several times, and then regained their foothold before they reached the raft and safety. With much care, the men crossed the river without further incident. The return trip was a bit trickier; there was no weight to hold the makeshift raft down and steady.

"We'll be okay," Pansy said. "I do believe they have it under control now."

"I hope you're right."

"I am dear. It can't be any worse than waiting here for those Indians to come for us. Mark my word. This is the lesser of two evils."

Emily had to agree.

Before they attempted another excursion across to the other side, two more ropes were tied to the raft to ensure it wouldn't get washed away.

Emily, along with Mr. O'Leary, helped Marian Aderley and the boys onto the raft when it was their turn.

"Hang on to your boys, Marian. I'll come along and give you a hand in a moment."

Marian nodded. She clutched her sons, her face contorted with pain. Emily admired the woman's determination, not wanting her sons to see the effort it took not to scream in pain with her own broken body. It took energy, and Marian had little to spare.

Emily joined them and gathered the youngest boy, still in a deep sleep, into her arms and held on tight.

The raft bounced wildly at first, but the men controlling the rope soon had it under control. At the water's edge, the wounded were carefully lifted onto the dry bank.

"Thank you," Emily said after one of the men lifted her out and carried her through the river to dry land.

She rushed to Marian and her children, hoping to be of assistance. She wrapped Jonathan in one of the blankets the men had retrieved from the train. The days might be extremely hot, but the night air held a chill. The boy needed warmth.

On and on the passengers and trainmen made their way across the churning river. Once on the other side, everyone gathered in a massive huddle, bedraggled, wet, tired, and muddied from their ordeal. They were safe for the moment. Not sure what to do now, they waited like corralled cattle.

Exhausted and frightened, no one spoke; the tension thick.

Total darkness set in.

"No fires," someone shouted in the still night air. "We don't want to alert the Indians."

Emily remained huddled on the ground next to Elizabeth, Marian, and their children.

The conductor made his rounds, passing out additional blankets and water, asking everyone to remain calm.

"As soon as we get organized, we'll climb out of the ravine and make our way to Silver Springs while it's still cool. Do we have any volunteers to stand guard tonight?" he asked. "We'll go in shifts."

A number of trainmen, the conductor himself, a few engineers, as well as the porter and several passengers volunteered.

"Everyone else get some rest," the conductor told them. "Try to keep as quiet as possible. If the Indians do come before we get started, they won't see us along the river bank. They'll most likely take what they want from the train and go back about their business. If we don't interfere, no one will get hurt."

Emily found sleep impossible even though she felt a bit safer knowing someone kept watch. She stared into the night and listened as the loud gurgling water rushed over the large stones and the frothy rapids splashing against the shore. She longed for Charles and her family. She tugged the blanket tighter around her shivering shoulders and huddled against the cold ravine wall. She looked up into the darkness of the night, surprised to find the big expanse of sky filled with nothing but twinkling stars. It would have been a wonderful night for sitting on the front porch with Charles by her side, swinging together, and wishing on each and every star.

She might not be on a front porch right now, but she sent up a few wishes, anyway.

As well as a few prayers.

Chapter Ten

Mason Aderley peered down at the engineers, the trainmen, and the brakemen.

"*Shit.* Between our men and the sympathizers, there must be at least five-hundred altogether. Including the tramps leeching in daily like mold on a crust of old bread," Aderley spat.

He shook his head and shouted. "Damn it to hell, Charles. It won't be long now."

Charley joined him at the window and looked at the gathering mob. People pushed and shoved each other with disregard, their tempers flaring. The scene below was far from under control. Three policemen worked the crowd. Charley looked toward Market Street where the Blue Bottle was already doing a stroke of business. Two more officers appeared on the scene. Huh. Two weren't near enough to contain the rowdy group congregated in front of the saloon.

Charley froze. *Dear Lord.* Did he just see Sergeant Mead swing his billy club and hit a man over the head? The poor soul had attempted to run across the tracks toward the roundhouse. Even from his vantage point, he could see blood ooze down the side of the man's face.

Sergeant Mead caught up with the man and hit him again. Another spurt of crimson shot from the man's face and splattered Mead's uniform. The man fell to the ground in a limp heap. Mead wiped at his soiled shirt, as if oblivious to the man he'd just bludgeoned.

Charley shuddered.

"God help us, Charles. It's begun." Aderley swiped his hands over his face and sighed.

Charley had to agree. No going back now.

The angry crowd shouted at Sergeant Mead. Charley could tell Mead had no intention of acknowledging them. He beat on another man who was attacking him. Within seconds, the sergeant was overwhelmed and forced to the ground. Three policemen rushed in and broke up the angry brawl. When they drew their clubs in the air to beat the crowd back, Charley turned away. He could watch no longer.

He sank into a chair at the same time Aderley dragged his out from under his desk and sat. He shook his head as if it would dispel the sight from his mind. He shut his eyes. Tight. Heavy-hearted, he took a deep breath.

Aderley struck a match and lit a cigar. He drew on it, then exhaled. He repeatedly drew in and exhaled several more times before he tamped the embers out in the ash tray. He shoved his chair back from his desk. Charley jumped at the sound.

"John," Aderley bellowed. "Get a message to Mayor Stokley right away. I need to talk to him. *Now!*"

He turned back to Charley, eyes blazing. "Stokley will know what to do. He has a way with mobs, and this one is out of control. The mayor led a police posse against the gas work strikers in '72. That alone got him re-elected back in February."

Charley didn't know what to say. Dazed, he stood while Aderley continued.

"John," Aderley called again, frustration ringing in

his voice. "Did you hear me? I said send a message to Mayor Stokley. Get him on the line. I want to talk to him."

Still no reply from Donahue. Aderley stormed from his office.

"Now where the hell did he go?" Aderley sat at Donahue's desk and pounded on the telegraph, then strode back to his office.

Charley stood like an invisible statue, not knowing what to do. How to proceed.

Aderley opened the bottom drawer of his desk and removed a bottle. He poured a liberal amount in a shot glass and handed it to Charley. Charley stepped forward to accept the token, waiting for Aderley to pour himself a shot. Not bothering with a glass, he tipped the neck up to his lips and drank. Back at the window, he stared at the scene below. Charley downed his drink, slammed the glass on the desk, and then joined Aderley at the window again. He hoped like hell things would calm down before long.

As night fell, a progression of cumulus clouds filled the sky, covering what moonlight managed to spill through. A great whisper of urgency surrounded the entire town that penetrated to his bones. He stood at the window with Aderley as the torch-lit night grew brighter and brighter as more and more people arrived. By midnight he figured there must be several hundred lined up along the tracks.

A shrill of a whistle filled the night, signaling the approach of an in-coming train. The engineer blew his whistle several more times to clear the tracks. No one stepped away. God forbid, there were men, women, and even children keeping vigilance on the embankment next to those tracks. They hooted and hollered as if they were welcoming the circus to town.

"Where the hell is Stokley?" Aderley hissed.

Charley had no answer.

By the time Mayor Stokley finally arrived, he issued a directive to the police sentries who had amassed in force. In a matter of minutes, they took charge and everyone scattered. The police cordoned off the depot.

But Charley figured it was too little, too late.

"I'll wire George McCrary for more militia," the Mayor, now standing beside Aderley, said. "We'll get additional troops in place at once."

"Is that necessary?" Charley asked the mayor. "Things look to be in control."

"Good God," Aderley exploded, his face mottled, his eyebrows raised. "I don't think we need to call in the secretary of war for help."

"We do for now," the mayor confirmed. "But don't fool yourself. It's only temporary. I've contacted General Hancock. The men will be under his command. I'll get in touch with the president and ask him to exert every constitutional power he has in order to restore and protect your property here. Once General Hancock arrives, he'll put this strike down in a matter of hours."

Aderley agreed. He had no choice if he wanted to end things as soon as possible. Aderley slumped in his chair, his head thrown back on the fine leather. Charley's own neck and shoulder muscles were tight, but nothing would give him relief anytime soon.

"They may block a few more trains from making their daily runs, but when Hancock arrives, his troops will take care of the situation," Mayor Stokley said, still looking out the open window.

Several hours later, all of them weary from lack of sleep and several shared shots of whiskey, Aderley stumbled to the window. Charley remained in his chair, wishing he were home with Emily. Then realizing she wasn't there, that she was out west, he closed his eyes.

The roar of the crowd rushed in through the open window like a cyclone. Charley jumped to his feet and joined the others.

"Look down there, Mayor." Aderley pointed out the window. "There must be over six hundred jammed elbow to elbow on Callow Hill Street Bridge."

They stood in silence as the mob grew and voices rose. People pushed and shoved each other; several brawls ensued. From the rear, a brigade on horseback pushed against the tight-knit crowd.

"Ah, here comes the militia as ordered." The mayor smiled.

Stunned, Charley couldn't believe his eyes. "How many do you think there are?"

"Should be the three hundred requested. Look at the crowd resisting down there. With the extra men coming in to help, it won't do them no good."

The mayor was right. The militia charged the group with raised clubs and loaded guns. More heads were bloodied. Many fell to their knees while others scattered like dust in a wind storm. A thick puff of dense smoke rose into the air.

"*Holy shit.* They've set fire to an oil car." Aderley turned, grabbed his black hat and clapped it on his head, then headed out the door. "Donahue," he barked, forgetting his assistant wasn't there. "Get the carriage. The whole station is under siege."

The mayor and Charley forgotten, Aderley rushed down the stairs. Charley followed, the mayor right behind him. Aderley disappeared around the side of the building toward his private livery.

"Quick, Otis, get my buggy ready," Aderley shouted. "There's been an accident on the tracks. I need to go see what's going on."

When Aderley's carriage rounded the corner, Mayor Stokley waved his hand for Aderley to hold up.

"Don't these men know how lucky they are to be having work at all?" Aderley mumbled as Charley and the mayor jumped aboard. He clicked on the reins. "If it wasn't for the trunk lines, they'd have been homeless long ago. No. Instead, they're down there burning their very livelihood."

No need for Charley to respond. He kept his eye on the crowd as the carriage bounded along the empty cobblestone streets. The Blue Bottle was empty for the first time in its entire existence, as if someone had put a cork in it and stopped the flow. The Women's Christian Temperance Union would be here with bells on if they only knew. Even old Jasper Groegen wasn't slumped over the hitching post outside, vying for space with the horses at the water trough after his usual indulgence at the bar.

A round of shots rang out in the afternoon air. Aderley's horse slowed, but Aderley wrenched on the reins, and the horse picked up the pace.

They couldn't escape the cries, the yelling and screaming. By the time his carriage stopped, the militia had forced everyone back, forming a hollow square around the inflamed oil car in order to protect the firemen and give them access. Black smoke billowed into the afternoon sky, thicker now, obliterating the bright blue overhead. Before Aderley could step down from the carriage, Charley was there.

"They've transferred six cars to safety but couldn't get to the oil car," he shouted at Aderley. "Damned contraption was blazing like hell. No one could get near the burning car. The militia just shot a bunch of men, too. Good Lord, the men were only trying to take care of the trains. They were doing their job. They didn't set the car a'fire."

Charley shifted from one foot to the other as if his feet were on fire. He glanced over at Mayor Stokley and gave the man a cautious look. An explosion filled the afternoon air. They both turned to see the oil car spit metal and flames a good fifty-feet into the air in slow motion. The loud explosion startled the horse, causing it to whinny and kick its feet in the air, the mayor still in the buggy. The horse bolted down the street several yards before Mayor Stokley had it under control, heading back toward Aderley's office.

The oil car flew into the haze of smoke, then landed with a sickening clatter spitting flames and metal pieces in all directions. Charley ran toward the commotion, elbowing his way through the crowd, Aderley by his side. Three men engulfed in flames like a wooden shack on fire yelled in wretched agony as they ran toward the crowd for help.

"Charles, get in there and see what you can do," Aderley yelled over the chaotic scene. Charley had already rushed forward. Another loud whoosh silenced the crowd. Charley stopped for only a split second before he ran to Johann Westmüller's side.

"Roll. Get down on the ground and roll," he yelled.

Fire crackled as flames licked at Westmüller's clothes, now covered in oil, burning them right off the writhing man's back. The stench of charred skin mixed with heavy smoldering oil filled the air.

Charley scanned the area. *God Almighty. He couldn't help them all.*

"Someone help the others," he yelled above the din, yanking his white soot-covered shirt off his back, the hand-sewn buttons flying off in all directions. "Fetch some blankets. Anything. Be quick about it."

Despite the hot flames licking all around Westmüller's body, Charley flew to his side. He grabbed his flaming, flailing arms and dragged him to the ground. The flames diminished, momentarily, but then flared straight through the thin cotton. A trainman shoved through the crowd and rushed forward with a blanket. Charley wrapped it around Westmüller, then rolled him on the ground until the flames died.

God, he hoped he wasn't too late. He'd be surprised if Westmüller survived. The flames, now extinguished, hadn't missed a single part of the prone man's body. Paper thin charred flesh hung from his arms exposing raw, red tissue and bone. Charley turned away and swallowed the bile that rose in his throat. The stench burned his nose.

"Get this man to the doctor," he ordered.

Several men ran to assist Westmüller. Charley wiped his hands over his face and sighed. He turned to see about the others and found Aderley standing just outside the ring of fire.

"See what else you can do here, then report back to me," he shouted at Charley. "I'll be in my office."

Charley nodded, then checked to see who else

needed help. He spied two bodies lying, charred, lifeless, and almost unrecognizable. Many stood by, stymied. Charley lifted his head as Aderley retreated. The boss had taken a chance coming to this area in the first place the way things stood. Right now, even Charley wanted to take a pop-swing at Aderley for letting things go this far. Without Westmüller's wages from the railroad, the man's family was gonna be heading for the poor house, thanks to the doctor's demand for compensation after this fiasco.

Not to mention the families of the other two dead men.

The damage done, the strikers started to disperse along the tracks. Weary now from the carnage, Charley leaned against one of the railcars. People wandered in a haphazard fashion down the tree-lined street. They got into their buggies and headed out. Still, plenty of others lagged behind and milled about as if they had no place to go.

The Blue Bottle would be finding it hard to keep up with business before long, what with so many militia and vagrants in the area. Tempers were still high. With all these sympathizers stoking the fires, wherever-the-hell John Donahue was right now, it was obvious the man had a big hand in all this.

****

Aderley paced his office while he waited for General Hancock and his staff to arrive. Mayor Stokley had put out the call over the wires as soon as he'd returned to Aderley's office. It wouldn't be long now. In the meantime, Donahue was nowhere to be seen. Charley knew Donahue instigated things at the tracks. *The dirty rat better not show his face right now if he knew what was good for him.*

By late afternoon, over a hundred marines from Baltimore rode the tracks into town. They set up positions along the bluffs and took control of the entire area. Charley sighed as Aderley continued to pace behind his desk.

"I have to get back to my office," Stokley said. "I've ordered a Committee of Safety, and they'll double the militia. By the end of the day, there should be another five-hundred armed men from the First Artillery. Order should soon be restored here."

Chapter Eleven

Jason Aderley took his last breath during the night while the others lay exhausted on the opposite side of Weber Canyon's raging river. Marian's haunting sobs awakened Emily.

How does one comfort a mother who just lost her son? What if it had been one of her children? Lord, she missed them something terrible. She should never have left home.

As much to comfort herself as Marian, Emily flew to the distraught woman's side and lifted Marian's head and placed it in her lap, brushing the woman's hair aside. She could do no more, for to envelope the already broken body in her arms would only cause more damage. No matter what people said, words did not help ease such pain at a time like this.

Emily hummed a lullaby. Her gentle voice drifted in the night through the ravine. Before long, others gathered around. Some joined in song for their own comfort; others sat close by listening. Word passed like a game of gossip informing everyone Jason Aderley had gone to meet his maker. The humming switched to hymns, heads bowed, hands clasped.

Touched by everyone's caring, Emily lay down beside Marian and let the spiritual glow from the strangers blanket them in healing. Jonathan moaned in his sleep next to his mother. His eyes remained shut. He would learn of his brother's death soon enough. The morning hours were not going to be pleasant for this young man who not long ago was so full of life.

The men dug a small grave for Jason in the morning hours. Sadness prevailed as the rest of the passengers and trainmen learned the Aderley boy had passed during the night. Before the sun rose in the sky over Weber Canyon, everyone had gathered to see the boy lay to rest.

"Such a shame," one passenger mumbled. "He was such a vigorous young man."

"What a terrible end to a marvelous adventure for him and his brother," another replied.

"A real heartbreak, for sure."

"Why, these things aren't supposed to happen," Violet Weaver complained in earnest. "They promised we'd be safe. Told us there was nothing to fret over."

Emily concurred. Once the trains crossed the vast countryside, the long journey wasn't supposed to be the torturous expedition it was turning out to be. How many other unsuspecting dangers lurked here in the west? According to a letter from Marybelle after she'd gone out west, people had starved, died of untold diseases, and even been attacked by Indians during the early days when the wagons wheeled across the continent. But those hardships were believed to be over. Especially, by railcar. No one anticipated a damaged trestle, let alone a fatal buffalo stampede.

"I say it's them Injuns what's to blame," Violet spouted.

"If'en we don't get going and get up out of this ravine, they'll be coming back looking for us soon enough," someone else agreed.

"We gotta get outta here. I ain't a'waiting for them redskins to come back for me." Violet muttered, agitated and fussing with her hands at her throat, her big bosom heaving dramatically.

"Now you just calm down. All of you," the conductor yelled to those kicking up a fuss. "Soon as we lay this lad to rest, we'll be on our way. Silver Springs is just over the rise a few miles. We'll get a good start before the sun rises too high in the sky so's we don't bake in the afternoon heat."

"I'm not walking to no town. It's too far," a portly woman protested.

"Ya can stay behind down here if ya want, but I be moving out with the others. Take yer pick," Mr. O'Leary said, which left the remaining passengers quiet for the time being.

Marian remained silent. Jonathan sat on the ground, mute, his broken leg stretched out in front of him. Mr. O'Leary said a few words over the grave before the last handful of dirt was tamped down. It was a sad group as they turned from the make-shift grave of the small boy to face the problems of the day.

They didn't dally.

Climbing up out of the rocky ravine was as arduous a task as the night before when they had climbed down. Filled with a panic to arrive at the top without delay, even though there was no sign the Indians had returned to the area during the night, the entire contingent of trainmen and passengers band together to forge up over the rugged rocky ledge.

Emily attempted to climb, but stumbled and lost her grip.

"Mrs. Carmichael. What are ya trying to do to

yerself?" Mr. O'Leary called over to her. "You be too weak to be climbing that hill all on yer own. Come. Ya should be using the lift along with the others."

Too weary to protest, Emily let Mr. O'Leary guide her to the lift. Along with the Aderleys, Mrs. Young, and the two sisters, Violet and Pansy, Emily waited her turn to be hoisted out of the canyon.

"Thank you, Mr. O'Leary," Emily said as the eccentric gentleman gave her a hand, assisting her onto the make-shift platform.

"Me pleasure, to be sure," he answered, then gave the signal for the men on top to get the pulley operation underway.

Next thing she knew, she was above the ravine and swinging over solid ground. Emily found the earth cooler now, almost cold, as she sat on the coarse sand waiting for the rest of the passengers. She sat next to Mrs. Young, who had come up before her. Emily positioned herself in front of the young mother who was in the process of trying to nurse her crying baby before they started their trek to Silver Springs.

As the others climbed up out of the deep cavern, Emily prayed for their safety. One by one, heads appeared over the rim. Along with the trainmen, Mr. O'Leary helped lift the passengers up. Several of the younger women didn't bother to wait for the lift, wanting only to get out of the canyon. Emily prayed harder after witnessing one woman, whose dress got caught and wrapped around her legs, making it cumbersome to draw her legs up over the side. The long skirt and petticoats clung to her ankles. Her shoe caught in the hem as she swung first one foot and then the other up onto safety. In an undignified grab, Mr.

O'Leary urged the woman away from the edge. The two rolled head over heels several times before coming to a quick stop, at which point the woman righted herself, giving Mr. O'Leary an ungrateful look before she strode away. Emily wanted to laugh but held back. However, she did smile when Mr. O'Leary's fedora, still fastened to his head, shifted over his left eye.

The rumble of gravel, stones, and even loose boulders sliding down and landing at the bottom of the ravine mixed with the whimpers, the cuss words, and the chanting of prayers as several passengers slid back down only to have to start the climb again.

Two and a half hours later, the chill of the night was gone, and the sun began to climb into the bright blue cloudless desert morning sky. The group, exhausted already, had a long walk ahead of them.

"There's a mesa over yonder," the conductor said, pointing west. "We're headed there. Must be about five miles or so. We'd best get walking now before the sun gets too high overhead. Don't look like there's much shade to be had between here and there."

They were given a few minutes to collect themselves, but time was sparse. The fear of an Indian attack made everyone anxious to get underway.

Several of the burly men had already made a make-shift litter with blankets tied to two long wooden poles taken from the raft. Marian and Jonathan were helped onto one, while Elizabeth Young and her baby onto another. The two older sisters refused to be coddled and insisted they were more than able to walk.

Regardless of their disposition, Emily figured she would be able to keep up with Violet and Pansy, seeing as they were more apt to keep a slower pace. She chose to walk alongside them.

Slow and steady, the contingent spread out across the plains. No one spoke. Before long, fatigue set in.

"I can't take another step," a woman wailed. "We have to rest. My feet are paining me."

Violet, the feistier of the two sisters leaned over to her sister and muttered "If'en she'd worn a more comfortable travel shoe instead of those high-heeled pointy things they wear in the city these days, her feet would be just fine."

"Now Violet, just think, the good Lord is using her to do us good. We're all in need of a rest," Pansy chastised.

"Don't I know it?" Violet sounded contrite. "Miss Emily, you must be near dragging yourself. Soon as we catch up with the others, we'll have a good sit down and rest, too."

"I am a bit weary." Emily managed a weak smile at her companions who hadn't uttered a word 'til now. "My feet are getting hot and tired as well."

"At least I'm glad to see you wearing sensible shoes, my dear. Quite serviceable. Quite," Violet said, nodding her head.

Emily's shoes were nothing to write home about. She could only imagine how uncomfortable it was to be wearing the kind of shoes several of the other women sported.

The sun had risen higher, and the heat was scorching. Beads of sweat trickled down everyone's foreheads, streaking the dust on their faces like irrigated fields they had passed back in the Midwest. The trainmen offered everyone a drink from several canteens they had filled with water. Emily sank to the gravel-covered ground where tufts of prairie grass lay scattered about.

"For drinking only. We need to save some for later," the man said. "We still have a long walk ahead."

Emily drank from the canteen, wanting to take a dram of Dover's powder, but she needed to stay awake. She laid her head down in her folded arms on top of her bent knees and closed her eyes.

"Mrs. Carmichael," Mr. O'Leary said. "Mrs. Carmichael. Ma'am. We've made room for you on one of the litters."

Emily barely registered the two men who helped her over to the litter where Elizabeth and her baby had been.

"If you will cuddle my baby, Mrs. Carmichael, I'll walk alongside for a spell." Elizabeth Young's voice cooed her words in the vicinity of the blanketed baby.

"Thanks. I could use the rest." Emily lay back, cuddled the infant, and closed her eyes.

Keeping a slow, steady pace so as not to tire everyone, the long trek took hours. When they stopped again, mid-morning, a tin of small biscuits and thin slices of salted ham were passed around. Water was doled out as well. But they didn't linger.

The sun had risen even higher in the azure, cloudless sky.

Mr. O'Leary took his heavy woolen coat off. Marian tilted her hat down over her face to keep the sun off and placed a thin shirt over her son's head for protection. Elizabeth Young took the warm blanket from around her baby and instead put a small lightweight cloth over the sleeping infant so she wouldn't be exposed to the sun. Others in the group were doing the same. Emily, although willing to give up her spot on the litter to one of the older women after her rest, was still tired.

"We're a sturdy lot, we are," Violet informed her. "Our mother didn't raise no weaklings."

"She's right. And we ain't near as ill as you are, my dear," Pansy confirmed. "You just lie still. Can't be much farther."

Emily thanked them, knowing she didn't have another step in her.

They stopped several more times during their walk to Silver Springs. The threat of an Indian attack was replaced with the danger of the constant heat from the hot sun climbing higher and higher overhead.

Before long, the travel-weary assemblage spotted the small town nestled at the foot of the tall, flat mesa.

"Don't be letting the distance to that town fool you," the conductor said, shading his eyes with his hands. "We have at least another hour before we get there."

The crowd was silent with the news.

"We can make it, sir," Pansy told him, stepping forward just to prove her point. "Can't be far if I can hear music drifting this way."

"Now Pansy, your mind's just so frazzled you think you're hearing things," Violet said. "Perhaps you should take a ride on one of them stretcher contraptions. Give your mind and body a rest."

"I can make it if you can, Violet. I'm not much older than you."

The challenge had been given. Neither woman let the other have the advantage.

Just the sight of the town up ahead gave Emily

hope they'd be there soon. Those who had lagged behind somehow found renewed strength to pick up their feet and stand a little straighter. Emily gave up her spot on the litter to the other woman whose shoes were causing her so much pain.

****

"New York's a mess," Charley gasped rushing into Aderley's office without waiting for an invitation. "They're striking in Buffalo and Hornellsville on the Western Division of the Erie. They refuse to let passenger trains go out. The Fifty-Fourth New York Regiment is posted at Canisteo and West Street Crossings in Hornellsville."

Aderley rubbed his hands over his face, his elbows rested on his desk. "What happened?" His words came out in a defeated sigh.

"A small passenger coach with about fourteen people, and four times the militia, rolled into the station close to ten o'clock. They didn't anticipate the steep climb of Tiptop Mountain. Can you believe they gathered up enough steam to try and make the climb? But the tracks were slathered with soap? The train didn't do nothing but slide back down those tracks."

"What about the militia? Didn't they do anything?"

"The crowd gathered along both sides of the track right down over the hillside like a sea overflowing its banks. Once the train lost speed, they all clambered aboard in a manic frenzy. Men, women, and children, yelled, shouted, scorning the militia who were ineffective. Even some of the militia started sympathizing with the strikers. Then someone uncoupled the cars and coaches. And that's not all."

"Don't tell me there's more?" Aderley shook his

head. "Go ahead, you might just as well get it over with and tell me everything."

Charley didn't think there was any reason not to tell Aderley at this juncture of the strike. The man needed to know what the trunk lines had started.

"Strikers axed the steel, and brake rods were bent. Wheels were damaged before the cars were run to ground. They stopped a train filled with troops who had set out for Buffalo. They boarded the train, expelled the militia, and sent the locomotive back to the yards. Another train heading out to New York City was ambushed and cleared of its passengers and crew. They stranded it half a mile away on the east side of town. If you ask me, Donahue has been aware of this right along."

"I'm beginning to believe you," Aderley mumbled. "I haven't seen him around, and he hasn't reported to work in several days."

The silence was almost piercing as they sat for a moment.

Aderley was the first to speak. "I'm sorry to hear things aren't going so well up in New York, Charles, but I've got to say, I'm glad things have calmed down here as well as in Pittsburgh."

"Once the militia took control it didn't take long," Charley agreed.

"Have you seen Westmüller lately?" Aderley enquired.

"No. I plan to visit him later today to see how he's fairing. Talk to the family, see if there's anything I can do."

"Keep me informed. And, Charles, stay alert. Let me know if there are any more rumblings going on down below."

****

Mrs. Flanagan proved to be a godsend. The house ran like clockwork, and Seth could concentrate on the farm. He even caught Catherine singing and smiling; something he hadn't heard in a long time. With Timothy helping with chores and the fields, and Michael and Robert busy feeding chickens, collecting eggs, pumping water for the kitchen, and carting wood for the stove, Seth was feeling right proud of the family. Madeline was a wonder with baby Sarah. In the evening, Mrs. Flanagan even found time to read to them at the kitchen table.

Anna Louise was missing out on a fine family.

"Have you considered selling some of your lace in town?" Seth asked Maggie one evening when they were all gathered around the kitchen table. "I could check in town next time I go and see if one of the dress stores might be interested in buying some. Perhaps you could display some samples at Mrs. Wentworth's millinery."

"Oh, these are just some pieces I crocheted for a special Sunday dress for your sister. She's been working so hard she deserves something nice. I'm sure the ladies in town would be wanting something a bit more delicate than this."

"Thank you, Mrs. Flanagan." Catherine's head popped up from reading her text book. "But Seth is right. Maybe you should let him take a few pieces into town."

"I'm thinking I need to go to town in a couple of days," Seth encouraged. "I'd be glad to take a few pieces with me. See what Mrs. Wentworth thinks."

Seth's eagerness didn't fool his sister if the smile

156

on her face was any indication.

"Well, if you have a mind to. 'Twould be a treat, Seth. You have such a head for business, ya do, always thinking up ways to make ends meet here at the farm. If ya don't mind, maybe I will. Just to see what comes of it."

"Oh, I'm sure he won't mind making a trip back into town, Mrs. Flanagan. Seth has business to tend to, I'm sure."

"What's that supposed to mean?" Seth glared at Catherine, a warning which didn't do much good. "Business is business."

"That's what you call it? Business?" She chuckled. "It doesn't have anything to do with Anna Louise, per chance?"

"Per chance, yourself. Mind your own business."

"Ah-ha. You are sweet on her. Ever since last year at the fair you haven't been able to stop talking about her. When are you going to do something about it?"

Her smile teased him.

"Leave me alone," he grumbled.

"Oh, my. Did you two have words? Did she reject your advances?"

"Leave it be, Catherine," Seth said, scraping the chair back preparing to leave.

"She did, didn't she? I saw her with Mr. Linsky. Oh, Seth, is that what's bothering you? I'm so sorry…"

"I said leave it." Seth grabbed his hat and stormed out of the house. He was going to prove them all wrong. Anna Louise just needed time to get used to the idea of marrying him. He didn't need an excuse to go into town. If he wanted to go court Miss Anna Louise, he would.

Who was to stop him?

****

Seth hadn't counted on the weather. Rain poured down in buckets the next day, and the two days following. The creek beds rose to flooding, and the road down off the hill washed out. When he and Timothy checked the crops in the fields, Seth stood and shook his head.

"Unless this rain stops soon, we're going to lose the buckwheat."

"How can we stop mud from sliding down the south slope into the potato field below?"

"I don't know, Tim." Seth brushed the hair off his forehead and sighed. The two new crops he'd planted earlier in the year were a wash out. He figured the rain had just cost him two acres of buckwheat alone and about another of potatoes.

"Can't you replant?"

"Only if the rain lets up soon. I'll see if I can get more seed from the mill. See if someone over in Richford has any potatoes I can buy."

"At least you have the herd of goats."

"Yes. We'll be okay. But I'd hoped this would be a success."

His herd of goats was producing milk like the rain falling from the skies. Even if he wasn't money ahead from the crops, the farm had no debts owing at the moment, thanks to his tin-eaters.

However, once the bad luck started, nothing went right. Michael slipped in the mud and broke his arm the day after the rains let up. The eggs he'd been carrying from the hen house broke right along with his arm. With no eggs in the kitchen, Mrs. Flanagan had to use her imagination to create meals for the day.

But the real problem involved getting Michael down the washed-out road to Doc Wooster's to have his arm set. Catherine and Mrs. Flanagan wrapped a towel around his arm to keep it from swinging on the trip to town. Catherine rode along to help out and remembered at the last minute to take some of Mrs. Flanagan's handmade lace.

Maneuvering down the dirt road was a slow process as Seth steered the horses through the muddy ruts, which had only gotten deeper with the flooding. The ride was bumpy to say the least. Several times the wagon skidded toward the steep bank on the right. Seth reigned in the horses just in time to keep them from going over the drop-off into the creek fifty feet below. The back wheel broke loose, and Seth had to get out in the mud to fix it before they finally turned onto the turnpike and were heading toward Candor. The Ithaca and Owego Turnpike trail, however, was just as muddy and washed out from all the rain. The going was slow. At least there were no hills to speak of, and they moved ahead at a steady pace.

By the time they got to Candor, Michael's staunch pride dissolved as he writhed in pain. Doc Wooster was in and able to care for Michael immediately.

"I'll give him a dram of laudanum for the pain. Just enough to ease the discomfort while I set his arm. He's too young for more."

Doc Wooster administered the vile tasting liquid. Michael made a face but was in too much pain to fuss.

"Help me get him up on the table, and we'll lay him down."

The table was a large wooden affair that had seen

many medical procedures in its time. The room he was taken to was tidy, clean, and smelled of lemon oil, antiseptic, and kerosene.

"Miss Carmichael, if you will just hold young Michael's good arm. Seth, you might want to hold his shoulders down while I set this."

Michael didn't even blink as Doc Wooster undid the towel and straightened out the arm. Within a matter of minutes, the arm was splinted and wrapped, then tucked tight against his rib cage to help keep it in place.

"Let him stay here and rest for a bit. I'll keep an eye on him to make sure he's not in more pain when the laudanum leaves his system. I'd say two to three hours."

Seth and Catherine walked on down the street and dropped off Mrs. Flanagan's lace at Mrs. Wentworth's store.

"Such wonderful lace. My dear, of course I'll purchase some for the store. You tell Mrs. Flanagan to send more."

"I'm sure she'll be pleased when I tell her," Catherine said.

Saying goodbye, Seth followed Catherine out of the shop.

"How about we stop at the Candor Creek Inn for a bite to eat?" Catherine suggested. "It's all the rave these days."

"I've never had the opportunity to stop in."

"Then let's go."

Walking into the Candor Creek Inn was like walking into a large kitchen, only there were many more tables and chairs. The tables were large, round and sat ten, easily. Instead of white pristine tablecloths, a round revolving tray on a small spindle held an assortment of condiments in the middle of each table. Simple curtains hung in the windows, and the waitresses wore plain white smocks over their dresses. The Inn was a no-frills establishment where the young people gathered to socialize. The smell of pan-fried food filled the room, along with the noisy crowd.

Catherine led Seth past several tables surrounded by people Seth didn't know. "There's an empty table in the corner. Let's sit over there," she said. "I want to try one of those fried beef sandwiches. They smell delicious, don't you think so?"

"Yes. I'll have one as well." Seth sat and glanced around the room. "Where did all these people come from?"

"You really need to get off the hill more, meet people your own age."

"I do get off the farm. And I do meet people."

"Just those old men on your agriculture committee."

"It's an important committee if you're a farmer, Catherine."

"I suppose. Oh, look. Anna Louise is over there in the corner with her friends from the Women's Christian Temperance Union."

Seth's head shot around. Sure enough. Anna Louise sat across the room with a group of young ladies, their heads all bobbed together toward the center of the table, real intent on something. As usual, Anna Louise was a sight. She was all smiles. She simply glowed.

"Go over and say hello, for heaven's sake," Catherine nudged. "She won't bite."

"She's busy with her friends. I don't want to disturb her." Seth wanted desperately to talk to her, but not while she was with her friends.

Catherine caught their eyes and waved a hello in their direction. "Don't be rude, Seth. Smile and wave."

Seth gave what he considered a friendly smile and attempted a wave. He nodded, then listened as the ladies tittered while they outright stared at him. Embarrassed, he glared at them in an effort to show his displeasure. They turned back to their own business as if he was invisible.

All except Anna Louise.

She still looked his way.

Anna Louise smiled.

Heat radiated up Seth's neck as if he had a fever.

Seth took hope once again.

Chapter Twelve

"You just walk right between us, Ma'am. We'll see you come to no harm," Violet said.

Emily walked beside the two sisters the last half mile into town. A collective sigh of relief washed over the bedraggled group as sounds of the pounding of metal on metal from the local blacksmith hammering away carried over the humid afternoon heat.

"Listen," Pansy said. "That there hammering is music to my ears."

Several small shack-like buildings appeared on the horizon. Lined up on either side of a wide road big enough for two wagons to pass each other, hitching posts and water troughs stood ready at various intervals along the way. Entering the town limits, a lone rider and his horse trotted down the center of the town, kicking up a dust trail. Grains of sand flew at the small contingent, and everyone quickly covered their faces 'til the dust swirls settled.

Emily looked around and sighed. Silver Springs didn't look like much. No flower boxes rested under the windows like back home in Candor. No bushes or trees planted next to the buildings or lining the streets. If there was an establishment where one could have a meal, get a good night's sleep for the entire contingent, Emily doubted one could be found in this lone town.

"Now, my dear, don't you become discouraged.

This town only looks deserted," Pansy said, stoically. "Why, even if it's naught but a ghost town, we'll have it all to ourselves. They'll be plenty of beds to go 'round, I'm sure."

It resembled an old mining town gone bust Marybelle had written home about. A little one-horse town they were called, places where it proved impossible to grow anything in the hard compact soil, or had lacked the water needed to survive. Once the spring rains ceased, the hot summer drought settled in.

Tufts of dry weeds leaned up against several hitching posts. Two horses were tied in place outside a storefront. The window advertised they bought and sold gold. The streets were empty.

As they entered the town proper, Emily spotted what resembled a stable of sorts, and a barn. Both looked as if they had been put up in a hurry and would only need a slight gust of wind to blow them over. Neither would keep out the rain.

At the further end of the street stood a two-story building boasting the Bottoms Up Saloon. A balcony, painted moon-yellow, circled the upper floor. It was by far one of the best kept buildings in town. Emily considered any fool without an education could tell what the place was about.

The tall, thin-hipped man wearing a Stetson rode up to greet them. The badge on his vest indicated he was the local sheriff. A double holster hung low at his hips, and a Winchester in his left hand was slung over the horse in front of him. At first sight, he looked threatening, but at second glance Emily found him to be handsome. His blue eyes, although cautious, held a spark of warmth.

"Howdy, y'all. Who's in charge?" He sat very still on his horse. His steady, guarded eyes scanned the crowd in front of him, his back ramrod straight. He took in each and every one of them, sizing them up. He spoke like a gentleman and tipped the brim of his hat back in acknowledgment at the bedraggled bunch.

Emily heard a soft sigh and turned to find Elizabeth Young, baby in arms, captivated by the local sheriff. A slight rosy flush crept up the young woman's dirt-stained face. Emily smiled as Elizabeth's mouth formed a stunned 'O'. She wondered just how long ago Elizabeth Young's husband had died.

One of the men from the train stepped forward and addressed the sheriff. The two proceeded to shake hands, and then separated everyone into small groups.

Emily, Elizabeth, her baby, Marian and her son, Jonathan, were ushered to one side, along with the two sisters and the woman who had complained about her sore feet.

"Doctor Shay's place is over yonder," the sheriff said. "As soon as I get the rest of you sorted out, I'll escort you ladies there myself."

Elizabeth's expression hadn't changed, except for a darker shade of rose staining her cheeks, her eyes never leaving the tall, handsome sheriff.

Mr. O'Leary and several of the other single gentlemen were herded off toward the yellow building.

"There's plenty of rooms over yonder," the sheriff said, pointing the way.

The trainmen and other employees of the railroad were sent to the livery and the blacksmith's shops where they were assured they would be comfortable for their short stay.

"You're all welcome at the Bottoms Up Saloon for a meal. The cooks will have everything ready in about an hour's time."

The sheriff gathered the small group of women together and motioned them forward. Elizabeth hadn't taken her eyes off the sheriff, and the sheriff's eyes kept coming back to rest on her, as well.

"Howdy, ladies. Son." He tipped his hat. "The name's Coulter. Levi Coulter. If you'll follow me, I'll see you get to the doc's house. His wife is real friendly and will make you feel right at home. I see we have some who need tending. Ol' Doc'll fix you up real fine when he returns."

No one spoke as they followed Sheriff Levi Coulter like metal to a magnet, afraid to be left behind. As if sensing their trepidation, he turned and confronted them.

"Now, don't worry none 'bout those Injuns. They might steal a bit of paraphernalia now and again, but they don't hurt no one in these parts. Ol' Red Eye and I are acquainted and have great respect for one another. You're all safe here in Silver Springs. Matter a'fact, Red Eye's sure to be in town tomorrow to sell some of his buffalo hides to send back east to New York. Fox and wolf pelts, too. They're worth a tidy sum. Don't you fret none, though, ol' Red Eye does his trading behind the livery pretty early in the morning so he don't scare no one. You won't even know he's been 'round."

Emily shivered to think they had traveled by foot all this way to escape the Indians, and here they were trading in the same town they had just retreated to for safety. Was this trip never going to stop surprising her? Had they gone through all this trouble walking through the desert for nothing?

"Here we are now," the sheriff said as they drew up to a large sturdy-looking home. A small porch with railings painted white to match the house circled the front and one side. "The doc and his wife will take care of you while you're in town. It'll be a couple of days before the train comes this way and can take you on to San Francisco."

The handsome Sheriff Coulter helped everyone up onto the front porch. He held Elizabeth's hand just a trifle longer than necessary. His arm circled her waist. She pulled her baby close, while her appreciative smile could have burned down the town. The sheriff didn't seem to notice the dirt-streaked face of the young, slim woman as he looked down into her eyes. Elizabeth didn't seem to remember or care that her face was a sight.

Emily smiled and waited outside while she gave a listen to their conversation.

"I hope your husband won't be too worried when you don't show up in San Francisco as planned," Sheriff Coulter said. "Out here all alone with a baby to look after won't be easy for a young lady like yourself. You can telegraph him after you clean up and rest a bit. Old man Lester, who runs the telegraph office, will be there later today. If you like, Ma'am, I can drop by later and escort you to the telegraph office so's you can get one sent off to him."

"Thank you." Elizabeth waved his offer aside. "But no one will be meeting me in San Francisco. I'm a widow. I'm traveling on my own. But I do appreciate your concern."

"How brave of you to travel all this distance by

yourself," Sheriff Coulter said, hat in hand.

From the corner of her eye, Emily could see his keen interest in the news. She had come to care for the young mother and her baby and was concerned with the immediate attraction between the two. How would she feel if this was her Catherine? She would do much more than eavesdrop. More than likely, she would intervene immediately.

Thinking of Catherine made her think once again of her family. For a short moment, her own trials and tribulations were forgotten. Lord, she was worn-out. She wanted a drink of water and a place to lie down and sleep. A bath would be nice, too. Even a bucket of rainwater would be welcome. Anything to rinse the desert dust away.

This wasn't at all what she had expected when she left Candor. How could she write home with this kind of news? It would upset Charles. He had enough on his mind with the strike. She would have to be careful what she telegraphed back when she did arrive at Marybelle's.

The doctor's wife opened the door to greet them. She was a short portly woman, her gray hair knotted at the nape and held back with long black straight hairpins. She was dressed with a simple crisp white, full apron covering her brown gingham dress and her ample chest.

"Come, come. Sit," Mrs. Shay coaxed. "I've rooms at the ready. Never know when my husband will need to keep people over while he's tending them." The woman scurried around the sitting room, helping everyone find a seat.

"I'm sorry Horace isn't here right now. He's

tending a family up in the hills yonder. The Missus Foster is having a baby. Might be a couple days 'til he comes back down. Babies come when they have a mind, don't you know. I'll make you all real comfy until he returns. How's about I make us all a nice cup of tea?"

"I'll be going now," Sheriff Coulter said after he helped settle Mrs. Aderley and her son in one of the larger rooms closest to the parlor. "I need to make sure everyone else has found accommodations." He slapped his hat on his head and let himself out. His dusty boots hit the wooden steps, then silence.

Emily joined the others in the front room where Mrs. Shay set a tray of tea and sandwiches on a small table covered with a dainty stark-white starched scarf. An easy silence filled the room while everyone ate as if they hadn't seen a meal in months.

They were just finishing up their tea when the sheriff knocked on the door and entered. Elizabeth jumped to her feet, then sat back down, hiding her crimson face in her empty tea cup. He cleared his throat and looked down at his hat, once again dangling in his hands.

"Thought I'd stop by to make sure you ladies are all settled." He turned to Elizabeth. "I'll stop back a bit later to escort you over to the Bottoms Up for an evening meal. My deputy will be taking care of the others."

He hung back, then with an easy smile nodded, turned, and fled.

"What a handsome young man," Pansy said when the door shut behind the sheriff. "Why, he must be all of six feet tall without his hat. Now, if I was a might bit younger..."

"Oh, give it up, Pansy," Violet interjected. "The sheriff would never look your way what with Miss Elizabeth sitting right here."

"There you are, my dear." Mrs. Shay entered the room, interrupting the conversation." I have just the room for you and your babe. Come along, Mrs. Young, and we'll get you and that sweet thing settled. Mrs. Carmichael, I can show you to your room now, as well."

Elizabeth and her baby were put in a room farther down the hall where the baby's crying wouldn't disturb the Aderleys. Emily's room, although sparse, was adequate and very welcome compared to her sleeping arrangements on the train. Mrs. Shay led the sisters to their room next door. Each of them was provided wash cloths, towels, soap, and a pitcher of water. They were also provided with a clean, starched robe and instructions to hand over their dirty clothes for cleaning.

Once washed and robed, Emily lay down on the bed. She wasn't worried about food right now. The tea and sandwiches had gone a long way to keep her from starving. She was bone weary, however, and the cool, clean sheets and soft mattress were a welcomed pleasure. She sighed once, and then fell fast asleep.

Emily woke to the smell of fresh coffee and the sound of a giggling baby, making her think she was home. She swung her legs to the side of the bed, disappointed to find she was still stranded in the small town of Silver Springs. Lordy, had she slept the afternoon and night away?

To her amazement, her clean clothes were draped

over the only small chair in the room. There was fresh water and towels in the wash basin. Mrs. Shay was a true wonder to her husband for sure.

Emily washed and dressed, then followed the aroma of coffee, and now bacon, to a mid-sized kitchen. Like all the rooms in Mrs. Shay's house, this room was spotless and welcoming.

"Good morning, my dear. Now sit right down. Everyone's been taken care of except you. You've all had a hard time of it, but that's all over now. The sheriff has sent wagons back to the river to bring your belongings. I only wish I could help the Aderleys with their pain. I'm afraid Horace has taken all his medicines with him. He won't have more until the train arrives from San Francisco. I've made them as comfortable as I can and gave them some Sassafras tea."

"Thank you, Mrs. Shay. I'm sure they're grateful for the bed and clean clothes. Coffee does smell delicious, though."

"Help yourself to all you want. I normally keep the pot going all day for Horace. Never know when he's going to be wanting some."

"How's Elizabeth Young this morning?"

"Oh, she's doing just fine. I made her a pram of sorts to take the baby for a stroll in the fresh air last night. Sheriff Coulter stopped by and said he'd walk them around for a while before they settled in for the night; keep them safe from the riff-raff here abouts. A young lady is sure to get attention she might otherwise not be wanting around these parts. Most of the young girls in town work over at the Bottoms Up, if you know what I mean. Others are smart enough to just plain pass on through."

The next day, Elizabeth Young and Levi Coulter spent a lot of time together. Marian remained quiet, and Jonathan kept to himself as well. Emily, well rested and in much better spirits, visited their room several times and helped Mrs. Shay with their care. By the second day, Emily was beside herself with worry. The Aderleys had been given nothing for their pain, and Doctor Horace Shay had not returned yet. Two days was a long time for them to be without medical care.

Emily left their sick bed and joined Elizabeth in the parlor.

"You're looking radiant today, my dear. The weather here seems to agree with you. And your darling baby is looking healthy, too. She hasn't giggled so much during the entire journey."

"I feel so much better since we arrived. And Sheriff Coulter has been very helpful."

The young mother wrung her hands, then bent over to lift her baby out of the make-shift pram. From the anxious look on the poor girl's face, something was certainly amiss.

"Is something wrong? Is the baby not well?" Emily asked.

Elizabeth looked down at her daughter. "No. My baby is fine. Can we sit down over here, Mrs. Carmichael? There is something I would like to discuss with you if you don't mind."

"My dear, of course you can talk to me. I know we've only known each other a short time, but you remind me of my own daughter, and I've been worried about you. You seem so lost. Does this have anything to do with your husband?"

Emily joined Elizabeth on the long Victorian settee

next to the fireplace.

"In a manner of speaking. You see, I don't have a husband."

"I know, dear. You said he is deceased. I'm so sorry for your loss."

"No. You don't understand. I tell everyone I have a husband so they won't think unkindly of me. But I never had a husband."

"Oh, my. This *is* your baby, isn't it? She so looks like you, my dear."

"Yes, she's mine. But her father refused to accept she's his."

"Oh, my," Emily said again. "What happened, if you don't mind me being so bold as to ask?"

"My parents disowned me when they found I was pregnant. I had no place to go." Tears filled her eyes. "I made up my mind to make my way out west to start over, some place where no one knows of my circumstance."

"You're a brave woman, Elizabeth. How could a mother turn her own child in need away? I'm so sorry my dear. But what about the father?"

The distraught mother's tears spilled over onto her pale cheeks.

"Here. Here," Emily soothed, dabbed at the young mother's damp cheeks, then took the baby into her arms. "Now sit back down and tell me what happened." Emily absently patted the baby's back, now positioned over her shoulder.

Elizabeth hesitated only a moment before opening the floodgates.

"I come from a large family. It was hard making ends meet. I had to find work to help out at home, so I kept house for the Taylors." She sniffed back tears and then went on. "They had a wonderful rice plantation. I did enjoy working there. The Taylors paid their workers well and treated them with respect."

Elizabeth hung her head and twisted her handkerchief. She hesitated before looking up at Emily. "I've never told anyone this and hope I can trust you with my secret."

"Of course you can, my dear. I swear your personal business will go no farther than this room. I can see there must be something more serious by the looks of the poor hanky you've just about got tattered to pieces."

Elizabeth looked at the hanky, smoothed the wrinkles out, and then looked back up at Emily.

"I became very attracted to their oldest son. He flirted with me, telling me how lovely I was. I wanted to believe him even though I knew it wasn't true. Then one night I met him as I was walking down the long drive on my way home. He said he wanted to walk me home. He took my hand and made me feel special. I even let him kiss me. After that first night, he often walked me home. Well, one thing led to another, and I truly believed he loved me." Tears streamed out from between the distraught girl's closed eyes and slid down her pale cheeks in silence.

Oh, lordy, Emily knew what was coming next. She wrapped an arm around Elizabeth to comfort her. "Get it all out, my dear. Then you can go on with your life."

"Of course, he denied it when I told him I was with child. Said it couldn't be his. When I tried to convince him I'd been with no other, he didn't believe me. Said if I told his family, he'd ruin my family. See that they didn't have work and that he'd make sure they weren't welcome at any of the local businesses. Wouldn't have mattered if I'd said anything or not. The Taylors wouldn't have believed a nobody like me. So I kept quiet, not wanting to worry my folks. But there was no way to hide the fact. When I told my parents, my father ordered me to get out because I'd disgraced the family. My mother took my father's side. She didn't try to stop me when I left."

Elizabeth paused. Once started, however, she was unable to stop.

"I was able to put some money aside while I was working. Wasn't much. Just enough to buy this ticket west, as it turned out. Get me to the California Territory with the baby. Start a new life. Find work. I made up the story about my husband being dead so no one would think unkindly of me."

"I'm sorry to hear about your misfortune. I had no idea. Please forgive me."

"There is nothing to forgive. Why, it is what I've wanted people to believe. I want no pity. I only want to get on with my life."

Emily rose with the baby in her arms. "You are a very brave woman, Elizabeth. You did the right thing to leave those uncaring, horrible people behind. Now, I want you to come along with me. I'm sure Marybelle will be delighted to have you stay with us."

"Oh, no. I can't impose. I didn't tell you all this to elicit your sympathy. I just wanted to let you know I won't be continuing on to San Francisco with you and the others. I needed to tell someone, and you've been so kind to me. And I do so feel better now I've confided in you. I hope you don't mind."

The poor girl, to have kept this tucked inside her heart all this time. To be hurting so with no one to see how bad she was hurting. Emily dabbed at her own eyes. She cuddled the baby closer to her chest.

"Does this by any chance have anything to do with the nice young Sheriff Coulter?"

Elizabeth's eyes sparkled, her cheeks turned a light shade of pink.

"I hope you know what you're doing, my dear."

Elizabeth looked away, then with a new-found determination, she stood taller and faced Emily. "Yes. I'll stay on here with Sheriff Coulter," the young mother said, fidgeting. "He's offered me a job keeping house at his ranch just south of town."

"Are you sure this is wise?" Emily's heart cried out to the young mother. If she had been Catherine, she'd be talking her out of staying, forcing her to change her mind. "After all, you've only known the man for a few days. You don't know much about Mr. Coulter even if he is the sheriff. And what do you know of the ranching life? I've only lived on a farm a couple of years myself, and I can tell you it's hard work."

Emily rocked the baby back and forth, wondering if someone were holding her own babe back home and taking great care to see she was rocked and cuddled in loving arms. Was Catherine tending well to her little one?

"I wasn't really keen on living in a big city, but I just didn't know what else to do, where else to go. All I know is that living on Sheriff Coulter's ranch, I won't have to worry about people wondering if I was married or not. As far as anyone knows, Mr. Young is dead."

Emily had seen another side of life out here in the middle of nowhere called Silver Springs. Signs of hardship were everywhere. If Levi Coulter had a successful ranch, for sure the homestead had to be quite a distance away, because Emily had seen nothing resembling anything other than desert for as far as she could see.

"Are you sure you know what you're doing?"

"I'm sure of one thing, Mrs. Carmichael. I'll be able to have my baby by my side all day, and I won't have to beg for work to survive. Being a housekeeper isn't all hard work."

"You're a fine looking young lady, Elizabeth. I'm sure Mr. Coulter hasn't let that fact slip past him. I have a feeling he'll be wanting more than housekeeping from you before long." It was none of her business, but the young woman had already been through a lot. Silver Springs didn't seem like the kind of town that would be kind to a young woman as pretty as Elizabeth Young.

"Sheriff Coulter is an honorable man. He offered me a home for as long as I want. The only stipulation is to be his housekeeper. I don't even have to do the cooking. He already has someone to cook for his men. An old cattle hand who he said has been on one too many cattle drives and has seen his last and is willing to stay behind to keep everyone fed."

"You sound like a very capable young woman, Elizabeth. Should the opportunity and need arise, you confide in Sheriff Coulter as you did me. I hope the sheriff can see past your unfortunate incident and be kind to you. If you've made up your mind to stay, then I wish you happiness."

"Thank you. I have."

Emily handed Elizabeth her baby, then gave her a quick hug. Sheriff Coulter knocked at the front door, opened it, and stepped into the sitting room. Emily saw the question on his face.

177

Elizabeth didn't hesitate. With the baby in her arms, she went to his side. "I'm staying," she said.

Relief was evident in the young man's eyes. A fraction of a smile on his anxious lips proved he was more than satisfied. A warm glow spread across his face.

Emily prayed Elizabeth Young would come to no harm.

Chapter Thirteen

The Fourth of July dawned bright and sunny. Like many small towns around the country, Candor was just as patriotic as the next in their celebration of the country's independence.

Seth made his way to the barn to do morning chores and ready the buckboard for the trip to town and the celebration. He hadn't given up on his intention of winning over Anna Louise. She was meant to be his bride. He couldn't wait to see her at the fair and have another chance at convincing her they belonged together. Only this time he needed to be more polite, show her he had manners. Just because he was a farmer, didn't mean he didn't know how to treat a lady. She'd see. He might not have money like Mr. Linsky, but what did it matter when love was involved? Farming was not an occupation to be ashamed of, after all. As long as people had to eat, he'd keep selling his goat's milk products, potatoes, and buckwheat to the markets in the big cities while he was able to keep up with the demand. He was confident he would be worth a fortune before long.

She'd see.

As the day got underway, the household woke and everyone started their daily morning chores. Seth and Timothy returned from the barn, washed up for breakfast, and then dressed for the day's festivities.

Catherine and Madeline helped get Sarah, Michael, and Robert ready for the trip to town. Maggie took care of the kitchen, and then gathered her hatbox full of lace she'd almost forgotten to take to the fair to sell.

"Careful with those cherry pies, Seth," Catherine cautioned on her way out the door to pack the buckboard. "I want a fair chance at winning the prize this year. Old Betsy Macken won it last year. With her being confined to her sick bed this year, I just might have a chance. I have one for the pie-eating contest and one for the auction basket as well."

"Oh? And who are you hoping will purchase your basket this year? Timothy Thompson?" Seth teased.

"Of course not. Don't be silly. Timothy only has eyes for Coreena Maison. If you must know, I really don't care. I have school to think of. Not marriage."

"If you say so," Seth quipped. Catherine hadn't quite gotten over her crush on Zachery Lettington in Philadelphia. He enjoyed teasing her every now and then anyway.

"And what about you?" Catherine threw back. "Going to try to win over the fair Anna Louise today?"

"I'm going to enter the pie-eating contest," Michael chimed in, making it unnecessary for Seth to answer his sister. "I hope I get your pie, Sis. It sure does smell good. You make the best cherry pie."

"Why, thank you, Michael." She ruffled his newly clipped hair and beamed. "It's mother's recipe, of course."

The mention of their mother caused a strained silence from the Carmichael family now gathered around the wagon. Catherine lifted Sarah from her pram then rolled the small carriage over to Seth to load into the wagon. She drew her baby sister in for a hug to reassure her everything was normal.

Seth liked that about Catherine. His sister had a way of comforting everyone without so much as a word. She'd make a fine teacher. Of course it went without saying they all missed their mother. No one had talked about her much since the day they'd seen her off at the station.

"We need to talk about this, Catherine," Seth said. "We can't just go on thinking everything is jim-dandy around here without her."

"Seth. Not now. You'll upset the boys."

"They know what's going on as well as you and I. Don't think they don't. It doesn't make it any easier for them. Does it boys?"

The three younger brothers stood to one side of the wagon peering over the top of the railing at them, eyes wide, heads nodding.

"Maggie is good to us, but we miss Ma," Michael whined.

The others nodded again.

"I know you do sweetie. We all do," Catherine confirmed. "But we must not dwell on it. So, Seth, get this pram loaded. I'll go see what's keeping Maggie and Madeline."

"We're right here, we are," Maggie Flanagan said, unaware of the exchange, her usual cheerful face aglow.

"Here, Mrs. Flanagan, let me help you with those," Seth offered.

"Why, how sweet of you, Seth. Come along Madeline."

Madeline tagged behind dressed in red gingham with a flounce around the hemline, and a white bib-apron which wrapped around her body with a huge bow tied in back. Her matching bonnet hung around her neck, her red pigtails resting over her front shoulders. Unlike her mother, Madeline's face lacked a smile. Seth figured the girl still hadn't gotten over moving up to the country and living with strangers.

"Somebody take a hold of Sarah while I place the blankets down on the seats so we'll be more comfortable on the long journey into town. We can use them this evening when it cools and the children fall asleep on the way home. I've put pillows under the bench seats for later, too."

"Is there room for my boxes?" Maggie held a couple more boxes she'd run back in the house to fetch and was now clinging to tightly, her chin resting on the top box to keep it from tumbling over.

"There's plenty of room under the bench seats on either side of the wagon. We even have room for the pies, and the two large picnic baskets filled for lunch at the park," Catherine said.

"Good," Seth said. "Let's get it all loaded, and settle everyone in the back so we can get underway."

Catherine climbed up into the back of the wagon with Sarah and the others, leaving Mrs. Flanagan to sit up front with Seth. Once everyone was settled, Seth clicked the reins, and the horses maneuvered the wagon out of the yard and down the steep hill.

Catherine started everyone to singing, and by the time they were half-way to town, Seth was pleased to hear them in a merry mood once again. Even Madeline had the makings of a smile.

Yep. Catherine was going to make a good teacher if she ever got the chance.

As Seth steered the wagon into the village and rounded the street next to McCarthy's store, they fell in line with other families coming in from the countryside to join the festivities. Finding an empty spot next to the athletic field where the day's events were already underway, he nudged his horses and wagon into the tight spot. A quick jerk on the reins and they were there. Seth jumped down, tied the horses to the iron ring in the hitching post, gave the horses a gentle pat on their heads, and then put a hand up to help Mrs. Flanagan down.

Timothy, Michael, and Robert didn't waste any time. They jumped from the back of the wagon and ran off to meet their school chums they'd already spotted. Seth took a moment to scan the open park until he found the one person he was looking for—Anna Louise. She was standing behind a table at the Woman's Christian Temperance Union's booth where people were already lining up to purchase some of the society's baked goods.

"She fancies you, you know," Catherine said when they were alone again, Mrs. Flanagan and Madeline having run off to join the throng of fair-goers and set up their own booth to sell her crisp, white Irish lace. Sarah was tucked snug around Madeline's pudgy frame, while Maggie carried her boxes of lace like a proud owner of precious Tiffany glass. Catherine and Seth carried the cherry pies across the fair grounds at a slower pace.

Seth sighed. "I aim to ask her to marry me today," he confided, not bothering to meet Catherine's eyes while they made their way to the tables where the pie contest was to take place.

"Didn't you already ask her?"

Seth kept his eyes on Anna Louise the whole time, hoping she'd look his way.

She didn't.

"I did. Guess I did it all wrong."

"If you weren't so stupid when it comes to courting a lady, Seth Carmichael, you'd figure out how to do it proper. Let her get her teaching certificate, and then go after her. What's the rush? You've a farm to run."

"Gads, Catherine. When it comes to love, I don't think you're an expert yet, yourself. Besides, in between milking cows and goats, and plowing fields my mind has been patient long enough. What I need to figure out is how to win her away from that lumber tycoon, Mr. Linsky."

"Tycoon? I don't believe Mr. Linsky falls into such an elite category." Catherine stopped and glared into Seth's eyes. "Perhaps they're just friends. And maybe, just maybe, Anna Louise is using him to find out just how serious you are about wanting to marry her. And from the looks of you, I'd say it's working. You're jealous."

"Jealous? *Jealous? Me?*" Seth hissed between clenched teeth so no one else would hear. He glared back into Catherine's sparkling eyes. Dang it. She had the nerve to laugh right in his face. Shucks. Maybe she was right. His sister had a knack of always being right. He took a deep breath and sighed, and then turned to continue across the noisy, crowded fairgrounds with Catherine, holding a cherry pie in each hand.

"I am not jealous. There is something about Mr. Linsky that doesn't seem right. I'm only worried about her getting involved in something illegal."

"You are jealous."

"I am not."

"Yes. You are." Catherine laughed.

Seth stormed off ahead of her toward the pie booth, ending the conversation.

Once the pies were delivered, Seth walked back to the wagon to get the two picnic baskets. He carried them across the field, along with a blanket he threw over his shoulders. He found a place along the far side of the festivities where they were sure to have an excellent view of the hot air balloon set to go off at one o'clock. He spotted Madeline rounding the last booth, Sarah in tow, heading his way.

"Where's your mother?" Seth asked, taking Sarah in his outstretched arms while Madeline helped spread the large quilt out on the grass.

"She's still at her booth. There were lots of people buying her lace."

"Good. I hope she gets plenty of orders, too." He handed Sarah back to the young girl once she was settled on the ground.

Catherine walked across the field, talking to a young lady he didn't recognize. They stopped for a moment, spoke, and then waved to each other as they turned to go their separate ways. From a distance, the girl was a might taller than Catherine. She was thin looking, wore a long skirt of blue denim, and her dark hair hung in a long single braid.

"Who were you talking to?" he asked as Catherine drew near.

Catherine knelt on the quilt and took the tablecloth out of the picnic basket to spread it on top of the blanket before she answered.

"An acquaintance from school, Cassandra Strang.

Her family lives on the farm over the hill from ours. I'm surprised you haven't met her father at one of your farm meetings."

"Of course. He's big in the Agriculture Society. I didn't know he had any daughters."

"Just one. I doubt if she's going back to the Academy in the fall though. She's too busy wanting to raise and train horses. I would have introduced you, but I figured the two of you had already met. She seems to know you. She's a very nice lady."

"It's not important." Seth looked over to where Cassandra Strang stood with her family, quite at ease with herself.

Catherine lifted fried chicken, potato salad, cheese, pickled beets, hard boiled eggs, and watermelon wedges out of the basket. The tantalizing smells reminded Seth just how hungry he was. He looked down at the great feast laid out before them and forgot about everything except his stomach. He figured his brothers must have a natural homing device for food because they appeared out of nowhere.

All around them, other families gathered with their picnic baskets and blankets and settled on the green lawn. Tiny violets grew among the clover and a few dandelions added a touch of sunshine with little mounds of yellow. A variety of colorful parasols also dotted the park to protect the women from the hot noontime sun. A cheerful afternoon, Seth's mood was light and positive. He sat back while everyone enjoyed the festivities. Even baby Sarah was on her best behavior, and Madeline's smile had grown a tad wider.

Seth scanned the picnickers in search of Anna Louise. Not able to locate her, he figured she was still busy at the Women's Christian Temperance Union's cake-wheel booth. He checked his pocket watch.

"Is it time for the balloon man to take off?" Timothy asked.

"It's taking an awful long time to get the dang-blasted contraption up in the air," Michael spoke up.

"According to the schedule, the balloon should have already been in the air, flying high over the field," Catherine said.

"Be patient," Seth scolded. "Let's eat while we wait. It shouldn't be long now."

They finished eating, stowed everything back in the baskets, and still the hot air balloon lay limp on the ground. Many of the other families started packing up as well, and were beginning to mill about, chatting, while their children ran off. Several balls appeared and a game of baseball got underway. Timothy joined in, but Michael, with his broken arm, and Robert stood to the side. Mrs. Flanagan and Catherine were engaged in conversation with several of the other women, while Madeline remained on the blanket with Sarah, playing pat-a-cake.

Seth spotted Mr. Linsky across the way talking to the owners of the two major mills in the village. Perhaps now was his chance to go visit Anna Louise's booth while everyone else was otherwise occupied.

Mustering the nerve, Seth had only taken two steps when the band struck up a few loud notes, followed by the thunderous percussions, preparing everyone for the biggest event of the day. The balloon was finally about to lift off. Children ran back to be with their families, and the entire crowd turned to observe the multi-stripped colored balloon take form and rise upward.

A man with a big black top hat, a black tuxedo complete with long tails, and a white starched shirt climbed into the basket, which was attached to the balloon with thick ropes. It was all held fast to the ground where another man was frantically running to each corner in an effort to untie the anchors so the basket would lift evenly. The basket jerked forward, then dragged along the ground like a drunkard, bumping, leaning, and lifting in a staggering motion while flames shot up inside of the balloon. Several bystanders, too close to the balloon, were knocked over, only just managing to roll out of the way, unharmed. The balloon finally took flight into the perfect blue sky in a dramatic sweep. The crowd burst into a cacophony of cheering and clapping. Kids jumped up and down, while adults craned their necks to watch the spectacle. The balloon hung in space for a few more seconds and then rose higher and higher, then drifted over the nearby homes along Main Street. Another round of clapping and cheering erupted as the great colorful spectacle floated up, up, and away. And disappeared out of sight.

Without seeming to worry about where the balloon was going to land, people settled back on their blankets to listen as the local band play several marching songs. Some settled in to chat and enjoy the remains of their picnics. Catherine picked up Sarah, settled her in the pram, and wandered off toward the pie contest booth. Seth and the boys took the empty baskets back to the wagon. Once they were stowed, the boys set off at a dead run to meet up with their friends once again.

"Don't leave the park," Seth yelled. "We're all to meet back here so we can go to the church for services and dinner later this evening."

The fair in full swing, the crowd milled about participating in the day's various events. Seth figured Timothy and Robert were off to take part in the ring toss and the three-legged races. Michael, more than likely headed for the pie-eating contest hoping he'd get Catherine's pie. With his siblings entertained, Seth took the opportunity to finally go in search of Anna Louise.

At first, he didn't see her, and his heart dropped clear down to his boots with a thud of defeat. He was too late. What was he to do? He'd come prepared to be a perfect gentleman and show Anna Louise how much he truly cared. Had he missed his chance to tell her things had changed at the farm? Now that Maggie was there to help his sister, she no longer had to worry about helping him with his family.

Seth turned around, head drooping, and walked back toward his wagon in disappointment. Not paying any attention to where he was going, he was surprised when someone called his name.

"Seth. How nice to see you," Anna Louise trilled, a welcoming smile covered her beautiful face.

Seth stopped and stared. Anna Louise looked like a Christmas present on the Fourth of July. Her white dress was ruffled with a big red bow around her waist and hung clear to her hemline in the back. Her long ringlets flowed from the crown of her head with another red bow keeping all those lovely strands in place. And Seth spied the tips of her red shoes peeking out from under her gown.

His heart picked up a beat, and his chest hurt with the speed. His mouth dry, he had to say something, but was speechless. Yet, he didn't want this chance to pass him by.

"You look lovely today, Anna Louise," he stuttered.

"Why thank you, Seth," she replied, bobbing her head, and then making eye contact.

If Seth's heart didn't stop doing a dance in his chest, he'd make a fool of himself when it popped right through in front of his shirt for everyone at the park to see.

He hoped his face wasn't red. Men didn't blush. But dear Lord, being this near to Anna Louise made him warm all over. It was a hot afternoon, yes, but this heat had nothing to do with the weather. On the other hand, perhaps she would presume the bright color of his face was the result of sunburn.

"Can I walk you to where you're going?" he asked. "Here, let me carry your basket."

"Why thank you. How kind of you to offer," Anna Louise said, handing him the basket and tucking her hand through his right arm.

Seth's heart picked up speed once more. Did this girl have any idea what her touching him did to his heart? Men didn't swoon, but he was pretty close to falling to his knees.

"I'm just back from getting one of my spice cakes to take back to the cake wheel booth. I made it myself."

"I'll have to take a chance, then. I love spice cake."

Which wasn't altogether true, but if Anna Louise made it, it had to be excellent. Perhaps he'd come to like spice cake.

Anna Louise smiled, her eyes as blue as a robin's newly laid egg and just as bright as the noonday sunshine. Lost in their depths, he almost dropped the cake when he lost his footing, catching himself only when he looked straight ahead. Her hands tightened on his arm, and he didn't think he was going to survive the experience.

Was Anna Louise flirting with him?

Confident things were looking up, to his way of thinking, Seth presumed this to be the right time to put his proposal forward again.

The smell of lavender wafted up to tickle his nose. He closed his eyes for only a moment to savior the essence of Anna Louise. He opened them to find Mr. Linsky approaching.

Seth's heart took a dive. This time, doom had just struck a blow. The spell was broken.

Mr. Linsky fell into step on the other side of Anna Louise.

Ill at ease, Seth was determined to keep pace and deliver Anna Louise's cake as promised. The three of them walked together to the cake-wheel booth. In silence.

If he didn't have a hold of her basket, he'd turn tail and run. Yep. He was a coward. So what? He couldn't stand the man.

There were words he wanted to say to Mr. Linsky, but he had vowed to be a perfect gentleman in front of Anna Louise today. As much as it tore at his heart, the best thing to do was leave without making a fool of himself once again. Instead, he begged his leave.

The day wasn't over. There might be other opportunities to be alone with Anna Louise. He would be patient.

Dejected, Seth searched for the others. Mr. Childs, the photographer, and his son were taking photos today.

He had saved enough money so he could have a photograph taken of the whole family. Catherine had suggested they send one to their mother so she could see they were all doing well, especially baby Sarah.

Seth rounded up the family with the help of Mrs. Flanagan, and they waited in line for their turn for Mr. Childs to snap their picture. Sarah started to fuss, and Catherine took charge of her, walking her back and forth. The boys made funny faces, hoping to make her smile.

Seth wondered if Mr. Childs was ever going to get around to taking their picture before everyone was too grumpy to smile when it was their turn. Mr. Strang chose that moment to stop by and strike up a conversation. The Strang farm, as Catherine had mentioned, was only a few acres over the hill from their land.

"I hear the trunk lines have officially reduced wages by ten percent," Mr. Strang said. "The B&O line is holding back. Don't know when things are going to blow around here, but I hear it's building up and could be any day now. Sounds like Pittsburgh is the worst."

Seth had been told the general strike scheduled for June twenty-seventh was cancelled because of dissention in the union ranks. For now, all was quiet here in Candor, and he could relax and concentrate on matters closer to home.

"The trains are still running. A good sign," Seth said.

"They're starting to hold back. Some have started running double headers. A group of us are getting together to voice our concerns. Going to form a cooperative. I like what I've been hearing about you,

Seth. You're doing good things up on your hill. A good head for business. Why don't you join the cooperative, too? We're meeting Thursday at the Town Hall. Two o'clock sharp. Why not join us?"

"Thank you, sir. A cooperative sounds like a good idea. I'll be there."

Mr. Strang shook Seth's hand and walked on. To be accepted by the local farmers was a big step forward in Seth's mind, but to be asked to join the cooperative was an even bigger feather in his cap. Many of these farmers had been around for a long while and didn't take kindly to some of the new-comers. He would attend the meeting, dang it. Getting involved in community affairs would prove to Anna Louise he was somebody. Just like Mr. Linsky.

Mr. Childs called to Seth. It was their turn to gather in front of the camera. Sarah sat still while the photographer fiddled with the picture machine, a smile on her face. When the camera flashed, Sarah wailed, and Robert rubbed at his eyes. Catherine soothed them, but a commotion to their left of the field caught everyone's attention, and Sarah stopped fussing.

The two fire departments, Alpha and Alert Hose were getting ready for the hose contest. Once the spray of water shot into the air, the contest was on. Hooting and hollering filled the afternoon as the hose companies sprayed water across the field at each other, each trying to outdo the other. Everyone standing within several yards of the event got soaked from the spray. This year the Alpha Hose outdid the Alert Company by a large margin, their water supply running out sooner. Afterwards the two companies competed in their annual baseball game. This time the Alert Company won.

Seth and Catherine took the children to look over the hand-made items at the various booths set up on the opposite end of the field where women sold their jams and jellies, canned or baked goods, and even Mrs. Wentworth had her hats on display next to Mrs. Flanagan's Irish lace display. The two ladies chatted amiably. Wand's Glove Factory and the Blanket Factory also had a booth selling some of their more recent articles of clothing and horse blankets.

Seth spotted Anna Louise several times throughout the afternoon. Each time, he held out hope she would look his way and smile or wave. But Mr. Linsky was always at her side. He couldn't get their kiss out of his mind. She had returned his kiss. Hadn't it meant anything to her?

Was there any hope?

To Seth, the day dragged on until it was time to gather everyone once again to go to the church for the evening reading of the Declaration of Independence and the community's traditional ham dinner. Catherine and Mrs. Flanagan helped him gather the family together and load everyone into the wagon. Seth waited for them to get settled before he clicked on the reins and instructed the horses to head down Main Street to the Federated Church.

"Seth, guess who won the pie-eating contest." Robert smiled up at him.

"You," Seth said, taking his brother's thunder away.

"How'd you guess?" Timothy asked, the dismayed look on his face comical.

"You have cherries on your face."

"Oh." He reached up to wipe it off.

"I got second place for my age group," Michael said. "I didn't eat fast. It was too good to gobble down."

"Did your pie win this year, Catherine?" Seth asked.

"It sure did," Maggie chimed in, beaming just as bright as Catherine.

"And who won your basket?" Seth asked.

"I don't know. I didn't bother to find out. I told you I didn't care."

"If you say so."

"It was Jimmy Leonard," Timothy snitched.

"Come on, everyone, let's get going. We have a dinner to go to." Catherine urged everyone along, taking the spotlight off her for the time being.

The sun had been bright overhead all day and had recently descended over the hillside toward Spencer. The smell of fresh baked ham circled out through the church's kitchen window and lingered down the street

Seth's stomach rumbled.

He did a quick sweep of the church lot as he drew the wagon alongside the street looking for a place to hitch the horses. Anna Louise was nowhere to be found.

"She'll be here," Catherine whispered in his ear. "I'm sure she's inside helping in the kitchen, as usual. This is her family's church."

Seth gave Catherine a withering look. His sister's smile firmly in place, he turned to concentrate on finding an area wide enough to hold both horses and wagon. When he found one, he maneuvered them into place, then jumped from the buckboard to hitch the horses to the post.

Seth threw on his finest church-going jacket he'd tucked under the front seat of the wagon and slicked back his hair to make sure it hadn't come undone during the afternoon. Satisfied he looked presentable for Anna Louise, he proceeded to help everyone down from the wagon. Together they filed into the church's side entrance.

Catherine was right, Seth noted as they paid for their dinner and found a seat. He spotted Anna Louise through the pass-through window in the kitchen. She wore a crisp white apron over her day dress. He was even more surprised when she was the one who waited on their table after they were seated. And even more pleased when Anna Louise and her family sat behind them during the reading of the Declaration of Independence held in the church meeting room after dinner.

He could smell her sweet fragrance and wanted to turn around to drink in her beauty. He held himself back from wanting to do nothing more than run his hands through her magnificent blonde ringlets which bounced every time she shook her head. If they weren't sitting in the middle of the church with everyone surrounding them, he would love to untie the red bow in her hair and let those wispy strands hang loose. He didn't even feel an ounce of blasphemy because they were in a church and he was thinking such thoughts. Being this near to the love of his life was driving him mad. Like a kid, he fidgeted in the pew, his long arms dangling between his knees.

Dear Lord. He should be praying. Instead, he wanted to cuss his father out for sending his mother west and putting him in this difficult position. Anna Louise was right. Who in their right mind with dreams within their grasp would want to take over the running of a ready-made family, run a household, and deal with a nobody farmer like himself?

Seth had hoped to make strides with Anna Louise today. Instead, she was right in many respects. Perhaps he wasn't the person she needed. She needed someone like Mr. Linsky who could take care of her, pay for daily help, and even a nanny when the children came along. Seth pictured her, a leader in the community, walking down the street and being held in high respect in many social circles. If she were to marry him, he could only see her as someone who would grow bitter with lost opportunities. But it didn't stop him from loving her and wanting her to love him in return. They could work something out. He was sure of it.

Bowing his head and closing his eyes, Seth sent up a prayer. *"Dear God in Heaven, please forgive me for asking for your help with Anna Louise, but I don't know what I'm doing wrong. I'm sure you mean for her to be my wife only she don't know it yet. Please help her to see the light."*

Seth opened his eyes. Guilt washed over him, and he bowed his head again. *"Please look out for Ma way out west and help her heal so she can come home and be with her family. Oh, yes. And help Catherine to pass her exams. Amen."*

By the time the oration ended, Robert and Sarah had fallen asleep. A gentleman in the back row snored to beat the band, and his embarrassed wife nudged him in an effort to make him stop. Mrs. Flanagan and Catherine carried the kids and herded the others from the church into the cool evening. Seth lingered near the vestibule to have a word with Anna Louise before she left. He caught her arm and drew her aside.

"Do you have a minute, Anna Louise? I'd like a word, please." Seth held his hat in his hand, his shoulders slumped.

"For you, Seth, I can make time. Shall we go to the alcove near the stairs," Anna Louise said with a hint of concern.

Her eyes hooded, she followed him.

He didn't want her pity.

Seth cleared his throat. He looked down at Anna Louise. She was so beautiful; he almost lost the courage to speak. But this was important, and he had to get through it.

"I, um…,understand why you can't see your way clear to consider my proposal, Anna Louise. So, I want to put your mind at ease. I won't pester you to reconsider my proposal I made the other day." Seth squeezed the hat in his hands while he gazed into Anna Louise's brilliant blue eyes. This was goodbye. He had to let her go.

"Seth…,"

"No. Let me finish," he said. "I know you have dreams, and they don't include me. I'm sorry. I want you to know I do love you, not because I need someone to help me out with my sisters and brothers, or the household, or the farm. The situation at the time prompted me to act irrationally. Too soon, as it turns out."

"Seth…"

Seth didn't give her a chance to speak. He drew her behind the alcove and wrapped his arms around her, pulled her in close, and kissed her full on the lips. He let her go, turned, and walked out of the church.

And wiped at the tears pooling in the corners of his

eyes. He was glad the sun had disappeared behind the hillside. He unhitched the rope from the post and got into the wagon where his family had already settled. He was thankful everyone was tired on the ride home and no one was up to talking as the night grew more dim. Even Maggie Flanagan. He didn't think he could keep up a conversation, his heart ached so. He'd likely bite their heads off if they started.

Is this what loving someone did to you? Turned you into a sorry sap?

Seth moaned, clicked on the reins, and drove the wagon into the night.

Chapter Fourteen

It'd only been a week since the oil car incident, and Charley's attempt to pacify the workers had no effect whatsoever. Meeting with the trainmen and the engineers did little to defray their concerns. Fight after fight broke out among the men once again. Sides were taken. It was time to talk to Seamus and find out just what the hell was going on, why the men were still all worked up.

"Donahue's been seen at the rails sparking the rift again," Seamus said, combing his fingers through his hair. "He's keeping the men agitated. Now he's nowhere to be seen. The coward. He hasn't been near his office, neither, far as I know."

"I told Aderley he should have fired him a long time ago. The weasel uses his position to fuel the fire. I think he keeps Aderley in the dark about a lot of important facts in regards to the true situation on the other rail lines and the strike. I'll eat my hat if they've really given out pay raises anywhere in the entire nation."

Charley clutched his fists at his sides. It was getting harder and harder to keep his loyalties on both sides of the matter. Fact was, he sympathized with those whose wages were next to nothing already. The entire strike could have been prevented if Scott and the other big bugs hadn't cut wages in the first place.

"How can I tell Aderley he hasn't gotten anywhere with those talking Union?" he asked Seamus. "I have to go in there now, report to the man himself, and see what I can do."

"Good luck to ya. I pray he listens this time, or we've got big trouble heading our way."

"I don't like this one bit, Seamus. Not one bit. I've been nothing but a sorry friend to the men. I've been stupid to stand by and let things go on without standing up for you and the others."

"You've been in a hard spot. Can't be easy."

"No. But I plan to tell Aderley, and even Scott if necessary, where my true loyalties lay. More than half the city of Philadelphia's moral majority has already figured out where their loyalties fit."

Charley walked along the tracks leading to the station and Aderley's office. Damn the rails. Child labor issues had surfaced during the last meeting. Nothing had been resolved. No way in hell did he want his children working in such dangerous conditions alongside him day after day. The other poor Joe and their sons busted their hides for the number of hours needed to earn a respectable wage. And in the end, it didn't make a damn bit of difference in their everyday lives. Working conditions were bad enough, and many of the young boys ended up injured. Still, he understood why men let their children work. They needed the wages. But it still didn't make it right. Or safe.

But dammit, Seamus was right. If they didn't stand up for what they believed in, then the corporations would win. *Again.*

Charley entered Aderley's office to find him at his desk, head held between clenched fists. An eerie keening noise filled the room. Charley stood just inside the doorway a moment longer, not sure what was going on. He'd never seen the big man in such bad shape. Had Westmüller died? Had there been more bloodshed he didn't know about? What had happened to put Aderley in such a pathetic state? Charley wasn't aware of anything happening involving the strike that would cause such a reaction. But for sure, it had to be something big.

Charley cleared his throat and entered the room as if nothing was amiss, hoping to catch the man's attention. Aderley didn't bother to lift his head or hide the tears streaming down his ashen cheeks. Instead, he gave a great sniff, cleared his throat, and wiped at his face with large trembling hands.

"He's dead," Mason Aderley keened. "Oh, my God in heaven, Charles. He's dead." The big man's voice shook with the news.

"The man made it through the fire," Charley said, sure Aderley referred to Westmüller. "I was sure God would've saved the man's soul after all he suffered through."

"No. Not Westmüller, dammit," Aderley yelled, pounding his fist on the table.

Charley jumped back at the outburst.

"Not Westmüller. If only it was. No. God almighty, Charles, my son. I just got a telegram from some god-forsaken place called Silver Springs. There was an accident. The train my wife and boys were on got detained on the other side of the Rockies. A damaged train trestle, of all things. A buffalo stampede. Indian hunting party chased them across the plains. My son. My son, Jason, was trampled in a buffalo stampede.

He's dead. I sent them away from harm, but instead, I sent them right into it."

The man bowed his head in his hands again and sobbed deep gut-wrenching sobs. Charley rushed to the desk, opened the bottom left-hand drawer, and took out the bottle of whiskey. He detached the cork and handed it to Aderley.

"Here, drink up."

Aderley didn't need to be told twice. Oblivion was the only way to handle this kind of news on the back of the oil car disaster. Right now Charley didn't give a damn about the railroad or the strike. It was all a big poisonous cauldron anyway. Aderley's pain went much deeper than any of those problems.

Charley sat down on the other side of the room and waited as Aderley drank himself into unconsciousness.

Charley jumped from his chair and started pacing. *Holy Mary, Mother of God.* Emily had been on that train, too. Her telegram hadn't said anything about a stampede. As soon as he took care of Aderley, he'd head on over to the telegraph office and contact Seth and find out just what had taken place. Find out if Emily had been hurt.

Damn trains. Damn strike.

Aderley's head lolled forward, then hit the desk with a thud. Charley grabbed the bottle of whiskey, took a long eager swallow, plunked the bottle on Aderley's desk, and walked out.

Strike be dammed. He prayed Emily was okay.

****

"Mrs. Aderley is asking for you," Mrs. Shay said. She rushed into the parlor, her face flushed with concern. "I assured her I'd fetch you right quick."

"Oh, my, is she okay? Is something wrong?" Emily followed Mrs. Shay down the hallway to Marian Aderley's room where she and her son had been cloistered since they'd arrived in Silver Springs. Emily prayed the poor woman wasn't on her death bed.

The afternoon sun was hot and the air dry. Emily shuddered as she entered the dark room, humid and musty from lack of fresh air. Marian's still body lay hidden under a heavy handmade quilt of muted shades of blues and greens from many washings and hangings in the sun. Emily approached the bed as quietly as possible, but it wouldn't have mattered if she'd tapped her heels across the bare hardwood floor. Marian looked to be dead to the world. Emily's heart raced.

"Marian?" Emily put her hand on the woman's forehead. Despite the hot room, it was cool to the touch. "Marian. It's Emily Carmichael," she tried again. "Mrs. Shay said you were awake and calling for me. How are you feeling?"

Marian opened her eyes to mere sunken slits. Emily sighed at the effort it took for Marian to focus her tired, pain-filled eyes. The woman was much too frail. The once vibrant woman, glowing with health, now gazed at the ceiling in the dark, wasting away.

"Let me open the curtains to let some sunshine in so you can enjoy this glorious day."

Not waiting for a reply, Emily rushed to the window and drew back the heavy curtains. She was surprised the doctor's wife hadn't already opened them on such a bright warm afternoon. Within seconds the room glowed with warmth.

Marian's son, Jonathan, stirred. Emily turned to find him huddled in a chair in the corner, leg propped up, head lolled sideways. Even in sleep the boy looked sad, sullen, and subdued.

"Are you in pain, my dear?" She turned her attention back to the boy's mother.

Marian blinked several times, then uttered a few words in a strained voice Emily had to draw closer to hear.

"Not if I lay still," Marian mumbled.

"What can I do for you? A drink of water, perhaps? A cool cloth?"

Marian's whisper was weak, as if the mere motion of forming words caused her lips to hurt. "The ache in my heart is much worse than any pain I suffer in either my ribs or my leg."

"I'm so sorry," Emily soothed, stroking the woman's brow, aware there was most likely nothing she could do to alleviate the woman's agony. There was no cure for heartache. But she had to ask just the same. "Has anyone sent word to your husband? Will he be joining you in San Francisco?"

"I've had word sent. But Mason is much too busy with matters of the strike back east to worry about me," Marian uttered as tears rolled over her pale cheeks. Her thick, black lashes spiked from the wetness against her chalk-white skin. The woman resembled a waif adrift at sea.

Emily's own cheeks were a bit damp as well. She took Marian's hand in hers and patted it gently.

"I'm sure your husband will be concerned. As soon as the doctor returns, I'm sure he'll give you a dram of laudanum for the pain. I pray it will be soon."

Emily walked to the dry sink, found a large but dainty white fluted bowl with roses circling the rim. Mrs.

Shay had filled it with fresh water. A pristine white cloth and hand towel lay in a tidy pile next to the basin. Emily dipped the cloth in the lukewarm water, wrung out the excess, then returned to Marian's side. With gentle strokes, she swabbed Marian's brow.

"Your son needs tending, as well," Emily soothed. "I'll check with Sheriff Coulter to see if he knows of someone who can be of help until the doctor returns. Perhaps Mr. O'Leary from the train might be willing to stop by. He was very helpful while we were at Weber Canyon."

"Please, if you would be so kind to take care of my son. Tend to his needs."

Jonathan stirred, moaned at the mention of his name, and then opened his eyes. He looked around the room in confusion. Emily wanted to take him in her arms and comfort him.

"Don't you worry now, Marian. I'm glad to be of assistance anyway I can. You rest."

Emily drew the coverlet down to allow air next to Marian's inert body. There was no need for her to be so bundled. She made her way around the foot of the bed and approached Jonathan.

"It must be hard for such a young active boy like yourself to be stuck in this room with a broken leg all day. I'll see if I can find someone to carry you outside where you can get some fresh air and enjoy this sunshine." Emily pointed to the window, but Jonathan didn't bother to look, his eyes focused on his mother. "The Shays have a wonderful front porch." Emily tried to coax a response from the young boy. "I'll just go see if Sheriff Coulter can find someone to help get you outside without damaging your broken leg further."

Jonathan looked at his mother as if waiting for her approval. Emily waited, too, and was soon rewarded when Marian nodded her head. Good. The young man needed to get out of the dark room. The sooner the better.

Emily left to search for Sheriff Coulter. Walking down the boardwalk, she lifted her freshly laundered skirts, thanks to Mrs. Shay, and stepped down to cross the dirt street to where the Bottom's Up Saloon was full to overflowing with business already. She spotted Sheriff Coulter coming from the jail, three buildings down. She waved to gain his attention.

"Sheriff Coulter. We need your assistance, sir. Young Jonathan needs to be taken outside to take advantage of this beautiful sunshine and get out of his dark sickroom. Could you do us the honor of finding someone to help transfer him to the front porch?"

Sheriff Coulter tipped his hat. "I'd be happy to, Ma'am." He followed Emily back to the house where Mrs. Shay stood, waiting for them on the front steps. Together they managed to get Jonathan situated in a chair tucked in a corner of the porch where they propped his foot up on a pillow.

"I know just the thing for you young man," Mrs. Shay said, her finger pointing up in the air, her head bobbing sideways. "A nice tall glass of squeezed lemonade. I had a delivery of ripe lemons the other day and kept them in the root cellar for just such an occasion."

Mrs. Shay spun around and entered the house to fetch the lemonade. Emily turned once again to Sheriff Coulter.

"Could you do one more kindness for us this morning, Sheriff? Mrs. Aderley is in need of a pain killer.

My supply of Dover's powder has dwindled. I wondered if perhaps you would check with the others, see if someone might have some laudanum on hand. The poor woman's broken ribs are extremely painful. She isn't able to get the rest she needs, and I'm afraid Dr. Shay took what was left of his supplies with him."

"Leave it to me, Ma'am. I'll see what I can do."

Levi Coulter tipped his hat, then sauntered back across the street toward the saloon where many of the stranded had been filing in for a noon-time meal. Although off limits to women in the evening, the Bottoms Up Saloon served a grand spread during the day for the stranded passengers and trainmen.

"That should quench your thirst, young man," Mrs. Shay said, returning with a glass in hand and a smile on her rosy face. "Now, you just call out if you need anything else. I'll go inside and tidy up your room and check on your mother."

"Looks like everyone is heading in for a noon-time meal," Emily stated the obvious to the Weaver sisters as they came out of the house.

"Yes," Pansy replied. "We were just off to partake."

"Would you like us to bring something back for you?" Violet asked.

"Thank you, you're very kind, but I'll make my way over in a bit. I'll sit here with Jonathan and keep him company for awhile."

The Weaver sisters preceded down the steps, then crossed the dusty street, arm in arm. Mr. O'Leary opened the swinging doors for them and then disappeared inside.

"Why don't you get yourself something to eat, Mrs. Carmichael?" Mrs. Shay said. "I'll keep an eye on this young fellow now his mother is all settled."

"I'll send something over for Jonathan. A growing boy has a hunger needing to be satisfied. He looks to be wasting away."

"I'll be fixing some broth for the boy's mother, don't you worry about her."

"Thank you, Mrs. Shay. You've been too kind to us already."

"I've enjoyed your company. We don't get many visitors way out here. Now, you just get on over there and get yourself something. You need to keep your own strength up. You worry about others more than you do yourself."

Emily didn't hesitate to cross the dusty street. She paused in front of the saloon's swinging doors, not feeling right entering an establishment full of rough men. But she couldn't deny the townspeople had welcomed them all with open arms. They'd even kept the night-time escapades to a minimum until after the passengers from the train finished their evening meal.

She swung the doors open, entered, and then cautiously stepped inside. The din of conversation and rattle of china and utensils filled the large room. Emily scanned the open space, and spotted Mr. O'Leary, who immediately spotted her. Like a gallant, kind gentleman, he came to her aid.

"Well now, Mrs. Carmichael. Will ya be joining us for some lunch? 'Tis not much, to be sure, but 'tis not bad for having to feed the bunch of us." He tucked her arm inside his and led her across the bare planked floorboards to his table.

Emily wanted to lean on him and let him carry her burden, he was such a gentleman; a truly caring person. However, with all the sleep and rest she'd indulged in over the past few days, she had gained a bit of strength and was determined to walk on her own two feet.

"What be bringing such a sad look to yer sweet face, me dear?" he asked.

Emily stepped aside. She forced a smile for his benefit.

"Mrs. Aderley is still not well. Her son sits on the front porch and is in need of some nourishment."

"Of course. Of course. We will see he gets a heaping plateful. Now, Mrs. Aderley. What can I be doing to help her?"

"Her pain is still fierce, I'm afraid. She isn't sleeping very well, nor is she eating as she should. Mrs. Shay is preparing broth for her."

Mr. O'Leary pulled out a chair for her. "You will eat. You look to be ready to pass out yerself. I will arrange a dish from this bountiful spread these kind folks have laid out for us and send it over to the lad."

"Thank you. But I wonder, Mr. O'Leary, do you know of any of the passengers who might have something for pain? The doctor is not back yet, and he might not return for a couple more days. I am afraid Mrs. Aderley's mental well-being is deteriorating because of her unfortunate incident. I've given her a touch of my Dover's powder the last two days, but, like I said, I have little left for myself. I would have asked right away, but I thought the doctor would have arrived before now. I'm sure he'll be able to prescribe something for her when he gets back to town, but in the meantime I don't have much left to share, and she does need something to ease the pain ."

"To be sure I can help. Ya see, my dear lady, I can be of assistance m'self as soon as I have something sent over for the boy. You sit here and relax a wee bit and eat."

Mr. O'Leary, with his twitchy long beard and Irish brogue, made his way to the far end of the room and returned with a cup of hot tea. He then returned with a plate piled high with a thick slice of ham, baked beans, and fried potatoes.

"My land, sir, I don't think I can eat all this. Perhaps you should send some of it back."

"Nonsense. Do what you can. I've found someone to take a plate to the boy."

Emily took the fresh, warm biscuits apart and savored the yeasty aroma as the steam rose up to meet her nose. She smeared a dollop of butter on top. The taste was as divine as they looked and smelled. The people of Silver Springs had come out and done a fine job of taking care of everyone, making sure there was enough food and lodging. Perhaps Elizabeth Young would do well here, after all.

"I didn't know you were a doctor, Mr. O'Leary," Emily said when he returned and sat down with his own full plate. "I would have called on you sooner. Mrs. Aderley will be grateful for your help."

"Oh, my dear lady, 'tis not a doctor I am, but a bit of a chemist. To be sure, I can provide some medicinal help that might reduce the fever a wee bit and even ease the pain, 'tis all. T'will make her comfy 'til the doctor arrives. Now, you just sit here and finish your meal. As soon as I finish, I'll get me bags and step across to visit Mrs. Aderley. Don't ya be a worrying, now. She and her son will be just fine."

Emily did worry. Was Mr. O'Leary one of those traveling salesmen who peddled snake oil and other ointments which promised to cure everything coming down the pike but didn't? For Marian Aderley's sake, she hoped not.

She finished eating then returned to Marian's bedside to find both she and her son resting comfortably. She tiptoed from the room, then made her way back out to the front porch and settled in one of the comfortable rockers. She closed her eyes and wondered how her children were fairing. Was Catherine taking good care of baby Sarah? And what of her own young boys, wild as the wind? Oh, how they would love the West and enjoy the experiences Emily had gone through. Just like Marian's boys had until their unfortunate mishap. And her Charles? Emily sighed. She missed him most of all.

Emily woke to the sound of a player-piano plunking out a rollicking tune across the way. Both male and female voices sang *Oh! Susannah* at the top of their lungs, as off key as the player piano. She stretched, then leaned against the white railing to look toward the Bottom's Up Saloon. Like a beacon in the evening sky, the saloon was all lit up for the night, calling to every man in town. Several of the trainmen swaggered through the swinging doors. No sign of a single Women's Christian Temperance Union member protesting outside the establishment like there would have been back in Candor.

At least not here in Silver Springs.

Since the trains had joined the east coast to the west coast, Emily figured it wouldn't be long before the Temperance Movement inched its way out through the desert, too. Candor's ladies met at the Town Hall on Main Street. Emily knew several of them, and although she had no liking for those who imbibed, she didn't have the time or the where-with-all to join with those who rallied against the bottle. She blessed the saints above she was fortunate her Charles wasn't one to over indulge in such spirits.

A loud commotion exploded across the street. Emily's heart set to pounding. Her hand flew to her bosom. The saloon door burst open, and several men tumbled out, voices raised. It wasn't hard to discern a couple of rowdy locals had taken exception to a few of the trainmen sharing their brew. And more than likely their ladies. She spotted Sheriff Coulter saunter down the street to her left. He fired a couple of shots into the air. The men separated. The trainmen, huffing and puffing, had held their own. The others were in no better shape.

Sheriff Coulter took care of the incident and rallied one of the men toward the jailhouse on the corner. Once again, the evening quieted.

The nighttime sky hung wide open, appearing larger than life. No single cloud obstructed the view of the twinkling stars. One could get lost in such a place. The Wild West was beautiful country if the hardships that many endured could be overlooked. Emily hoped Elizabeth Young would be able to see the beauty of it, and the good sheriff would keep the young mother safe out there on his homestead.

The noise from the saloon drew her back down to earth as another fistfight broke out. This time Sheriff Coulter corralled the culprit and didn't hesitate to strong-arm the man and drag him off to jail.

Emily turned her back on the ruckus and walked to her room at the back of the house without disturbing the others. Lord, she was anxious to leave Silver Springs behind. She prayed they'd be on their way tomorrow.

She changed into her long, white night dress and rinsed her face and hands in the washbasin next to the window. She braided her hair, took a dram of Dover's powder from her skirt's pocket, and washed it down with a glass of water Mrs. Shay had placed on the night stand. Hopefully, the medication would help her get a good night's sleep despite the commotion still coming from the Bottom's Up Saloon.

Chapter Fifteen

Dr. Shay returned to Silver Springs during the night. Just in time to confirm the Aderleys were in good shape to continue traveling by train.

"Mr. O'Leary's new Elixir of Paregoric seems to have done the trick, along with the Willow Bark tea my wife administered while I was away," the good doctor informed them.

Mrs. Shay beamed with his praise.

"I'll talk to the man myself and see if he has more," the doctor said. "Perhaps he will continue to administer to her on the ride to San Francisco."

"I'm sure he won't mind," Emily said. "I'll see they both are looked after."

"I understand you are almost out of your own medicine. I've prepared a packet for you to carry in case you need it."

"Thank you. It is almost gone."

"Sheriff Coulter stopped by earlier and informed me the depot received a telegram this morning saying the train will be arriving tomorrow," Mrs. Shay reported. "I'm sure everyone is looking forward to moving on."

"Yes," the Weaver sisters chimed in as they entered the sitting room.

"It's been rather a long journey. Harrowing for some. I'm sure everyone is looking forward to arriving at their final destination," Pansy said.

"I'm afraid the Aderley's broken bones will heal sooner than their broken hearts," Mrs. Shay said.

"Yes, I do not envy their circumstances," Emily addressed Mrs. Shay. "Thank you for your care and kindness. You've made our stay here more comfortable."

"My dear, I will miss the company more than you know. It isn't often passengers stop by and stay for a spell. It's been my pleasure."

True to Sheriff Coulter's words, the train screeched into Silver Springs at 1:05 in the afternoon the following day. Emily stood alongside the trainmen and passengers on the depot platform clapping and cheering the train's arrival. For some, their welcome in Silver Springs had worn thin. It was past time to leave.

"Sorry for the delay, folks," the new conductor called, stepping down from the long black passenger car as steam hissed out from around large silver iron wheels.

"A bit of a problem with the strikers stopping all trains coming and going. We were lucky our train was able to get out before things really het up."

An hour later everyone rallied to get on board.

Elizabeth Young, her young babe in arms, and Levi Coulter were there to wave them off.

"You take care, now," Emily said. She hugged the young mother and kissed the baby. She looked up at Sheriff Coulter and smiled. "Keep her safe. I don't want to hear she's been mistreated."

"Yes, Ma'am. I'll look after her, for sure. Trust me."

"I hope so."

Emily lifted her skirt to step up into the train. Sheriff Coulter stepped forward and took her hand, guiding her up the steep steps.

"Have a good journey," he said. "I'll make sure Elizabeth contacts you before long."

"I'd like that," Emily replied. He let go of her hand. She found her seat just as Pansy and Violet Weaver waved from the back of the coach, catching her attention.

"Come, my dear. Come sit with us. They've taken Mrs. Aderley and her son to the sleeping car where they will be more comfortable."

"Thank you," Emily accepted their invitation. At least the rest of her journey would be entertaining.

Although resting on this train wasn't any easier than it had been on the one they'd traveled on coming from the East, Emily managed to get a modest amount of rest in between the two sister's continuous disagreements. Lord, couldn't these two agree on anything once in awhile?

The noise of the wheels clacking along the track, the cranking engine combined with the puffing and smell of the smoke from the fire, and the unsavory aromas of cheap cigars made Emily nauseous. Not able to take any more, she excused herself and made her way out to the observation car to get some fresh air. Emily settled at the far end of the open car, remembering the last time they had been in an observation car. She'd never forget the sight of those thundering buffalo and the high-pitched calls of the Indians as they raced across the desert. She closed her eyes and let the rocking motion of the train soothe her frayed nerves and lull her to sleep.

The train made several stops at small stations along the way, leaving Silver Springs far behind. Emily joined the others as they disembarked to enjoy a drink of fresh water, use the facilities, and walk about. The stops, although too short, were a reprieve from the closed proximity to the Weaver sisters who still at this late juncture of their travels found something to argue about. It also gave her a chance to check on the Aderleys, who were still finding it difficult to deal with their injuries and their loss.

The final morning of their journey, clean, wet wash towels were handed out. Emily washed up, then helped the Aderley's prepare for a short stop and their morning meal. Once accomplished, Emily took her leave to go to the observation car. Pansy and Violet had decided to do the same.

"We're almost there," Violet said to anyone who was listening, her voice filled with excitement.

"Well, not quite," Pansy injected a bit more pessimistically. "I can't smell the ocean yet."

"You don't know what an ocean smells like," Pansy assured her in no uncertain terms.

"I'll know it when I smell it."

They were in the California Territory now. She couldn't smell the ocean either, but the train had passed over mountains and valleys. There were fields of vineyards growing in profusion everywhere; orange groves and fields of vegetables unlike anything Emily had ever seen before. The vastness of these farming pursuits was beyond her imagination.

"It's lovely landscape, nevertheless." Emily smiled at the two sisters.

Thankfully they agreed, and to Emily's chagrin, the

two spent the rest of the time in peaceful solitude viewing the grand sights before them.

Two hours later the train slowed as they approached their final destination. San Francisco was a big thriving town, and the train station was impressive for a western territory. Goods from the other eastern trunk lines were transported by way of a different route not affected by the strike and were being unloaded onto waiting wagons. Mail was taken into the station through a special entrance. Mr. O'Leary helped Marian Aderley and Jonathan off the train and whisked them away before the platform and station became over crowded. The white-gloved porter helped Emily and the sisters off the locomotive. Once Emily stepped onto the platform, she quickly caught up to the others.

"Mrs. Aderley," Emily called. "I pray you and your son will receive proper medical attention, now you've arrived to stay with your sister. Your husband will be very anxious to hear from you, I imagine. I won't keep you a moment longer."

"Thank you for all your help, Mrs. Carmichael," Marian said. "And, of course, you too, Mr. O'Leary. You have both been so kind. I don't know how I can ever repay you. If either of you need anything, please look me up. I hope wherever you're going, Mrs. Carmichael, someone will look after you as you've looked after us."

"My cousin Marybelle is expecting me, as you know. I'll be in good hands. She'll be here soon, I'm sure." Emily gave Marian a quick, but gentle hug. She bent and gave Jonathan a hug as well.

"You help take care of your mother, young man. She needs you to be there for her as much as you need her."

Mr. O'Leary took her hands in his and gave them a gentle squeeze.

"If ever you are in need, I hope you will call on me," he said. "I'll be remaining in this town for some time, ya know. I'll be making sure Mrs. Aderley and her son are settled in with her sister. 'Tis the least I can be doing."

"Good luck to you." Emily smiled, at odds with her happiness between leaving with Marybelle and having to leave her new friends behind.

"My dear lady, 'tis been my pleasure, to be sure."

The three of them took their leave, disappearing along with the others inside the station. Emily sighed, straightened up, and went in search of her baggage now stacked with the others on the platform.

"Emily, land sakes, lady, look at you?" Marybelle called. "Why, I'd recognize that family nose and high cheekbones anywhere. Pure Irish O'Malley's to be sure. Turn around and let me look at you. Why, other than looking like you're about to fall off your feet, and the fact you're a little disheveled from riding the rails and the frightening ordeal you've suffered, you look to be able to mend. You are a sight for sore eyes, I can tell you. With the delay in Silver Springs and that confounded buffalo stampede, I about had a heart attack right then and there, I did. Glad to hear there were no serious injuries. Indians have been no problem the last few years, but you never know when one will go wild."

Emily looked at the tall woman standing before her. She couldn't believe her own eyes. If this was Marybelle, she'd eat her hat. For all she knew the darn hat could be back in Silver Springs laying in the desert somewhere, she didn't know where it had gotten to.

"I'm glad to finally be here."

Over the past ten years, Marybelle had grown into a stocky, solid, woman. Once dressed in city finery, and as small and petite as any young girl out east, this Marybelle wore men's breeches and a flannel shirt stretched across her ample bosom. Her oversized hat hung down her back on a neck string. She had a bolero around her neck with a large turquoise stone the size of a twenty dollar gold piece. Her shoes, dusty, man's work boots and just as worn, were laced up around her ankles. She wore her clothes with pride, and no one took exception to Marybelle's dress. Her auburn hair, brushed back in a long thick braid shone squeaky clean in the late afternoon sun. A smile with full lips spread across a face full of freckles that ran into each other, and a set of deep green eyes sparkled with merriment. Emily couldn't help respond to this woman's infectious laugher.

"My gawd, Emily, it's good to see you," Marybelle hugged her so tight she was in danger of her own rib cage breaking. Emily caught the scent of pine and a hint of dust just before she was planted back on her feet.

"Let's grab your satchels, and we'll put them in the buckboard before we go find William. I've arranged a hearty meal, a wash, and a rest for the night before we head out in the morning. William and I have a room just down the hall from yours. Now don't say a word, Em. Let's get you settled, and then we can talk a blue streak and catch up on all the chatter what's been happening back east. This strike isn't going to help us out here any more than it's helping people elsewhere. A lot of people are upset with the Chinese around here and are starting to stir up trouble. You've made it here in time. They're just about to stop trains from going out. No matter. You're here now. That's all that counts."

"I need to send a message to Charles to let him know I've arrived," Emily said, finally able to get a word in.

"Now, don't you fret. The telegraph office is going to be so busy for the next hour or two, we'd be standing in line forever and a day if we tried now. We'll relax first, then send a message to Charley-boy. Here, now, watch your step, we have real nice boardwalks here, but the streets in between are positively dusty and even worse when the rains come. Might be a few puddles still, as we just had some rain the other day after a real long drought. Wouldn't want you to get those fancy shoes of yours dirty. Might just have to be getting you some sturdy boots while we're here. Why, where we're going up in the hills into lumber country, it ain't no place to be prancing about with thin, soft shoes, like yours. No, siree, Em, we'll get you fixed up real nice before we head out tomorrow. There's a few good shops in town, might just as well outfit you here, as to try to find what we want in Wolverine Pass. We stock up while we're in town, so we'll be taking some supplies back with us for our own camp store. We live about twenty miles out from the nearest town. We run a small shop at the camp and stock supplies and equipment for the men who work there. Sometimes other lumberjacks stop by to pick up a few things, too."

Emily didn't need to bother to answer. Marybelle was doing a fine job keeping the conversation going on her own. Besides, Emily was too tired to talk. Within minutes they were across the street at the Fleur-de-lis

Hotel. The exterior was simple, but when they entered, Emily was surprised to find a unique, opaque blue ceiling, Fleur-de-lis wallpaper with gold stripes separating the pattern, thus the name of the establishment. On the left corner, mahogany wainscoting stood out, waxed and shinier than any she had ever seen back east. White damask tablecloths flowed over round tables, and fresh cut flowers decorated the center. Emily, for all she was dressed more appropriately than Marybelle, was still uncomfortable knowing they both looked out of place in such an elegant establishment.

"Don't you fret, none, Em. Follow me. We'll get you in the back and cleaned up real nice. I expect you have some clean clothes in your satchel."

Marybelle led Emily to the back of the building down a narrow hallway to a room with fresh water for bathing. The room had a washstand, a few hooks to hang her clothes on, and a comfortable looking bed with a matching dresser. There was a settee too pristine to sit on. Emily was so tired she sat anyway, unlaced her shoes, and took them off.

"Now you take your time and do a nice slow wash down. I'll wait for you in the dining room. I'll order us up some grub while you get yourself taken care of. It'll be waiting for us when you get done. Just leave everything and come on out. Poor, Em. You do look all done in. You'll be real comfortable here tonight."

"Thanks, Marybelle. I am weary beyond belief."

"You can tell me all about your travels on the way to camp tomorrow. Wait 'til you see our homestead. It's real comfy. Overlooks the ocean. You'll have nothing to do there but put your feet up and relax and get well.

Lord, Em, it's good to have you here."

Emily opened her bag and took out a simple, wrinkled, but clean frock Mrs. Shay had laundered before she left Silver Springs. She washed, changed, and then joined Marybelle and William for dinner minutes later.

****

Bright and early the following morning after a breakfast at the Fleur-de-lis befitting royalty, the trio climbed up on the wagon packed full of various provisions. William managed the loaded buckboard as it bumped along the rutted hillsides. The horses knew their way as they kept a steady pace and wound up the steep slopes and down into the low valleys. They had been traveling similarly for most of the morning, and Emily had lost track of time. Her head bobbed up and down and from side to side, having nodded on and off several times. The rocking motion kept her from falling asleep completely. Her bottom ached. She was sure she'd never be able to sit down again once she got to Marybelle's. Even the train ride hadn't been this bumpy and uncomfortable. She suspected her teeth were in danger of falling out from all the jarring before they arrived at Wolverine Pass. Thankfully, the Dover's powder helped relieve the headache.

The scenery was more beautiful the closer they got to Marybelle and William's homestead. They rode through thick wooded land covered with tall pristine pines and even taller redwoods. Emily breathed in the deep, pine scent and welcomed the shade they provided. They had traveled through valleys where homesteaders had planted vineyards, some of which were great expansions of fields with what looked to be hundreds of rows of grape vines. But none of this beauty prepared Emily for the sight as they dipped over the final hill. William and Marybelle's home stood perched on the next hillside nestled between a grove of tall redwoods. A structure to rival a southern mansion stood out against the bluish-green shades of the majestic cedars high on a sheer cliff which dropped right down into the ocean far below.

Marybelle's 'shanty' turned out to be a large rambling dwelling. Emily couldn't help but wonder just how wealthy William was to be able to afford such an opulent home. Why, the veranda on the second floor wrapped clear around the side of the house with a wrought-iron staircase leading to the back and a sprawling lawn. Spanish grillwork decorated the outside porch on the first floor as well. The large windows were adorned with sturdy shutters the likes of which Emily had never seen. They were large, warm, and welcoming. The roof peaked in the center with smaller windows outlined with more ironwork. The lumber business must be very good at Wolverine Pass, indeed.

Emily didn't have a chance to utter a word as William, a quiet man, yanked in the reins, and the horses stopped in front of a large portico entranceway on a drive patterned in red brick. Marybelle jumped down from the wagon and turned to help Emily down.

"Now, Em, you pay no never mind to the size of our shanty. You won't have to lift a finger to help keep her clean."

"It's such a grand place," Emily whispered in admiration when she finally was able to catch her breath. "Why, this place must take forever to keep up.

There's just no other way I can repay you for letting me recuperate here, Marybelle."

"Gosh, Em. No need to thank me. We're glad to have you. Margarita lives in and takes care of everything, so you needn't fret 'bout a thing. I just haven't the time to keep up with it all, and she does such a magnificent job. She's a great cook, too. You won't have to worry. We'll keep you fed real good. Wait 'til you try her fresh grape pie. We'll get you fattened up. You're looking much too thin."

"I'll need something to occupy my time while I'm here. I can't just sit around and let you wait on me day and night. I won't have it. You're kind enough to let me stay. I need to earn my keep."

"Don't fret. We'll talk about it later. Right now, you need a wash, a rest, and a meal. As I do. Come. Let's get you to your room."

Marybelle led her through the wide entrance of thick, double pine doors. Stunned, Emily stopped in the middle of the foyer. A curved staircase dominated the area seeming to sweep clear up to the sky; the banister of polished honey oak. A deep, dusty, rose-flowered runner carpeted the stairs and the hallway leading to either side of the house and the upper floor's wide hallway.

"I've given you the southwest wing so you can watch the ocean when the sun sets. It's a beauty of a sight, Em. Real restful. You can sit at the desk by the window and write in the evenings. Just wait. You'll see what I'm talking about this evening. You have your own indoor plumbing of sorts. A new-fangled contraption set up, but dang if it don't work just fine. There's some fresh water in the taps in the washroom, too. Just take your time and relax. I'll send Margarita up to fetch you after a while. We'll have our evening meal on the veranda next to the garden before the sun goes down. Fresh air will do us good."

Marybelle shut the door on her way out. Emily walked to the window, and sure enough, the ocean pounded on the rocks below; a loud roar and a mighty spray of white foamy water the likes of which amazed her. The ocean stretched out to meet the sky and the late evening sun sparkled off the water in the distance.

It was as peaceful as Marybelle said it would be. The sight of it alone was worth the trouble she'd gone through to get here.

If only her children were by her side.

If only she could share all of this with Charles.

Chapter Sixteen

General Hancock arrived in Pittsburgh with little pomp and circumstance, unlike his men who had arrived the day before, swooping down in a thundering sea of blue and a cloud of dust from the clomping horses. General Hancock and his staff of four rode into town, tied up just outside the station, then entered the building and knocked on Aderley's office door. Charley sat in one of the leather chairs next to the mahogany desk, where Aderley had slept, slumped in a drunken stupor the night before. He looked like hell this morning—still under the influence of the effects of the bottle. Charley raised his brows watching Aderley stand at attention on steady feet as the general entered. He had to hand it to him, the man never wavered.

"Come in, General. I've been expecting you." Aderley offered his hand.

Charley detected a slight gravel in Aderley's voice, muffled with a deep sigh. Charley stood and shook the general's hand as well.

"Sir, it's a pleasure."

"We had an awful mess here yesterday and don't want to see a repeat," Aderley stated. "The whole town erupted into a frenzy. Thanks to your men, things are under control now. Have a seat." With his hand, Aderley indicated a chair close to his desk.

The general's aide pulled the heavy leather chair

forward. General Hancock sat with purpose, his back ram-rod straight. He lifted his hat and set it on his lap.

"Glad we could be of help. Where's Scott?" the general asked.

"He left for Pittsburgh to take care of some messy business. Sorry, I can't go with you to see the damage in our yards right now. I'm running a bit behind, but my good man Charles Carmichael here will take you down and fill you in on what's been going on."

Aderley nodded to Charley, a pleading look in the man's bloodshot eyes. Charley nodded in silent understanding.

"I'll have my carriage brought round," Aderley said. "I apologize. I do, however, have a meeting with the engineers later this afternoon I must prepare for. Perhaps you'd care to join us. See what we're up against."

"I'll be there," General Hancock confirmed. He stood and placed his hat on his head. "Perhaps my presence will help calm the men down, and we can put an end to things."

"Let's hope so."

General Hancock turned to Charley, who quickly stood.

"Shall we proceed, then, and see what needs to be done?" Charley suggested.

He and General Hancock rode to the rail yard to view the damage caused by the oil car fire. Hancock's staff followed behind on their horses. Never one to feel comfortable around horses, Charley was impressed with the way the men sat tall in their saddles. Hopefully, it would impress the workers as well.

A small contingent of militia had the area

surrounded by the time they arrived. As General Hancock approached, the soldiers snapped to attention, saluted, and then stood aside to let him pass.

"We've ordered troops from the east and the north to stop here when they come through," Hancock told Charley as they walked toward the charred train.

What a sorry sight. Oil smoldered, filling the air with a strong stench. It reminded Charley of Westmüller lying in the hospital, his skin blistered from head to foot. He could still detect the faint sickening stench of burnt flesh. The taste of creosol mixed with petroleum from the burning ties, and the smoking oil tinged his lips. Heat from the smoldering fire warmed the air.

"What the hell happened here?" the general boomed.

Charley thought the general's eyes were going to pop out, they bulged so wide. He proceeded to relay the events leading up to the explosion.

"Your troops managed to turn the townspeople away, but they'll be back to see for themselves what happened," Charley replied. He hoped the strikers wouldn't rally again quite so soon. But if things didn't go well at the meeting this afternoon, they would be back in force.

"Mr. Aderley will be following Mr. Scott's order at the meeting. He's not about to give in to their demands. He's going to need all the help you can give him come morning," Charley advised.

"We're not going anywhere. He can count on us."

Charley was relieved to hear it. He left General Hancock talking to his men. He strode over to talk to the trainmen huddled together on the other side of the tracks next to the roundhouse.

"What's going on?" he asked.

"We ain't backing down." Michael slammed his fist down on the side of a rail car. "I've said it before and I'll say it again. We have nothing to lose."

"Michael's right. If they cut our pay, we'll have nothing a't'all. They might just as well shoot us and get it over with."

"But is it worth dying for?" Charley asked.

He was met with silence.

"What about your families? What's going to happen to them?"

"We can't feed them now," Michael said.

The men all nodded.

Charley knew their dilemma. It was why he'd taken his family north. He patted his pockets for a smoke. Empty. He shook his head and gritted his teeth. He didn't blame the men for not wanting to back down.

"I'll talk to Aderley before the meeting. See what I can do. In the meantime, don't do anything rash to blow this thing wide open."

"No promises, Carmichael. We're going to do what we have to do, no matter whose side you're on."

The men turned from Charley and walked away. He was on his own. He wished he were anywhere but in Philadelphia. He wished he'd gone west with Emily. He sorely needed her comforting arms around him.

Charley couldn't stop thinking about the conversation with Aderley. Aderley had been distressed because he hadn't been there to comfort his wife in her time of need. He had also confided in Charley that there'd been several kidnapping threats against his children, the main reason he'd sent them to San

Francisco in the first place. Where they were supposed to be safe.

But their conversation had also centered on the strike. Mason Aderley and Tom Scott were adamant about enforcing the wage cut despite the events so far. They anticipated being able to replace every single one of those striking with others who needed work. They weren't aware the community was supporting the strikers. No one was going to cross the line and fill those jobs.

With all the reinforcements coming to town, they were going to be outnumbered. God Almighty, they didn't stand a chance.

"They want that meeting," Charley told the general when he'd finished talking to his men. In his opinion, the general wasn't much interested in what the men wanted.

He shook his head and followed the general back to the carriage.

Later, in Aderley's office, Charley listened as the room full of disgruntled engineers and trainmen were informed—strike or no strike—the reduction in pay would stand.

"If you don't want your jobs, there are others who do," Aderley said.

The room broke out in a rash of angry shouts and raised fists.

"Damn it, we're starving now," someone yelled. "If you cut our pay, we won't be able to feed our families or pay the rent."

"Yeah. We won't be able to pay the rent. We'll be put out of our homes, we will."

"We'll be forced to live like the hobos who hop

rides on the rails."

"Think about what you're doing to us. We can't afford another cut in our wages. We're underpaid now. We'll become tramps."

Other cries erupted from the crowd as Mason Aderley, General Hancock, and a few militia guards looked on, not knowing how to respond. Charley kept to the side. He didn't want to appear loyal to the railroad, but he didn't want to look as if he was siding with the strikers. He was a coward, but it was the only way he would still be able to talk to the men afterward to try and help calm things down so the sorry fools wouldn't lose their jobs. He might be able to help Seamus, but he couldn't help everyone and their families. The best he could do was keep their tempers from getting the better of them. Didn't the poor fools realize that if they didn't have their jobs, they would be out on the street before the week was out?

Charley's mind shifted to Emily. The room hummed with tension and fear. He'd gotten definite word from San Francisco. Emily was okay and recuperating at Marybelle's. There was nothing to worry about. He sent up a silent prayer, grateful she was okay.

But, word was, a strike was a'brewing in San Francisco, too.

Loud shouts rang out. Charley turned his attention back to the meeting. General Hancock raised his voice over the din. Aderley stepped back in charge.

"Mayor Stokley has organized a Committee of Safety. He promises to do everything necessary, regardless of the law, in an effort to make sure there is no more disruption of the peace here in Philadelphia.

Just look around. The police force has been doubled. More troops arrived last night. There is nothing to do now but go back to work and forget about striking. We don't want any more bloodshed here."

Charley could see the engineers weren't appeased by Aderley's statements. In fact, they were more riled than before. Having troops, the mayor, and everyone else jumping down their backs and running all over the place did not bode well. The men were fired up over the oil tanker explosion, the deaths of the two men, the loss of their wages, and now the fact no one was listening to their demands. The angry looks on their faces told their own story. They were a sorry looking lot. Tired. But not beaten.

Yet.

The meeting over, General Hancock left to join his troops stationed nearby. The engineers and sympathizers left, heads hanging, shoulders drooping, and at odds with themselves over their next course of action. Seamus nodded from across the room. They needed to talk. But Charley needed to talk to Aderley first.

The eerie emptiness and quietness in Donahue's office outside Aderley's chambers surrounded Charley. His footsteps sounded loud to his own ears as he walked across the solid wooden floorboards. There was no need to knock. The door stood open.

Aderley sat behind his desk, his chair swiveled so he was staring out the window into the clear blue late afternoon sky. He addressed Charley without turning around.

"Sit down. I'm not sure what to make of this meeting. What do you think?"

"I'm not sure, either. I think they were holding their emotions under control. They were a bit dejected when they left. I don't think they're about to give up. I'll meet with them later to find out what I can. Try to find out what they have in mind."

"Let me know as soon as you can. I can't believe they would try anything else after the oil car explosion. Or with all the militia and other forces in town."

"How many do you figure?"

"I don't know," Aderley turned toward him. "There's more than a thousand armed police, about four hundred firemen, seven-hundred United States Regulars, and a hundred or so Marines. I should think there are a couple thousand special police and a good handful of men of the Veterans Corp."

"I don't think we have anything to worry about right now. Besides, the men will need to regroup and pass the information they received this afternoon along to the others."

Aderley looked pensive. The news from California and the results of his having drunk too much again the night before was still obvious. The day wasn't going well. Charley didn't care any longer. Too many lives depended on him.

"What's happening in San Francisco? There's some sort of uprising underway." Charley put his hands on his knees and leaned forward, shoulders hanging low. He tilted his unshaven face up and looked Aderley in the eyes.

Aderley looked down at his hands lying still on the shiny mahogany desk for a few long, quiet seconds and then looked across his desk at Charley. Determination reflected in the man's eyes, and in his body language.

Still, Charley couldn't read the man in front of him. Was he or wasn't he going to confide in him?

"California has been suffering a drought for some time. Their grain crop failed. Cattle are dying. Scott tried to get his Texas & Pacific branch into California. Californians blame the Chinese for their economic troubles." Aderley lit a cigar, handed it to Charley, and then lit another for himself. He leaned into the bottom drawer for his bottle, lifted it out, and placed it on his desk with a thump. Empty. He tossed the bottle in the trash can next to his desk.

"More than fifty-thousand Chinese were let go by the other railroads after they were built," Aderley said. "About twelve thousand settled in San Francisco and are now farmers. Some of them found domestic service, many opened laundry shops, and others found jobs in factories. They started living together in overcrowded "rookeries." Squalid at best. They're known for their exotic dress, gambling, opium addiction, and worse—prostitution. Can you believe the overall worst thing they did was to work longer hours for much less pay than the white workers, making the white workers look lazy? Seems it riled them up a bit."

Aderley stood and started pacing the hardwood floor. His loud footsteps echoed in the large opulent room. The state of the Chinese was no news to Charley, but he let Aderley expel his frustrations while he waited for the man to get to the bottom of the real problem.

"I understand there was a meeting on a vacant sandlot next to San Francisco's City Hall. Can you believe, in sympathy for the conflagration in Pittsburgh? About eight-thousand people gathered. A bunch of hoodlums, no doubt. The meeting lingered on into the night before someone shouted for the discharge of the Central Pacific's Chinese workmen despite the fact it was supposed to be an anti-coolie rally. Anyway, to get to the point of the matter, one of the hoodlums knocked down a Chinaman at McAllister and Leavenworth Streets. From there, all hell broke loose. Rioting and looting and burning have been taking place, mostly within the Chinese district, hitting many of the laundry shops. Thank God this took place in a different section of San Francisco than where Marian is staying."

"Is there any word from her since she arrived in San Francisco?" Charley asked, sitting forward, understanding now what Aderley was getting at.

"I got in touch with her while you were with Hancock. She's doing as well as can be expected. They both are. Marian says Jonathan feels guilty over his brother's death." Aderley took a moment before he continued, jammed his thumb and forefinger over the bridge of his nose and closed his eyes. "As soon as this business here is over, I plan on going out there myself. We've been apart too long. I should never have sent her out there alone with the boys."

"Are things still in an uproar out there? Has the strike affected other towns?" Charley was worried about Emily's safety.

"Word is, there was one last disturbance. A wash-house sacking of some sort. The police have gotten things under control. They've got a veterans brigade with Union and Confederate's and about two-hundred United States Marines, along with the police. Put them in their place. Things are as close to being back to normal out there as can be expected right now. We can be thankful our wives got there and settled in when they did."

Charley couldn't relax; he was still concerned about Emily. The sooner he could reunite with his own family and walk away from the railroad, the better. After seeing the damage this strike had caused already and the treatment of the rail workers, he was more determined than ever to leave and walk away. God knew he wasn't a farmer, but he'd just have to work harder alongside Seth, and became one.

Now was the time to make his stand with Aderley.

"You might feel our wives are not in any danger now, but my family has been split apart, too. As soon as this strike is over I plan to set things right." Charley stood and paced the room, his hands held behind his back, cigar dangling between his fingers. His back straight, his eyes never left Aderley's all the while he walked back and forth in front of the shiny desk where Aderley now stood.

"The railroad companies have done nothing to help their workers, including yours. It's about time they understood my loyalties may have been with you during this uproar, but by God, my heart has been with the strikers. They're starving. Why do you think I sent my family out to the country two years ago? Even *my* wages aren't enough to support them. I've tried my best to keep things quiet here in Philadelphia, but even the citizens and local police sympathize with the engineers and trainmen. Just why do you think that is?"

Charley stopped in front of Aderley's desk and stared at the stunned expression on the man's face. He wasn't deterred by the look.

"Are you so blind you can't see the way people are living; trying to survive? Are your pockets being lined as well as Scott's and the others to the point your heart has dried up to what really matters? You've just lost a son, nearly a wife. Put yourself in their place, dammit. How would you feel if they were the ones starving?"

Charley pointed his finger at Aderley. "You said you would reward me for staying loyal to you and the company. Well, I have been. And I'm here to collect. After this is over and the trains are running without a hitch, I want a ticket home to see my children to make sure everything is all right with them. Then I want a ticket to go to California to get Emily, and one for the both of us to come back home."

Aderley stood, face to face, with Charley. He looked just as defeated as those who had left his office not long ago.

"You're a good man, Charles. You're right. I do owe you. And I keep my word. As a matter of course, I too, like I said, will travel to San Francisco to be with Marian and my son. She has dealt with our son's death on her own long enough. As for this strike, I fear I have no more control than you. Tom Scott calls the shots. I'll be meeting with him when he returns from Pittsburgh. I'll see what I can do."

"I'll go talk to the men and see if I can keep them from rioting a bit longer, at least. Any sign of Donahue?"

"No. And let me tell you, if I ever lay eyes on him again, I'll fire him on the spot. You were right about him. Not only did he keep information from me, he's been altering the books and stealing right out from under my nose."

"Do you think he had anything to do with the kidnapping threats?"

"I've given his name to the locals. They're investigating him now. And to think I sent him to my home to run errands for my family."

He never liked John Donahue, never trusted him.

****

Two days later Tom Scott arrived in Philadelphia. He and Aderley spent most of the day behind closed doors. Charley wasn't surprised to learn Scott had called in all his I.O.U.'s.

"Aderley told me Scott's invited House Speaker Samuel Randall to Philadelphia so he can ask him to talk to President Hayes on his behalf," Charley told Seamus as they sat across the table from each other at Seamus' house. "He wants him to write a proclamation to put down the strike."

"What does that mean for us, Charley? If the President says we can't strike, can Scott cut our wages anyway?"

"Aderley said Randall refused to speak on Scott's behalf. Seems a citizen from Cincinnati wrote advising a federal intervention would only provoke a nationwide revolution. After President Hayes met with his Cabinet, he refused Scott's request."

"Then that's good news?"

"Yes, but I need your help letting everyone know we need to stand down 'til we see what happens, Seamus."

"I'm not sure they'll trust you."

"Tell them I informed Aderley I chose sides. And it's not the trunk lines. I know it's coming a bit late, but it's where my heart has been since the beginning."

"They'll be happy to hear you're with them. They think you're a good man."

He wasn't as good a man as his friend thought. If he was, he would have spoken up for them much sooner.

As the days wore on, Scott's promise of a wage cut remained adamant, although he didn't put it into effect. Charley and Seamus talked to the men; things remained calm. Aderley had been informed other trunk lines had already rescinded their cut wages and had called their men back to work. He hoped Thomas Scott would rescind their cut in wages as well.

Chapter Seventeen

July continued to be a good month for calving. Seth helped deliver three newborns toward the end of the third week. Hay was tall enough for a second cutting, and Seth enjoyed watching the long strands flow back and forth in the afternoon breeze. He took pride in the abundant crop. The potatoes were doing well despite the flood in June. He should still have a good crop for harvest in late September, early October.

After the rains, a slight beetle problem had invaded the potato fields. He'd checked with potato growers in Richford and caught the infestation in time to deal with it right away. Come fall, he would have to round up a couple of hired hands in order to get all the crops in come harvest, as well as maintaining the milking and other responsibilities of running the farm. Of course, his sister and younger brothers would pitch in, but they could only do so much. Digging potatoes was hard work needing many hands. The potatoes couldn't be left lying in the field, or they'd end up with sunspot damage from the sunlight. He was well aware of the stench of rotten potatoes from their own family supply. Storing them underground to keep cold didn't guard against a rotter. All it took was one decomposed potato for all the others to go bad. He couldn't afford to lose an entire crop of stored spuds due to one rotten potato.

Seth had dug out and extended the root cellar next

to the house beside the woodshed. He lined the walls with fieldstone, using the flatter stones for the floor. The cellar was deep enough so the potatoes wouldn't freeze during the winter months. They could store other tuber vegetables and canned goods there, as well.

Seth had a ready market for the potatoes. If the trains stopped running due to the strike this far north into harvest time…well, he didn't know what he'd do.

"I've telegraphed the markets as far east as New York City, north to Syracuse, and west to Buffalo along the Erie Canal," Seth told Catherine, as they sat across from each other at the kitchen table late one night. It was the first time they'd been able to sit and talk while everyone else had gone to bed.

"People in the cities are clamoring for potatoes, as well as my goat products. If we have a good harvest this year, I figure we'll be able to make ends meet through the winter months even if the strike continues and Pa don't have an income."

"What if the trains do stop? What are you going to do?" Catherine asked, wringing her hands in her lap.

"I don't have the time, equipment, or the help to transport everything myself. How much food have you and Maggie been able to put away so far?"

With his mother west, Mrs. Flanagan and Catherine had started putting away berries, fruits, and drying vegetables in anticipation of the winter months. He built shelving along one wall in the root cellar for the processed jars. Already there were several rows of brightly colored labeled containers, with room for more. He'd hung rope outside under an overhang for drying herbs in the summer heat. The fragrance of rosemary, thyme, sage, and lemon already filled the air.

"Maggie's been a great help," Catherine said. "Most of our garden will be coming on at the end of August and September. There's plenty. At least we'll have food on the table." Catherine hesitated a moment, closed her eyes, and then looked up at Seth. "Will we have enough money for my schooling?"

Seth nodded. "I've been putting some aside in case Pa doesn't come through. The strike is hurting us all. Have you been keeping up with your studies?"

"Yes. Maggie is a big help with the boys. And Madeline loves taking care of Sarah. I don't know what we would have done if she hadn't come up to live with us. The good Lord is smiling down on us."

"She has been a big help," Seth agreed. "So are you all set for the exams tomorrow morning?"

"Yes. Are you sure you can find the time to take me in to town? I can drive the team myself."

"I don't want you going by yourself. The hillside can be a bit tricky. I've given orders to the boys, and I'm sure Maggie will make sure things go as planned around here without us for one day."

Seth wouldn't miss taking Catherine in for her exam if he could help it. For sure Anna Louise would be there to take her exam, too. He hadn't seen her since the Fourth of July celebration, and he couldn't get the kiss they'd shared in the church vestibule out of his mind. Even though he'd left her standing there convinced he was letting her go, he just couldn't forget about her. Yes sir, he had big plans for tomorrow. A surprise he hoped would help change Anna Louise's mind about him once and for all.

****

Seth and Catherine arrived at the academy the

244

following day, along with others who rolled in on buckboards. A few walked over from the train depot across the street having come in by train. The academy's lawn was a hive of activity with twenty or so young ladies dressed in their Sunday finest, their hair combed up in dangling ringlets and their hats tied neatly under their chins. Although they were all pretty ladies, Seth considered as how his Anna Louise had them beat by a mile.

Catherine had also put on her best dress, a lavender and lace concoction Mrs. Flanagan had helped her sew for the occasion. She looked more like a schoolmarm than a farmer's daughter, and Seth had no doubts she'd do well on her exams today. She sure had studied hard enough.

Seth stepped down from the wagon, turned, and offered his hand to help Catherine down. He looked over his sister's shoulder and spotted Anna Louise coming through the iron gates surrounding the academy grounds. Dressed in a bright sun-yellow dress, Anna Louise carried a matching parasol in order to keep the hot afternoon sun from her fair skin.

"Good day, Miss Anna," Seth called as she approached. He tipped his hat slightly, then offered what he hoped was a beaming smile of welcome. "You're looking mighty fine today."

He was going to be a gentleman today even if his insides were tied in knots.

"Why, thank you, Seth." Anna Louise smiled. "Catherine," she nodded to his sister. "I hope you're both doing well."

Seth had made up his mind to clarify his position with Anna Louise as soon as possible. The light shade of pink on his true love's cheeks wasn't caused by her lovely rouge, or the reflection of the afternoon sun. He'd bank his crop of potatoes on it.

It was a very good sign, indeed.

"I wish you well on your exam," he said. "I hope you both pass with flying colors. I would be honored to have the pleasure of your company for tea at the Spinning Wheel when you're finished here today."

Seth smiled at both of them, thinking as how his speech was a bit overdone, but one Anna Louise would appreciate. Anna Louise twirled her parasol and turned even pinker.

Seth took hope.

Catherine's eyes twinkled at him. The corner of her mouth lifted a tad. He didn't care, dang it. His relationship with Anna Louise was worth any amount of embarrassment his sister chose to lay on him.

Before Anna Louise could respond, Seth continued, least she refused. "I will stop in at the Spinning Wheel and give them our reservations. I'll return and pick you both up later. In the meantime, I must be on my way to the telegraph office. Good day, ladies."

Seth tipped his best Sunday-go-to-meeting hat, bowed his head slightly, and then jumped up into the wagon. Before he could click on the reins, Catherine laughed. He didn't care. He smiled to himself as his insides danced with pleasure. The look on Anna Louise's surprised face had been worth it. He'd been a perfect gentleman. If Anna Louise wanted manners, he'd work real hard to accommodate her. He'd work real hard to do the best he could to impress the woman he loved. Even if it meant enduring a proper tea with others watching. Like Catherine said, all he needed was a bit of patience.

Seth's smile broadened as he drove his team out onto the main street. He'd just left Anna Louise speechless. And by Catherine showing up to take the exam, he hoped it proved to Anna Louise he didn't need her to help out at the farm; he was making do just fine since Mrs. Flanagan was there to help.

Seth had passed his own test. Another step in his attempt to win Anna Louise's heart. He couldn't wait to take them to tea.

Seth headed straight to the telegraph office across the street at the train station while he waited for the two-hour exam process to be over. He hitched his horses and buckboard to the post in front of Candor Hall across the street. With plenty of time on his hands, he walked down the street to the Spinning Wheel to set his reservations.

The afternoon was warm and sunny, and the sunlight twinkled through the leaves of the maples on both sides of the street. There hadn't been a single raindrop in a week, and dust kicked up as several wagons rolled into town. But nothing could waylay him today. Today he was going to have tea with Anna Louise. Of course, Catherine was going to be there, too, but she was aware he was in love with Anna Louise. She understood.

After making reservations at the Spinning Wheel, Seth headed back to the telegraph office to thank Mr. Benson for sending the telegram from his father. He had picked up the family photo taken on the Fourth of July from Child's Studios and wanted to send a copy to his mother.

"Morn'n, Seth," the man behind the ticket booth called when he entered the depot. "Come to send a telegram to your ma? I received one for you the other day. Seeing as no one was going out your way, I kept it right here for you. Figured you'd be coming in with Catherine for the school exam today. Other than a slight incident with the hoodlums and the Chinese riots out there, you're ma's just fine. Marybelle says your ma's health has improved. Says she's almost as good as new. Now, if I know Marybelle, Emily is in good hands. Always was a kind person, our Marybelle. Why she'd want to up and leave and travel way out west, I'll never know. Heard her husband found his pot of gold out there before going up north and getting involved in the lumbering business."

Seth smiled. No matter when Seth dropped in, Mr. Benson always had a story to tell and could recite the entire message verbatim.

"We were all surprised they didn't go way on up farther into Alaska like everyone else to do some panning," Seth replied, wondering when Mr. Benson was going to get around to giving him the telegram.

"Settling for a logging camp was sure a surprise to folks around here, seeing as lumbering is pretty big in these parts, too. Now, where'd I put that dang telegram. Ah, here it is. Tucked it away to keep it nice and fresh for you. I guess you'll want to be writing back later with Catherine's test results today."

Seth took the telegram, and as Mr. Benson said, his mother was fine. Not much more about the rioting in San Francisco.

"Yes sir. I'm taking Catherine and Miss Mitchell to the Spinning Wheel for tea after their exams. I'll stop by later."

"Miss Mitchell? Well, now, Seth, she's a right pretty little thing, our Miss Mitchell. Wasn't she seeing Mr. Linsky from Catatonk? Hmmm..." Mr. Benson scratched his head. The telegraph contraption started clicking away, and Mr. Benson turned, he and Anna Louise already forgotten.

****

Seth grinned from ear to ear all the way home. Catherine shook her head and covered her mouth. Still, her laughter rang out. He didn't care. He was happier than a flea on a dog's behind. What a lark. Mr. Linsky walking into the Spinning Wheel toting another lady on his arm. His eyes had just about popped out of his face a good country mile when ol' Linsky'd seen Anna Louise sitting next to him at a corner table. They sat so close together Seth's arm was draped across the back of Anna Louise's chair. The look on Anna Louise's pretty little face had been a picture, and it warmed his heart. She and Catherine had just been discussing the fact they had both passed their exams in the top five percent of everyone taking the exam. The smiles and twinkle in their eyes were a pleasure for Seth to behold. He had just been congratulating himself on being clever enough to plan this treat for them when the bell had tinkled over the door. And Mr. Linsky walked in. For a moment Seth had been ready to do battle. But when he'd seen the shocked look on both Mr. Linsky and Anna Louise's face, he wanted to stand up and clap and give himself a sound slap on the back. He could see Anna Louise hadn't anticipated Mr. Linsky's duplicity. And Mr. Linsky hadn't expected to be found out. In all, Seth figured it had been a very successful day, indeed.

"You didn't have to gloat so," Catherine admonished him as they sat in the buckboard riding out of town. "Poor Anna Louise. I could see she was crushed."

"Like a groundhog under a hay wagon wheel," Seth chuckled.

"Seth. How could you? You confessed your love for her, and you were trying to be such a fine gentleman today."

"Oh, hang it, Catherine. I know Anna Louise has feelings for me. I can sense it every time we're near enough to breathe on each other she can't take her eyes off me. I must say, I was trying to make amends and let her know that even though she didn't accept my proposal in the beginning, I truly wanted to wed her for all the right reasons."

Seth recalled how upset Anna Louise had been when she'd seen Mr. Linsky walk in with another woman on his arm. Seth had taken her hand in his and given it a gentle squeeze and then laid it on his lap under the tablecloth. Anna Louise hadn't looked at him right away, and he hadn't said anything. Without thinking, he had raised her hand to his lips and planted a tender, understanding kiss on the underside of her wrist. Thinking back, his gesture had been very romantic. Anna Louise had looked up, and he was shocked to see her dreamy blue eyes seek his in an exchange of mutual understanding. Her tender mouth quivered, her lips parted, and Seth wanted to do nothing more than to sweep her up out of the chair and out of sight of everyone in the room. He had wanted to be alone with Anna Louise. He had wanted to kiss her right properly.

"Well, I will agree Mr. Linsky was rather shocked to see the two of you together," Catherine said, hanging on to the buckboard as the wheels bounded along.

"If you ask me, the man was shocked because he got caught with another woman. Ha. I told you I didn't like the man from the beginning. Couldn't see why he was coming around Anna Louise in the first place. No doubt because her family has money."

"It doesn't matter now. Anna Louise has seen him for what he is. And more credit to you, I say. I could see she connected with you back there. I think you've hooked her good, Seth. Now just don't go ruining everything by being stupid."

"I love her, Catherine. I truly do. I guess I just don't know how to go about getting past all her hopes and dreams if they didn't include me."

"Keeping your mouth shut is a start. Your actions seem to speak for themselves."

"I'll keep it in mind." Seth looked at Catherine and smiled.

The remainder of the ride home was accomplished in companionable silence. They crested the top of the hill to the homestead to find Madeline and Timothy herding five cows along the road. Seth maneuvered the wagon up beside them.

"What happened?"

"Gab Hayland stopped by and told us he'd seen our cows grazing down the road in the hay field on the other side of the fence," Timothy said. "Not sure how they got out. What with you gone, and Madeline's mother up to her neck in baking and minding Sarah, we volunteered to round'em up."

At fourteen, Timothy was starting to turn into a

fine young man, and a big help on the farm. Without Ma around, Timothy had been a bit of a problem at first. Seth had a hard time getting him to help with chores, but once Mrs. Flanagan arrived, his behavior changed. He became more accommodating.

Brownie, the Collie, herded the cows as they meandered up the road like they were out for a Sunday stroll, their tails switching back and forth.

"Brownie's a good help," Timothy said. "He's kept the cows from heading on down the road and got them started up the hill toward the barn without a fuss."

The big brown dog wagged his tail and barked as if he understood and accepted Timothy's praise.

Madeline waved her long crooked tree branch at the cows, the leaves still clinging for dear life. She hit the dirt path with the bough in an effort to help the dog coax the cows back up the hill. If Seth didn't know any better, he'd think the girl had lived on a farm all her life; her smiles infectious. Timothy didn't seem to care that Madeline dogged his every step. In fact, Seth considered as how Timothy enjoyed the girl's attention. Seth would have to have a talk with Timothy soon. Madeline was only twelve.

"Catherine, take the reins." Seth handed the strands of leather to his sister and slid down, both feet hitting the dry dirt at the same time. I'll stay and find where they broke through the fence. Timothy, when you get the cows back to the barn, get the fencing tools and ride back on out here. We'd best take care of this before we lose a crop or two to more curious cows. I'm just thankful they didn't discover the potatoes and tromp all over them now they're doing so good. You two did a fine job."

Seth finished mending the fence long after suppertime, and then headed straight to the barn. Thankfully, Timothy had gone back earlier, and he and Madeline had fed all the animals, gathered the eggs, and made sure all the gates were locked. Seth set to milking, and then settled the cows and goats for the night. For the end of July, he was satisfied everything in his life was starting to fall into place. The only thing on his mind now was the strike in Philadelphia, and what it would do to his marketing ventures.

After today's events in Candor, Anna Louise was close to being his for good.

Chapter Eighteen

Emily couldn't believe how much strength she'd gained over the last month and a half. Marybelle's doctor explained to her how often times women experienced a state of depression after childbirth.

"My dear, your body has gone through some rapid changes," the older doctor said in a mild, caring voice. "What with moving your entire family to a new location, caring for your new baby, along with your other children, not to mention taking care of an entire household, you have no strength left for yourself so soon after giving birth." He patted her hand she held clasped in her lap.

"I have been tired," Emily confirmed. "When Doctor Wooster told me I suffered from consumption, why I had no reason to disbelieve him. And now you're telling me I don't have the dreaded disease?"

"My dear Mrs. Carmichael, of course you don't have consumption. Like I said, what you do have is a bad case of exhaustion. However, your doctor back home was right in his assessment. You needed complete rest and care. I'm glad you decided to come out west to your cousin's. It's plain to see she's been taking good care of you."

"Charley-boy was a wise man, Em," Marybelle said. "I'm glad he sent you my way instead of to one of those old stuffy institutions for the really sick people nobody wants. Surely your condition would only have worsened all closed up in such a place."

At Marybelle's, she was free to sleep and relax on the side veranda and take in the soothing breezes blowing in off the ocean all day if that's what she wanted to do. She drank plenty of fresh, cold lemonade, enjoyed hot Sassafras tea, and ate hearty meals she didn't have to prepare. Before long, the fever had broken, and she'd gained strength. Marybelle had suggested she start taking walks in the afternoon, something she had never had the opportunity to do back home. What with the children, there'd always been too many things to do—scrubbing, laundry, cooking, and picking up after everyone. Looking back, her doctor was right. No wonder she had been so tired all the time.

Today she and Marybelle decided to take a stroll down along one of the old access logging paths.

"William and his workers cut this path months ago," Marybelle said. "It's turned into a nice lane for walking, don't you think, Em? It's good to finally get you to walk this far. I'm delighted you're feeling so much better. Won't your family be surprised to learn you don't have consumption after all? Did you notice how clean the area is? Sweet the air is? My William makes sure every scrap of wood is used. See those neat stacks over there? The camp uses it for firewood for the camp stoves. We'll take the bigger pieces for the winter months to put in our own fireplace. I wish you were going to be here in the winter months, Em. We don't get the ice cold weather like you do back home, but it's still cold enough to sit back and enjoy a nice log fire big enough to warm the soul."

Emily kept in step with Marybelle, surprised when

her cousin grew quiet.

Birds twittered overhead, and the sun dimpled in between the trees as if lighting their way in the forest.

"How do you manage, Marybelle?" Emily asked. "How do you keep up your strength to go on? You work hard around here. I've seen you manage the house and help William with the accounts. You run back and forth between the logging camp and the house and San Francisco."

"It's not easy, Em. Lord knows I thrive on it, though. The boys work with William all day, now they're old enough. If I sat around I'd go crazy like old Johnny Johns back east. Say, whatever happened to him? He was pretty old when I left. Can't be still alive now, can he? Poor old soul. Must be a relief for his family."

"He was killed in a horse and wagon accident right after you left. He didn't get out of the way fast enough, and a horse spooked and reared up and killed him. It was a sorry day. The whole town came out to support his family." Emily thought of Marion Aderley's son having ended up the same way as Johnny Johns. She wondered how Marian was doing.

"What's Candor like now? The country sure is a great place to be, isn't it? I'm not sorry I followed William, though. I've got to tell you, coming across the dry prairie was no walk down the lane. Yet, it gave me the strength I needed. My William was a big help throughout our long journey, yes sir."

"Like you have been for me. I do so appreciate everything you've done. Taking care of me these past couple of months has been a blessing."

"Ah, Em, I didn't do much. I'm just glad you've

regained your health and are ready to go back to Charley soon."

"Yes. But I was glad to learn Charles sent Mrs. Flanagan and her daughter up to the farm. Just knowing there was someone to help Catherine with the children was a Godsend. You know how much I've missed the children, Marybelle. It will be so good to see them again." Emily wiped her eyes. "Oh, dear. Look at me—acting like a blubbering fool."

"Now don't you be fretting about a few tears. You've been away from your children for far too long. Just wait. You'll be seeing them before you know it. Won't they be surprised? Come. Let's go see what William and the boys are up to. You can tell me more about what's been happening in Candor along the way."

Marybelle put her arms through Emily's, and together they walked through the sun-dappled forest of redwoods. The fresh scent of evergreen mingled with the breeze from the ocean as the two strolled along. Emily proceeded to tell her cousin about moving to Candor. In the distance, the sound of lumberjacks cutting down trees filled the air. Men called out 'timber' and trees pounded the forest floor, reverberating clear to her bosom.

A train whistle blew as it chugged to a stop at William's mill. She spotted it as she and Marybelle strolled over the crest of a small knoll overlooking the logging camp.

"Oh my," Emily exclaimed. "This is a much bigger lumbering operation than I expected."

Marybelle smiled. "William has fifty men working for him. As you can see, they all have different tasks. My William don't need to tell them what to do, neither.

They're reliable. William don't keep anyone who ain't reliable."

Men trimmed, cut, and loaded logs onto the small lumber train. Others cleared the area and stacked logs. As Marybelle said, not one man stood about waiting to be told what to do. And William and the boys worked right alongside his men.

"How do they do this day after day? It must take all their energy to cut such large trees."

"They do eat a lot at meal time. They need to keep up their strength. But it's a skill they've mastered. And with everyone moving west these days, there's a big demand for lumber to build homes. It is hard work, to be sure, Em, but it's provided us a very good living, as well as for the lumberjacks. No sir, you won't hear a one of them complaining."

"Maybe you should have kept panning for gold. Wouldn't it have been much easier?"

"Panning for gold is even harder work. Sometimes with little results. We panned for a short time and made a bit of money. We needed to be more financially secure with the children. And dredging day after day was long, hard, dirty, and tiring work, Em. I started cooking and doing laundry, and made more money than we made from our gold. We didn't have much to spend our earnings on in them days, so we put aside every penny we didn't need. When William figured out there was more money in logging, what with everyone moving in and needing a place to live, he gathered up a few of the down-trodden gold busted families and offered them a job. Within a year, we had more than enough to build our own home and expand William's business venture. In the meantime, we lived in a tent until the first winter. The nights got mighty cold. We about froze to death. Before the first snowflake fell, William built us a small shack with a fireplace. The other families did the same."

"You're so brave to have gone through so much and keep on going."

"We're not so different. Why, I bet you'd follow Charley-boy anywhere if he asked. You moved to Candor and survived, didn't you?"

"You're right. But I think my Seth is the true survivor there. He adapted so well to farm life, the rest of us just followed along."

"I'm sure you had a hand in making things easier. Think of your stay here as a much needed holiday. Everyone will be so happy to have you home. They'll bend over backwards to help you out from now on."

"I hope you're right. Just surviving the trip out here showed me how strong I really am. Poor Mrs. Aderley and Mrs. Young, they've had a much worse time traveling out here then I have in so many ways."

"Stop worrying about other people. You need to learn to take care of yourself first. You're going to be fine. Now, let's get back before William and the boys come home for dinner."

****

Seth arrived in Candor, walked inside the Town Hall on Main Street across from the train depot, and found a seat next to Mr. Strang. He nodded a quiet hello. The farmer returned the silent greeting. Many already seated were dairy farmers; others raised poultry or sheep. A few grew hops, while a good number grew buckwheat. The meeting had been called by several of the more prominent farmers concerned about the railroad strike and how it would affect them.

"If the strike continues for several more weeks, even a month, our harvests will be in jeopardy of going nowhere," Mr. Meadows said, after he called the meeting to order.

"What are we going to do about it?" someone from the back yelled. "If this here train stops running, we're gonna have to haul our goods to market by wagon again."

The room erupted. Seth sat silent, taking it all in, waiting to see if someone had a solution to the problem.

"We'll have to go back to the old ways of keeping our milk and cheese cold," one of the dairy farmers stated.

"And our slaughtered meats, we'll have to be doing animal drives again. I can just see it now, herding cattle, pigs, and hens cross country."

Several snickered.

"Order," Mr. Meadows called out. He pounded the gavel on the table to gain the men's attention in the back. "We have a potentially serious problem on our hands. Now, let's try to settle down and come up with a solution instead of bemoaning what might be."

"Biggest problem is spoilage," Mr. Tallow spoke up.

The entire room, including Seth nodded. Seth looked around at those assembled. Twenty farms in all were represented. His farm was small in comparison to the other's operations. He had a long way to go before he was in sharp competition with any of them, despite his large acreage. There weren't many who raised goats, so no competition there. Tobacco had become big in the area, but it required a fair amount of work. He wasn't sure he was going to continue growing the crop. Potatoes were easier, and except for having to dig them up by hand, he had a more ready market for them locally.

"What about getting the fertilizer and feed we need for our cattle and dairy herds?" Mr. Tallow asked.

"If the trains don't come into town," Jerome Little spoke up, "then we have a problem making sure our livestock survive the winter. It will sure cut down on milk production."

Harvey Strang stood up. "It's not just livestock. The womenfolk are concerned they won't be able to buy the necessary dry goods to keep their homes running. I say we meet in small groups to discuss the situation. Designate one from each group to be a spokesman who will report back for the group. Maybe we'll come up with a solid plan."

"You're right," Mr. Meadows said. "In the meantime, please try to remember this is only a contingency plan in case the strike continues. We aren't in a pickle yet."

"We're at least sure of one thing; we're all concerned about what effect this strike is already having around the country."

"You're right," Mr. Meadows replied again. "Form your groups. See what you come up with. Report back."

Seth was disappointed his group was unable to come up with a single solution. When the various groups got back together, the outlook was dismal.

"I can't believe not one of you was able to come up with a single suggestion." Mr. Meadows shook his head.

Harvey Strang stood again. "At least we all agreed

we can help each other. If we work together, we'll get through the worst of it. That's got to count for something."

Several nodded, others shouted out 'he's right, we'll work together.'

Seth agreed.

An hour later the meeting adjourned. The farmers filed out of the building. Several crossed the street to the depot to find out if Mr. Benson had any news about the strike.

"Seth, hold up a minute." Harvey Strang stopped him before he could cross the street to his wagon. "I want you to meet my daughter, Cassandra. Cassandra, this here is Seth Carmichael. His pa owns the farm up over the hill from us. He's been running the farm while his father works the rails in Philadelphia. Made a real nice job of the farm, too."

Seth hadn't seen Mr. Strang's daughter join her father; he'd been too busy thinking about Anna Louise. He tipped his hat to Cassandra. He remembered her from the fair. Up close she appeared taller, not too thin. Her eyes were a deep chocolate, almost black, and her dark auburn hair was combed up on top of her head in a riotous array of curls. She wore a pretty pink frock. Her well-worn boots sticking out from under her skirt added to her appeal. He couldn't help but smile.

"Why, hello, Seth. Pleased to finally meet you."

Her soft voice, like a caress, stirred his insides. If he wasn't already in love with Anna Louise, he might just be mesmerized by this young lady.

Miss Strang batted her eyes in his direction.

Seth stood motionless, transfixed. *Holy cow.* Was the woman boldly flirting with him so openly in front of her father?

Hands held behind her back, she swayed back and forth, her curls bouncing all about her sassy face.

"It's a...it's a...my pleasure," he stuttered. He gave her a brief nod and stepped back.

"Seth was just telling me his sister will be attending teaching academy starting in September," Mr. Strang said, breaking the spell.

The man's face was deadpan, but Seth was sure he'd noticed his reaction to his daughter's flirtatious manner.

"Cassandra, maybe you should be thinking about what you're going to do when you've finished your studies next year," her father said.

"I have no designs to work at teaching, Daddy dear." Her beguiling smile never left her animated face. "I've told you before. I simply love helping you out on the farm. Why, the young baby chicks, lambs, cows, and horses are simply the best. Just the best. Don't you think so, Seth? Aren't baby animals adorable? Just adorable?"

Seth nodded. He wasn't sure about adorable. Cute, maybe. Harvey Strang was one of the more wealthy dairy farmers who also raised beef. He could afford to indulge his daughter in her every whim. Even horses. If she wanted nothing more than to play with baby animals, who was he to care?

"Come, Daddy, we must be going. Mother will be wondering where we are." She turned her radiant smile and sparkling eyes toward Seth again. "Mr. Carmichael, it's been simply wonderful meeting you. Perhaps you will drop by for dinner some Sunday. It would be our pleasure."

"Thank you for the invite, Miss Strang," Seth managed, his throat restricted. He fingered his tight collar in an attempt to breathe. "I'm rather busy at the farm this time of year."

"Just call me Cassandra. Miss Strang is way too formal."

"It was a pleasure meeting you…Cassandra," Seth relented.

"I'll see you at the next meeting, Seth." Harvey Strang offered his hand in farewell.

Seth shook his hand, and then once again tipped his hat to Harvey's daughter.

"Miss."

Cassandra battered her eyes at Seth once more before she turned away to leave. Her father took her arm and together they walked across the dusty street. Seth turned toward his own wagon.

Darn. He had things to pick up at the mill before heading home to do chores. There was no time now to stop by and see Anna Louise as planned.

Seth drove into town several days later to stop at the telegraph office. Mr. Benson looked up at him with a wide toothy grin when he stepped inside.

"Saints preserve us; the strike has been put down. Just got word this morning. The lines are just a clacking with the news."

"That is good news," Seth agreed. "The Agricultural Society will be able to breathe a sigh of relief."

Now that the strike had ended, there would be no problem with transporting his produce.

"Just in time, I'm a-thinking," Mr. Benson said. "The mills in these here parts will be starting to gear up for the harvest season soon. We've dodged a near disaster in our farming community, I tell you. This calls for a celebration."

Seth couldn't agree more.

Chapter Nineteen

Though the strike hadn't been as bad in Philadelphia as in other towns such as Pittsburgh, a flare up might happen again. Donahue was still as elusive as ever, and Charley didn't trust him any more now than he did when he was working for Aderley and Scott. He was a weasel of the first degree. He'd been seen smiling his heart out at the edge of many of the strikers' crowded rallies. The rat had been pleased to see the men riled and defying not only the company, but the local police and militia as well. Charley hadn't seen him around much since things had finally quieted down.

Word from Aderley confirmed the strikes were under control on the B&O, the New York lines, the Fort Wayne & Chicago, the Illinois lines, the Alton & St. Louise, and the Canadian Southern lines, as well as those in Pennsylvania.

"The Committee of Safety has successfully kept law and order and the strikers at bay," Aderley said. "And the businessmen in San Francisco who had banded together to take down those anti-Chinese rioters are under control as well. The U.S. Naval fleet was called in to guard their harbor."

"What about New York City?"

"The Working Men's Party was surrounded by over a thousand police and the National Guard in

Tompkins Square. Thankfully many of the strikes were put down before they got underway."

Charley knew the militia and United States troops had forced open many of the roads to Pittsburgh, and some were operating with one passenger and mail car per train, per day, and freight was starting up again.

"Are they still striking in Harrisburg and Altoona?"

"No. Governor Hartranft stepped in and broke it up. The strike may have been broken by force," Aderley said, "but wages stay the same."

Charley left Aderley's office to tell Seamus the latest news. To be put down by force with a decree from the President of the United States was a far cry from being a successful strike for the working man. Even though the wage cut was rescinded, the strikers would have to reapply for their positions, along with others who were already out of work needing a job. There were too many needing work. Seamus included.

Seamus waved at Charley from across the rail yard on the other side of the tracks past the roundhouse. The evening was cool for the beginning of August, and Charley wondered at the sweat beading down Seamus' forehead and upper lip as it glistened under the lamp light. His friend kept looking over his shoulders; first to the left, and then to the right as if someone was following him. After the incident at Seamus' home, Charley didn't blame him one bit for being nervous. No sir.

"What's wrong, Seamus? You look sicker than a dead man," Charley asked as Seamus drew near.

"God Almighty, Charley. The man was crushed between the couplings like he wasn't even there. A miserable way to meet your maker, I can tell ya. They left him there to bleed to death. The blood drained out of him and lay like a pool beneath his dangling feet between the ties. I had to get the others to help me uncouple him. Lord, his innards were retched clean right out of him. Whoever did this had to be making a point, cause it sure was no accident."

"Who? Seamus. Who was it?"

"Donahue. God, Charley, even in the dark the scene was hard to look at. I left the men back there to deal with it. Said I'd go get the police."

"I can't say he didn't deserve what he got." Charley cringed. He rubbed his hand over his face, shook his head in disbelief. "He's been nothing but trouble. Still, it's a hell-of-a-way to die."

Seamus sat down on the end of one of the railroad ties he'd been walking on and put his head in his hands. He rested his elbows on his knees.

"May God forgive me. Yes. After the shock of seeing the man dangling there like a hog on a spit, I was relieved. I gotta tell ya, Charley, I've done nothing but look over my shoulder since the attack at my house."

"I'm sure you have nothing to worry about now. Donahue was the one who had it out for us, not his cohorts." Charley clamped his hand down on Seamus' shoulder in a reassuring grip.

More than a friend, Seamus was like a brother. Now that Maggie had settled in Candor, perhaps he could talk Seamus into making it a permanent move. Candor had two trains running through town, now. Maybe Seamus could find work on one of them. The New York lines hadn't suffered as much as the Philadelphia or the B&O lines had. Still, the strike had all caused considerable damage.

Aderley owed him for his loyalty. He was damn well going to call in a few favors for Seamus, as well.

"Listen, friend. I've been thinking. Why not go on up to Candor with your wife and daughter. You can start all over again up there. Get out of Philadelphia."

"Sure, and what would I be doing there? Living off my wife? Her sewing won't be worth much."

"You're not thinking straight. You're still in shock over seeing Donahue's gored body."

Charley wasn't sure he was up to witnessing such a death.

"Let's find our way to The Blue Bottle. Donahue isn't going anywhere. We'll get you a pint to warm you and get the blood flowing. Put some color back in your white hide. I'll get someone else to fetch the police. You need to get home and get some rest. We'll talk in the morning."

Charley helped Seamus to his feet. Getting his friend out of Philadelphia might just ease the man's memory of what had taken place here. Whoever Donahue had been working for, they weren't worried about taking his life, or how they accomplished the deed. Only a sick mind would think of doing such a thing.

Charley took Seamus to The Blue Bottle, ordered him a couple rounds of ale, set him up at a table in the corner, and left him there while he returned to the bar.

"Hey, Mac. I've run across a slight problem back at the yard. You want to find someone to get the police to take care of the body? Donahue didn't survive a gruesome accident."

Mac would know how to deal with this situation before it got out of hand. He had his own contacts.

Charley didn't ask any questions.

"Got himself in a fix, did he? Seen him talking to Salina The Pig just the other day. The man was getting sloppy being seen with that Italian. Just how did Donahue die?"

"Can't say he met his maker at all. More like the other way around, now I think about it. God may have been his maker, but the devil took over right after, far as I can see."

Mac poured Charley a drink and handed him the frothy glass.

"Here. This one's on the house. You look almost as bad as poor Seamus over there. He find the body, did he?"

"Yes, he ran across Donahue dangling between the cars; seared straight through. I'd appreciate it if you'd send someone to get the police while I take Seamus on home."

Mac was already calling in his help as Charley walked toward Seamus.

"Come on, friend. Let's finish this pint and get you home."

"What about the police?"

"Mac's taken care of the situation. We don't have to worry." Charley wrapped his arm under Seamus' shoulder and hefted him to his feet. The guy was short and weighed nothing at all. By the time Charley half carried him down the street to his house, the man was ready to drop from exhaustion and drink.

Charley put Seamus to bed, then made the necessary rounds, locking everything just to be sure. He checked the rooms, behind the doors, inside the closets, made sure all the windows were shut and locked, the curtains closed, and the back door locked. He checked under beds and every other little hiding spot even an ant could find refuge in. Once satisfied all was in order, he made himself comfortable on the sofa and slept with one ear uncovered so he wouldn't miss a sound. By now he recognized almost every night sound inside and out of the house; a tree branch rubbing against the window pane or a mouse scurrying across the floor. He hadn't gotten much sleep himself, but tonight he would. He was confident Donahue's cohorts wouldn't be back.

Now that the strike was over, Donahue had become expendable.

No man should have died the way Donahue had.

****

Charley had the coffee ready when Seamus woke early Saturday morning.

"How you feeling?"

"My head's spinning," Seamus muttered splashing cold water on his face.

"It's not so much from the ale, but from what you've been through." Charley poured two cups of coffee and handed one to Seamus. "Here. See if this helps."

"You're a real good friend, ya are, Charley. I don't know what I would have done if you hadn't been here. I've got to thank you for talking me into sending Maggie and Madeline up to Candor where they're safe."

"Then let's talk. You can start all over again if you go up to Candor with Maggie and Madeline. Two trains run through the town. You can see if one of them will hire you. With everyone having to apply to get their old jobs back down here, you just might have a better chance getting something up north instead. If not, there's always Owego or Spencer. Even Newark Valley might be needing someone."

Charley looked in Seamus' eyes. There was caring there, and an overwhelming amount of friendship shining back.

"Ah, Charley, you're a true and loyal friend. You've done so much already."

"Then let me do this one last thing for a friend. Something I can do. In fact, I'll be going to get Emily as soon as I talk to Aderley."

"I'm sorry I questioned your allegiance, Charley. It must have been hard to divide loyalty between your friends and the company. Somehow you managed not to compromise yourself. I hope Aderley realizes how strong your commitment is and rewards you right proper."

"As soon as I settle things with him, you can go with me to Candor. There are others who can do our jobs here. They won't be missing us."

"What do you mean, us? You're not giving up your position with Aderley are you?"

"It's time my family got to see a lot more of me. Not sure what I'm going to do. I'm not a farmer like Seth. Maybe they'll have a job on the rails for both of us in New York," Charley chuckled. "We'll see. But before I decide, I need to get my family back on track. I am not letting the trains get in the way any longer. Even if I have to learn to be a farmer."

Charley scraped his chair out from behind the small kitchen table to get the coffee pot.

"Here. Have another cup of coffee while I get us some breakfast going. No need to be thanking me. I haven't done much."

"What are you going to tell Aderley about Donahue?"

"The truth. The man is dead. I think Aderley will be just as relieved. Seems there's been kidnapping threats on his family just before the strike got underway. One of the reasons he sent his family out to California. The irony was he thought he had sent them out of harm's way."

Charley peeled potatoes while he talked to Seamus. Emily would be proud of the way he took his time to slice a paper thin layer of skin off the potato and then dice them into the pan with a slab of bacon drippings.

"Sad thing is, Aderley found out the day before Hancock arrived that one of his sons had been killed in a buffalo stampede. Aderley was in pretty bad shape just before the meeting with the engineers, too. I was about to tell him I couldn't support him and Scott, when he told me about the incident. How could I tell him I was about to walk out on him once I found out his son had been killed? I just couldn't add more to his worries."

"Like I said, Charley, you're a faithful friend."

"Go get yourself dressed while these potatoes finish frying. We've arrangements to make. I'll deal with Aderley, you deal with things around here. Start getting your things in order. I plan to be going home in a few days. I'd be glad of your company."

Charley visited Aderley later that day. His boss was in better spirits than he'd been since before the strike broke, and the news of his son's death. The sparkle in his eyes was still lacking, but he looked a hell-of-a-lot better.

"Afternoon, Charles. Glad you're here. Did you hear about Donahue? Me? I'd of taken my sweet time on him."

"I suspect the blood draining from his body took some time."

"Hell, the shock alone might have killed him right off. Anyway, I found proof he was the one threatening my family. I was cleaning his office drawers out the other day and ran across evidence, papers and another note he was getting ready to send."

"At least you won't have to be concerned about your wife and son coming back home, now. They'll be safe."

"It doesn't matter where you are, you're never safe. You can never fully protect your family no matter how hard you try, Charles."

"All the more reason to take care of them while you can."

"You're right. I'm heading out to California to take care of Marian and Jonathan. Spend more time with my son. He's going to need someone. Lord knows I need them."

"I know how you feel. I've come to ask for those favors."

"You were a faithful employee during this entire fiasco. I know you had loyalties to the workers as well. I don't know how you managed to carry out your job at the same time. It's what I value most about you. Anything you want. Ask."

"I'd like the company to help relocate Seamus up to Candor and get him a job on the rails there. He needs to be with his family, too. He's gone through too much down here to ever feel safe again. I'm sure Donahue and his thugs were the ones who attacked him at his own home. Seamus was the one who found Donahue dangling from the trains. He needs to put this all behind him. Besides, you know there are others who need the work here. There are too many bodies trying to grab hold of the too few available jobs. Rescinding the wage cut only put these men back to the same level they were before the strike."

"The company is floundering. Scott is having a hard time keeping things going, and this strike hasn't helped. There's even talk Scott's Empire Transportation is in trouble. He mentioned John D. Rockefeller is interested in buying him out and controlling the company with the Standard Oil Company in New York. Heaven help us, it will be the biggest monopoly the world has ever seen."

Aderley paused, looked out the window, and then turned back to Charley who was trying not to feel sorry for Tom Scott. The man was a true capitalist. Whatever Aderley could do for him and Seamus, he'd better be doing it fast considering Scott's predicament.

"Seamus is not a problem. Done," Aderley said.

Aderley lifted the carved humidor on his desk and took out a cigar. He rolled it between his fingers, and then as an afterthought, offered one to Charley. Something he didn't do too often. Charley took one and rolled it in his hands, as well, both of them savoring the feel, and the rich tobacco aroma. Aderley offered him a light, and then pulled out his bottom drawer.

"I restocked. Let's celebrate." Aderley poured two drinks and handed one to Charley. "Now, what about you?"

Charley didn't hesitate. "I need a ticket to go home

and then out to California to bring Emily home. She's doing well and needs to be with her family...our family. A doctor out there has somehow helped her overcome her illness, and she is well rested. Her cousin wants her to stay longer, but if I know Emily, she's ready to come home to be with her family. After the episode on the train ride out there, I want to be by her side during her ride back home. I *need* to be by her side to make sure she's safe."

"Done. Take the children out to her. She's been away from them long enough. I can't imagine what Marian is going through without Jason, now he's gone. Mothers need to be with their children. If you need anything while you're out there, you contact me at Marian's sisters. I'll give you her address in San Francisco."

"I'll be leaving for Candor the end of next week. Seamus will be coming with me. I'll need a few days to get the children ready for the trip."

"I'm leaving for California by the end of the week, myself. Scott will be back in his office and will manage things just fine without us for a while. Freight goes out day after tomorrow."

"We were luckier than Pittsburgh and some of the other mill towns," Charley said. He took a swig of the amber liquid and set the glass back on Aderley's desk. "They're going to have a hard time recovering. Some of the miners are still holding out, though."

"Won't last too much longer," Aderley confirmed. "Their grievances are different. Entire families are being buried alive in those mines. Kids never see the light of day."

"I hope it's resolved before too many more lives

are lost."

Mason Aderley placed his cigar between his teeth and grabbed his whiskey bottle with shaking hand. He poured a couple more shots for both of them.

"What happened to Westmüller? Do you know how he's doing?"

Charley hadn't forgotten about Johann Westmüller. He had visited Johann several times in the hospital and learned the man's body was starting to heal, although he was going to be scarred for life. Sixty percent of his body had been burned before Charley had been able to subdue the flames, including the left side of his neck and lower cheek. He had been luckier than the other two men who had burned to death.

"He's going to be okay. Scarred a bit, but he didn't lose the use of his hands and legs. He should be up and about in several months. The company ought to pay for his medical expenses. The family has nothing much to speak of, and these expenses will put them in the poor house for sure. God, he was one of them trying to save the car, not destroy it. He deserves some help now."

Aderley was silent. Charley held his breath. Had he stepped over the line with his demands? Was Aderley about to tell him to get out of his office and be glad with what he got? Would he take it all back and send him packing on his own? He couldn't quite meet Aderley's eyes. When he did look up he found them shut in contemplation.

"Ah, Charles, a true humanitarian. You drive a hard bargain, and you catch me at a time when family means a great deal. I'll see what I can do, but I'm not sure Scott will go this far. Tell you what I'll do, though. If the company won't pick up the tab on this, I will. I'll see Westmüller is rehired as soon as he's able to work. Now, there isn't anything else I can do for you, is there? Someone else you want to help?"

Charley looked at Aderley and smiled. "Would you help them if there were?"

"I think I'm out of favors for one day. Go. Start getting things wrapped up here. I'll see you before I leave. I have a proposition to put to you. I hope you'll agree. In the meantime, I'll go see Westmüller myself. Tell him the good news. Might just help his recovery some."

Charley stood, took the cigar out of his mouth with his left hand, and accepted another refill with his right. They clanked glasses, drained their shot, and then shook hands. The hand clasp lasted a moment longer than usual. Charley was grateful for the unspoken admiration Aderley's grasp implied. This was goodbye. Charley wouldn't return to Philadelphia any time soon.

"It's been a pleasure, Charles. A real pleasure."

Charley wished he could say the same.

Chapter Twenty

News of the strike being put down traveled fast, thanks to the telegraph offices and the newspapers spreading the word across the nation and Candor. President Hayes' announcement was unexpected but welcomed by many. Cut wages were rescinded. Some rail workers had fought for an eight-hour day and won. It would please his pa. The man worked too hard for the rails as it was.

Even with all the concessions made, however, Seth vowed he would never consider working for the rails. If his grandmother hadn't needed help at the farm in Candor when his grandfather died, and his father hadn't wanted to get them out of the tenement houses in Philadelphia, he'd already be working the rails right alongside his father. He'd have been involved in the strike, too. He'd heard from Mr. Benson at the depot that child labor had also been talked about during the strike. He hoped they were put into law as well.

Seth stopped by the depot to see if there was any word from his father.

"Why, yes, Seth," Mr. Benson smiled. "Your pa says he and a…, let me see…" Mr. Benson looked for the telegram on his desk, then held it up with a smile on his face. "Ah, yes. Here it is. A Mr. Flanagan is coming home with him at the end of next week."

"Yes. Maggie's husband."

This was good news. Having his father home would relieve some of the pressure of family responsibilities such as making sure Catherine's education was taken care of, making sure there was food on the table, and dealing with other family matters that arose. Mrs. Flanagan had been a Godsend, even though the bulk of the farming responsibilities rested on his shoulders. With his father home to take some of his worries away, he could concentrate on the farm itself. And of course he would have more time to concentrate on courting Anna Louise.

"Thanks, Mr. Benson." Seth smiled and reached for the telegram. "I'll be sure Catherine gets this as well. She and Mrs. Flanagan will be happy to welcome them.

"You take care, son," Mr. Benson called as Seth headed out the door.

Seth waved and then walked down the street to the Candor National Bank. He needed to withdraw money for a down payment on Catherine's tuition fees and take it to Professor Denison at the Academy.

Professor Denison gave Seth the names of three possibilities where Catherine might be able to board for the school year; one of which was Anna Louise's home. The other two were located on the outskirts of town on the south side of Candor Corners. Anna Louise's house was the better choice for several reasons. Not only could Catherine walk to the Academy with Anna Louise, but he would also be in a more favorable position to have plenty of excuses to visit Anna Louise.

He rounded the corner of Spencer and Mill Street and caught a glimpse of Anna Louise sitting on her front porch. A smile lit up her face when she spotted him. Her smile faded as he drew closer. But Seth had already seen the momentary pleasure in her eyes. Ah-ha, all would be well. He'd known she'd had feelings for him all along.

Seth found when it came to looks, Anna Louise had sassy Miss Strang beat. When it came to manners, Anna Louise's were gracious. There was nothing sassy about his Anna Louise. She was small and petite, Cassandra was full-bodied and tall. Anna Louise was blonde, perfectly groomed hair and sparkling blue eyes. Cassandra had deep, dark brown eyes and a head of unruly auburn hair.

He wasn't quite sure why he was comparing the two ladies, but when he stepped up on the front porch with confidence blooming inside, he walked right up to Anna Louise and forgot all about Cassandra Strang. He stopped in front of Anna Louise, looked down at her perfect face. He clasped her hands gently, tugged, and lifted her up and forward. He led her away from the white wicker chair where she'd been sitting. She didn't say a word; just followed. He was sorely tempted to take her into his arms and kiss her proper, but he hesitated.

She was a fine looking woman, any man's dream. She was *his* dream, and he hoped his dreams were about to come true. He didn't want to ruin things by acting too eager.

Anna Louise's eyes looked at him in expectation. His heart skipped a beat, heat started at the base of his neck and work its way up.

"Have you come to apologize, Seth?" Anna Louise asked, looking even more hopeful.

What? Seth froze. What was he supposed to

apologize for? What had he done?

Before he could think of anything he had done wrong recently, Anna Louise put him out of his misery.

"I do recall you taking the liberty of kissing me several times over the past month."

Her demure smile and tilted head melted his heart further.

"And if I'm not mistaken," she said, "you haven't contacted me once since our last encounter at the Spinning Wheel. I don't mean to be forward, Seth, but if we're courting, I need to know."

Seth swallowed, his momentum halted before he could utter a word. Why, Anna Louise was acting just as sassy as Cassandra Strang. *Oh, my!*

"What about Mr. Linsky?" Seth was sorry he mentioned the man's name the minute the words flew out of his mouth.

"Mr. Linsky is just a friend, Seth," Anna Louise said, her tone matter-of-fact. She waved her hand in a dismissive swing.

"My dear, Anna Louise. I've been waiting for you to tell me I can court you. Do you mean to say you're… yes?"

Truth be told, he wasn't sure what he had done right in courting Anna Louise, but it didn't matter. Anna Louise was his. She had just said so.

"Are you saying you're agreeing to marry me?" he tried again.

Anna Louise tugged her hands from Seth's and stepped back.

"Oh, Seth. You do understand I can't marry you right away. I have my teaching responsibilities, as you know. I can't change my plans now."

"I propose, then, we become engaged while you do your studies. We can court right properly and get married when you've finished." Catherine's words flew out of his mouth.

Several more emotions played across Anna Louise's petite, rosy face while Seth waited for an answer. He stepped closer, took her into his arms. She fit just right. He didn't give either of them a second to think about anything else. Before she could turn away from him again, he kissed her. Long and slow, and he didn't care if they were standing outside on her front porch where everyone could see. When he released her, her body sagged into his. His body reeled with the impact.

"Yes, Seth. You may come courting," Anna Louse pulled back and whispered, looking deep into his eyes.

Seth's jubilation knew no bounds. He grinned from ear to ear, took a couple of deep breaths, and then placed his hands on her shoulders and stepped away so he could look deep into her heavenly blue eyes. He gathered her up against his body again.

"That's all I can ask for now, Anna love," he whispered in her ear. "I will make a formal plea to your father for your hand. Perhaps at Christmastime we can make more serious arrangements for when you finish your studies in the spring. We can set a date." Seth wanted to run his hands through her hair. Instead, he cradled her head into his chest trying hard not to mess up her hair. He kissed the top of her forehead and then released her.

"Let's just keep this to ourselves for now, Seth," Anna Louise implored, her eyes looked no farther than his shirt buttons.

Her hand massaged his chest.

Seth gulped.

"Wait until Christmas before you talk to father. Maybe once he sees you visiting more often, he'll get the notion we're interested in each other all on his own. I'm sure he'll agree and not take it upon him to give you such a hard time when you do ask for my hand."

Seth hadn't anticipated her father giving him a hard time. Of course, she knew her father's way of thinking better than he did. He would concede to her wishes for now, and wait until after the Christmas season to approach him.

"Anything you say. Come, let's sit down over here. You've made me the happiest man in town."

He led her to the wicker bench instead of the chairs. Anna Louise patted her hair as if a single strand had dared to pop out of place. Dang. He'd been so careful, too. He took a closer look. Nope. Not a single lock was misplaced. His insides smiled. He couldn't wait for the day her messed up hair would be splayed all over their bed pillows. Then he could run his fingers through her blonde hair without having to worry about messing a single lock.

"Oh, my, Seth, you shouldn't have kissed me out here in the open," Anna Louise said, looking around to see if they'd been caught. "Why, anyone could have seen us out here in broad daylight. What would they think?"

"The truth. I'm in love with you. In fact, I wished they had."

She had blushed beautifully before, but her complexion now glowed. Perhaps word would get back to her father soon, and he wouldn't have to wait so long to approach him for Anna Louise's hand in marriage. He wasn't pleased about postponing things. But he was so happy Anna Louise had said yes, he refused to dwell on her request to wait.

Caught up in the moment, Seth had almost forgotten he had another purpose for his visit.

"Oh, Anna love. You do distract me so. I nearly forgot I had another reason for visiting you today."

Seth was delighted when Anna Louise sat very close. In fact, her lace-trimmed petticoat skirts covered his left pant leg, her hand draped snuggly through his left arm. When he looked at her, she gazed into his eyes and he almost forgot once again why he was there.

He cleared his throat, ran his finger inside the too tight collar around his neck. Without hesitation, he took a deep breath and covered her hand with his. The lady was much too beautiful. Much too distracting. Waiting until the yuletide was asking a lot. Once harvest was in for the season, he'd have more time to court her proper.

"Now, Seth. What else did you want to discuss?"

Anna Louise batted her eyelashes. Seth tightened his grip. She reminded him of Cassandra Strang. He wondered if all girls batted their eyes at men in such a seductive manner.

"If it's about Catherine, I was wondering if you would consider letting her stay with me this fall. She'd be such good company, and the two of us could walk to the Academy together."

Seth couldn't contain his smile. He simply beamed. He was so worried about asking Anna Louise this favor, and here she was posing the same question.

"Sounds like a solid arrangement, Anna, love. I'm so glad. Would you mind then if I stopped in to see

Catherine while I'm in town? To see she doesn't get homesick, of course."

"Only if you make time to see me while you're here." She batted her eyes again and patted his hand. Seth squeezed her hand in return.

"Would you like some lemonade? Macey made a fresh gallon this morning. It's better than anything they serve at the Spinning Wheel. It'll keep your thirst down on your ride home later. You don't have to rush off just yet, now, do you, Seth?"

"No Anna, love, for you I'll always make time."

"You wait right here, Seth. I'll be back in a minute."

Seth couldn't help leaning over to plant a kiss on her lips. It was a short kiss, but meaningful. Anna Louise was his. He could stop worrying now and concentrate on the farm. He hoped the lemonade was cold enough to douse the heat coursing through his body; just looking at her did that to him.

Ahhh, all was well. His father and Mr. Flanagan would be coming home in a week's time. His mother's health was much improved, and it wouldn't be long before she returned home and he'd be free to concentrate on farming and courting Anna Louise, openly. Catherine was all set for the fall semester. And Michael's arm was out of his cast and healing nicely. The strike was over. Things would be back to normal before long.

Yep. Things were certainly looking up.

Seth left Anna Louise standing on her front porch after another long and heated kiss. He hated to leave her, and if Anna Louise's reaction to his advances were anything to go by, she hadn't wanted him to leave, either.

Seth waved to several of his acquaintances as he rode down through town. He met Jerome Little and Mr. White when he rounded Mill Street.

"The strike is officially over," they yelled up at him, jumping up and down, waving to Seth and others who passed by. "The strike is finally over."

Others shouted and waved back, as well, passing the news along. Thank the good Lord, their transportation worries were over. He rounded the corner and stepped out onto the turnpike. Seth decided to stop on over at Harvey Strang's place, only a few miles out of his way over in Lovelyvale. Harvey would want to know the good news. He could swing up over the hill and still have plenty of time to do the evening chores when he got home. It didn't matter if he was late for supper, Mrs. Flanagan would keep his dinner warm for him, as usual.

Harvey's spread was easy to find. Their homestead was on the left side of the turn-off to Fairfield and occupied over three hundred acres either side of the road as far north to his own property. The road dissecting the property was the original drive to the farm, but over the years had given access to farms further up over the hillsides to the east. Harvey's home was two miles up beyond the first crest in the road and sat at an angle overlooking the small valley and creek bed flowing through his property. The large log home was handsome, sprawling and well kept. Flowers were in full bloom and green shrubs bordered the length of the porch. A walkway ran clear down to the fence posts lining the drive. A large barn with several different size pens were also fenced off, some already filled with dairy herds ready to be milked. He spotted a corral to the left with Cassandra's fine looking horses.

Seth reined his wagon in next to the house. Cassandra swung the front screen door wide and stepped out onto the porch. She looked as if she'd been expecting him. She waved her fancy handkerchief like an unmentionable blowing in the breeze on a clothesline. He put the brake on the wagon wheel in place and slowly stepped down. He took his hat off and made his way up the walkway to the house.

Cassandra Strang met him on the bottom step.

"Good evening, Miss Cassandra. Is your father here abouts?"

"Why, hello, Seth. What a surprise. Have you come for supper?"

"I'm sorry, no. I came by to speak to your father about the strike. Is he available?"

"Daddy's gone over to Mr. Yarrows' farm for a bit. Don't expect he'll be back for another hour or so. Why don't you just come on up here and sit for a spell while you wait. We can keep each other company. Ma is inside, so we will be properly chaperoned."

Unless she had something in her eye, Cassandra looked as if she were batting her eyelashes at him. Again. He wasn't about to get close enough to find out. And he certainly didn't want to encourage her. Mother or no mother for a chaperone, he wasn't about to spend time on Cassandra's front step waiting for her father to show up. There was something about Cassandra that made him uncomfortable. He wasn't ready to take the time to find out what.

"Sorry. Can't today. It's getting late, and I have to get home to do chores. Just wanted to let your father know the strike is over, so there won't be a problem with any of us shipping our goods come harvest."

"He'll be pleased to know. I'm sorry you can't stay longer, Seth. We could sit and chat, and find out more about each other. Daddy's told me so much about you. Why, according to him, you've just done wonders on your farm since your family took over. Is it true you single-handedly turned the farm into a successful business overnight? How wonderful. Your family must be so proud."

She sighed as if she'd just eaten a bowl full of freshly churned iced cream. He could almost picture her spooning a scoopful into her mouth. He could almost taste the thick heavy, frozen cream melting in his own mouth. He shook himself as if the iced cream had traveled down his throat. What in blazes was wrong with him? He'd never had these feelings before. Never. He had to do something about them, and fast. He had to let Cassandra know her actions were not proper. And that he didn't return those feelings.

"The farm's success is a natural growth of hard work and simple planning." Seth found himself twisting his hat in his hands as he stood there talking. "I'm sorry. I, umm…I can't stay for dinner. Thank you for the offer."

"I'm disappointed you can't stay longer."

Cassandra batted her eyes again and stepped off the porch. She walked toward him. Seth stepped back. The closer she approached, the more Seth didn't want her to come any closer. He didn't know what else to do. He had to be honest with Cassandra and let her know her flirting was for naught.

"Excuse me for being so blunt, Miss Strang. I think

you should know I'm engaged to Miss Anna Louise Mitchell. Fact is, I was just at her place, and she has accepted my proposal."

"You mean you've announced your betrothal?"

"Why, no," he hesitated. "We agreed to wait before I talked to her father and make an official announcement. Nevertheless, we are betrothed."

"I see."

Seth hoped she did.

She kept walking toward him in that sassy manner of hers, her hips swayed from side to side. He stepped back in an effort to put more distance between them. But Cassandra Strang just kept coming, batting her eyes and swaying her hips, her gingham dress rustling around her long legs.

"I suppose it means you can't even look at another woman now," she tsked. "What a shame. I had so hoped I would have a chance to get to know you. You know, just in a friendly way. What a darn shame."

Cassandra shook her head, and her massive curls swirled in all directions around her face. She stopped just short of the tips of their shoes touching as if a line had been drawn between them. Heat sizzled around his collar. Sweat broke out on his forehead. If he didn't leave soon, he was going to make a total fool of himself. This woman made him feel things even Anna Louise didn't.

It wasn't right.

"I guess there is no need to get to know each other, in any case, now is there?" he stuttered. "If you'll excuse me, I do need to get home to do chores. Please, tell your father I stopped by."

Seth put his hat back on his head and backed up

toward his wagon. "Good day," he said, and then turned and walked away from Cassandra. When he backed the wagon up to turn and head back down the drive, he didn't look back. But she was still standing there. Watching him. He could feel those dark brown, sassy eyes bore into his back all the way down the road until he was out of sight. Even then, he couldn't get her out of his mind. Especially, when he should be thinking about Anna Louise and their plans for the future.

Chapter Twenty-One

Charley and Seamus arrived in Candor on the afternoon train. The hot August sun was still high overhead, and the smoke from the train rose straight up to meet the sky. Passengers took their time as they disembarked and entered the depot to pass through to Main Street. If he knew Seth, his son would be waiting on Stowell Avenue behind the depot.

Charley didn't bother going inside. Instead, he stayed on the platform and waited 'til all the passengers were off and the train chugged toward Weston's hay barn to unload dry goods. He waited with Seamus next to his baggage, which had been already placed on the platform. What little Seamus had packed amounted to two large trunks with brass bindings and latches, and a brown oversize crate with Maggie's china and other well-packed household goods.

"We'll leave them here 'til the train clears the track. Seth will bring the wagon around."

"Would you believe I left a lot of Maggie's things behind? Some not worth packing up."

"Nevertheless, Aderley would have paid."

"It was good of him giving me extra to see my way clear to start over up here. Said to see a Mr. Benson about a job." Seamus took his cap off, scratched his head, then replaced the cap at an angle.

Charley appreciated what Aderley had done for

Seamus.

"Take a couple days to be with your wife and daughter, Seamus. Breathe in some of this great country air. Let it blow the grease and oil off. See what you've been missing. Ain't a single time I don't come home I don't appreciate what this great countryside has to offer. Only trouble is, Seth has everything under control. I just get in the way." Charlie smiled. It was the God's honest truth. His Seth made him feel worthless when it came to running a farm.

"You're a lucky man to have a son to take care of the farm while you're away. You should be right proud of him."

"I am. Don't know what I'd have done without Seth. And Catherine."

With the strike over, Charley now had time to appreciate how strong the bond was that tied his family together. Their sacrifice made Emily's recovery possible. It had also allowed him to concentrate on the strike in Philadelphia.

"Your Maggie was a big help. Now don't you feel you have to find a place in the village right away. I'll take my children with me to meet up with Emily. There'll be plenty of room left for you and the Missus at the house."

The train whistle blew. Slow moving, the black locomotive made its way along the track behind the businesses on Main Street. When it finally chugged along out of sight, Charley spotted Seth waiting.

Charley grinned. "Here's Seth now. We'll be home before long. Seth knows how to handle a rig. Just wait and see."

Seth drew the wagon up alongside the platform and

jumped out, landing right in front of his father.

"Hi, Pa. I hear the strike is over and everything's back to normal." He tipped his hat back on his forehead and smiled.

Seth shook his father's hand and turned to Seamus. "Pleased to meet you, Mr. Flanagan. Your wife and daughter have outdone themselves since they arrived. Madeline seems to enjoy following Timothy around and helping out where she can. I think she'll make a good farmer's wife one day."

"Better than being a rail worker's wife," Seamus said, shaking Seth's proffered hand.

Seth was acting more like a man now than when he'd left him back in June. The boy had the knack of surprising him every time they met at the station.

"Let's get things loaded so's we can get on the road," Charley said. "We can talk on the way home. Tell me everything; what's been going on while I've been gone? Don't leave nothing out."

Seth helped his father load Seamus' belongings on the wagon. Once everything was tied down, the three of them settled in and set off for the farm.

"How's Catherine? Has she passed her exams yet? Is she ready to start school come September?"

"Yep. She did right good. She's all excited, too."

"Good. Good. Did you have enough money to pay the fees?"

"A down payment. I was hoping you would be able to pay the rest."

"Yes. Mr. Aderley was generous. Does she have a place to stay in town come fall?"

"She's arranged to stay with Anna Louise Mitchell. You remember, her father owns Candor National Bank.

By the way, Anna Louise and I now have an understanding. I'll be courting her right proper after Christmastime."

"Is this the young lady you've been seeing all summer? 'Bout time you got yourself engaged to be married, son. Don't see why you have to wait so long to make it official. What's the hold up? The sooner you tie the knot, the sooner you can bring her home to be a good farmer's wife."

"She hasn't told her family yet. These things take time. I haven't asked her father for her hand yet."

"I see. You haven't asked for her hand yet, but you're going to court her."

"Anna Louise also took her exams and will be going to Normal School with Catherine to become a teacher. She needs time to concentrate on her studies. Just like Catherine."

Charley held his tongue. Things sure had changed since he'd courted Emily.

"Did I mention that Timothy has been my right-hand man, Pa? He's learned a lot about farming, especially the dairy end of things. We bought a couple of heifers to get him started, but he has a long way to go. He thinks we should switch everything over to dairy."

"Isn't the goat dairy prospering?" Charley asked.

"They are. But he's more interested in dairy cows. We've added to the herd, started out small to see how things go. The Agriculture Society has done research and suggests that's the way to go in this area. Hey, did I tell you Sarah is walking now?"

"I'll be," Charley exclaimed. "Bet she's a handful. Giving Mrs. Flanagan and Catherine a hard time keeping track of her."

"She got out in the yard the other day and started chasing the chickens until one of the geese spotted her and started chasing her," Seth said. "She'd like to have screamed the house down."

"She's not even a year old. How can she be walking already?"

"Everyone has been too busy to carry her around, so she just up and started walking all on her own. She whistles a lot, too."

"Well, I'll be. What about Michael and Robert? How're they doing?"

"They're holding their own. Mrs. Flanagan spoils them, even though they mind her. They gather eggs, feed the chickens and pigs, and even carry wood in for the stove. She's got everyone doing things right on schedule."

"That's my Maggie," Seamus interjected. "Always likes to keep things in order and on time, she does."

Seth gave the reins a snap and yelled "gee." The horses and wagon turned onto their road. Before long they were in front of the kitchen door.

The screen door banged open against the outside of the house and Maggie ran out to meet Seamus; Madeline close on her heels.

"Seamus. Oh, Seamus." Tears rolled down her cheeks. She ran to him, arms outstretched. Seamus jumped from the wagon and met her across the yard. Enveloping her in his arms, he lifted her off the ground and twirled her around. Setting her back down, he kissed her long and hard.

"Awww, Maggie, my love, I've missed ya. I ain't been the same since you left me, I haven't."

Seamus held her face between his hands, kissed her forehead, then looked into her smiling Irish eyes. "And who have we here behind you? That can't be my Madeline, now can it? You've grown since I've seen ya last, lass. What a fine lady you've become."

"It's only been a couple months, Pa. I haven't had time to grow." Madeline giggled and then ran into his arms and hugged her father. Seamus kissed the top of her strawberry blonde head.

"Well, then. You've blossomed into a fine young lady. Come, you can tell me all about your summer here on the farm."

"I want to hear about you and the strike," Maggie said as they linked arms and headed toward the house, Madeline in tow.

"It's over. Best forgotten," Seamus told her. "We're making a new start and a new life right here in Candor."

Seamus' smile grabbed at Charley's chest. He beamed at the happy reunion and thought of Emily.

He spotted his own children lined up along the railing on the front porch, baby Sarah in Catherine's arms. How to approach them? How to break the news? He wondered what their reaction would be. Hell, it was easier dealing with a bunch of railroad workers than his own children. Even speaking to Mason Aderley and Tom Scott had been a breeze compared to showing his love for this brood of kids living in his house. Being away and visiting home sporadically was no way to live, thanks to the railroad.

No more.

His family stared back at him as if he were a stranger. Starting today, right now, his family was gonna come first. Not the railroad.

Charley inched his way to the porch and stopped at the bottom steps, his worn work boot tapped the paint-chipped wooden boards.

"Children," he said, nodding in their direction. "I know I haven't been much of a father over the years, but I aim to change all that now. I've quit the rails in Philadelphia. How would you all like to ride the train out west to be with your mother? She'll be real pleased to see all of you, no doubt."

Michael and Robert jumped up and down clapping their hands. "We get to ride a train? Oh boy, oh boy. When do we go, Pa?"

"The end of the week," Charley said. His insides warmed at their excitement.

He couldn't remember when he'd felt so good inside—not since before he'd sent Emily west. When was the last time he'd seen his boys so excited about anything? He wiped the corner of his eye with a shaky finger. He had missed so much.

Catherine was the first one off the porch. She stood close to him. Her hair tied back in a chignon, her simple blue homespun dress crisp and clean, she looked lovely. All grown up.

"It's good to have you home, Pa," she said. "I know Mother will be very glad of your news, too."

"That she will. She'll be glad to see all of us." Charley took the initiative and wrapped his arms around Catherine and kissed the top of her head. "It's good to be back," he said.

Catherine hesitated, then wrapped her arms around his neck. He couldn't remember the last time he'd held his daughter in his arms. Most likely when she'd been a toddler. It was mighty good to hold her in a warm hug again.

"I understand you've passed your exams. So, you're off to school to learn how to become a teacher this September. Your mother will be very proud of you."

"And you, Pa? Are you proud?"

"Yes. I'm just beginning to see what a right-minded family I have here."

Seth secured the horses and tethered them so they wouldn't bolt while the wagon was being unloaded. The new, large, black mare, Midnight, was still a little skittish and tended to bolt if he wasn't reigned in properly.

"I have chores to do, Pa. Maggie and Catherine will have supper ready in a bit. In the meantime, I'm sure they'll have some coffee waiting inside."

Charley clapped his hands on Seth's shoulders. "You've done well here, my boy. I'm proud of you, too. You and Catherine have dealt with more than your fair share this summer. I'm sorry to have put you in such an awkward position."

Seth took the compliment in stride. Hearing his father finally admit he'd done a good job on the farm made his words all the more welcome.

"Thanks, Pa. I feel it's in my blood. Just like those trains are in yours."

"I'm mighty glad. I understand your ma likes it out west being with her cousin Marybelle. It's been good for her health. So, we'll join her out there. As soon as I settle things here and get everyone ready to go, we'll be on our way."

Did his father mean for him to go, too? To leave

everything he had worked so hard for and start all over again? And what about Anna Louise? He couldn't up and leave her behind. Surely his father understood what she meant to him. He'd already told him about their plans. And Catherine? What about her plans? Seth's mind raced as he searched for words to tell his father he didn't want to leave Candor. He wanted to stay and work the farm. He had such plans for improving produce, reaching bigger markets farther away, and even contemplated taking a position on the Agriculture Society Board. Buying more land. He was making a name for himself in the community. He couldn't leave now.

"Now don't get your knickers in a bunch, Seth," his father chuckled before Seth could protest. "I can see you haven't grasped what I'm talking about. Fact is, the farm is yours. I'll never be a farmer like you. Just don't have it in me, son."

His father shook his head and clasped his shoulder harder.

"Aderley promised to do good by me if I stayed loyal to the railroad during the strike," he said. He pursed his lips. "The man actually kept his word, by gum. He's agreed to pay for the rest of us to transfer all our belongings to San Francisco. Seems they need someone at the other end of the line to take care of the Pennsylvania Railroad's concerns. Mr. Aderley rode the rails out west to fetch his wife and bring his family back home safely. Things are growing by leaps and bounds out there, and he needs someone to keep things going at that end. They'll set up an office in San Francisco for me if I'm interested. I'm going to check it out while I'm there. I'll have an honest to goodness desk job. Won't have to spend much time at the tracks. And I'll be making a decent wage for a change."

"What about Catherine?" Seth wondered what would become of her teaching. "Like I told you, she's taken her exams and is already enrolled in the fall teaching program."

"I'll need her to help me with the children on the train, of course. It'll be a good experience for her. Give her something she'll be able to use in her teaching. She can spend time with us, then return home in time for the semester if she's a mind to."

Catherine, like Seth, was finding their father's ultimatum hard to swallow, if the tears in her eyes were any indication. Her large eyes stared past their father at the roof of the barn.

"Think of this as a well-deserved holiday for all of your hard work this summer," their father said, trying to soften the blow.

With his father taking all the children with him, Seth didn't know how he was going to manage without Timothy, or even Michael's help. Seth had depended on Timothy to be there every step of the way, and his brother hadn't disappointed. It was past time he told Timothy so. Seth didn't want Timothy to wait so long to be told how proud someone was of him and just how much his hard work was appreciated. His brother needed to know he was growing into a fine worker before he headed out west with the family. Darn it. This couldn't have come at a worse time. Harvest was fast approaching. He would need all the help he could get. He'd have to see who else besides the Hayland boys he could hire.

Timothy's indignation smoldered. Once a mild

mannered boy, Seth had seen the boy start to turn into a man over the summer. So he wasn't surprised when Timothy spoke up.

"I don't want to go west, Pa. I'll go out to visit Ma with the rest of you, but I'll come back with Catherine. She'll be needing a chaperone on her return trip. Seth needs me here. I like it here. What will I do out at a lumber camp anyways?"

"For one thing, you can help your cousin William with logging."

"I'm not a logger, Pa. I like farming just fine."

Seth looked from one to the other in the silence. He was proud Timothy had courage enough to speak up.

"I'm relieved to hear you say you like farming, Timothy," Seth said, then faced his father, unable to hold his tongue any longer. "I sure could use his help, Pa. Like I said earlier, Timothy has been a big help around here. Couldn't have managed without him. Don't know how I will if he goes. Let him go visit Ma, and chaperone Catherine on the return trip. As long as he's back before harvest. I'll be able to manage."

His father pondered the situation before he gave his answer.

"It seems my sons are growing up with minds of their own. Guess it was bound to happen sooner or later. Can't say I was counting on it happening so soon. We've all had to make difficult decisions on the heels of this damn railroad strike. Damned trains. They've taken too much out of our family as it is. I've gotta say starting over in the California Territory will be like a breath of fresh air."

"We're really making a go of it right here in Candor, Pa," Seth said, hands on hips, both feet planted firmly on solid ground.

Timothy and the others stood in silence waiting for their father to say something. For all his bravado of a moment ago, Timothy hung his head, his long, skinny arms dangled at his sides, his fists balled. Timothy wouldn't go against his father no matter how much he wanted to stay on the farm.

"Well, I suppose Timothy is old enough to make his own decisions. If the fool boy wants to stay behind, so be it. Can't force him to do work he don't like. Lord knows I've been at it long enough." He turned to face Timothy.

"If you want to stay behind and be a farmer, it's your choice," their father stated, his staunch features showing his displeasure. "Seeing as Aderley's paying the fare, you can come on out and visit your ma and return with Catherine. I like the idea of you chaperoning her on the return trip. Just can't tell about the West. I'm not liking the tales I'm hearing about young ladies traveling all alone out there and being abducted and never seen again." Charley nodded his approval. He faced Catherine, sighed, and said, "It's settled. We'll leave Saturday morning on the eight-fifteen train out of Candor. Should give everyone plenty of time to gather up your belongings and say your goodbyes."

Chapter Twenty-Two

The week flew by for the Carmichael and the Flanagan families. Seamus traveled to town with Charley to see about a job on the Delaware, Lackawanna, and Western Railroad in Candor. Mr. Benson received word from Mason Aderley, as promised, and Mr. Benson hired Seamus on the spot. Instead of having to ride the rails, Seamus was now responsible for the functions around the depot and station area, including signals and making sure the trains left on time. He was the go-between for the engineers and the station master. Seamus was glad of the work, as well, and before the week was out, he was on the job.

Charley rode to town to send a telegraph to Emily saying he'd be coming out to get her as soon as he tied things up at home. He didn't mention that the children would be accompanying him. He wanted to surprise her. She'd be over the moon with excitement when they stepped from the train for sure. Instead, he sent a separate telegram message to Marybelle so they'd know to expect the lot of them. He also told her he planned to be settling out west for good. Marybelle had offered her home to his family for as long as they needed to get back on their feet. With what Mason Aderley promised him in a pay raise, it shouldn't take too long.

While in Candor, Charley stopped at the Mitchell's

to thank them for taking Catherine in for the coming school semester and to make a down payment for her lodging once the winter weather set in. He had hoped to meet Anna Louise, but she and her mother were off attending a Women's Christian Temperance Union meeting at the Candor Town Hall. The girl sounded too highfalutin for Seth. However, if Seth loved the girl, then there wasn't much he could do. Seth didn't imbibe anyway, so it shouldn't be a fly in the ointment between the two of them. From the looks of her home life though, Charley couldn't picture Anna Louise living on a farm. That might be a speck of dust in the eye, if anything. Seth would have to figure that one out for himself.

Passage for everyone had already been taken care of, and the packing was coming along. Maggie had made sure the laundry was done and ironed for the overnight bags, and the rest of the children's belongings were packed neatly in her own trunks for Charley to use going west.

"The trunks can come back with Catherine and Timothy on their return trip, they can," she told him with a smile.

"That's kind of you, Maggie," Charley said. He pulled out a chair and sat at the kitchen table where Seamus was already seated. "You've done so much for my family already. I wish you were coming along. I'd like Emily to meet you. I'm sure she'd like to thank you personally for helping out with the children."

"Perhaps someday." Maggie shrugged her shoulders. She drew a fresh loaf of bread from the oven and placed it on a cutting board. "I'm not so anxious to leave my Seamus behind again for a while. Besides,

I'm not sure I could stomach the train ride for such a long period of time. If Seamus is happy in his new job with the trains here in Candor, then it's fine by me." She reached for the bread knife above the dry sink and the freshly churned butter.

The yeasty aroma filled the kitchen, and Charley's taste buds couldn't wait to bite into the crunchy goodness. "Some lines are more responsible for their employees than others," he said, helping himself to a slice and slathering it with the butter Maggie sat on the table. "In the end, Aderley found he actually had a heart and showed compassion for his workers. Be glad Seamus doesn't work as a coal miner. Their lives are far worse. They're still striking, and I don't blame them. Their children are dying alongside them in those cold, dark mines."

"It's too gruesome to contemplate," Seamus said.

Maggie set a cup of coffee on the table for Charley and her husband. Charley poured a good dollop of fresh cream in his cup and swirled it together with his spoon. Seamus did the same.

"You should be aware little Sarah might be a handful on the train," Maggie said. "Being cooped up in such a tiny space for so long, she'll need time to run around when you make stops along the way."

"I'm sure Catherine can manage," Charley said, then picked up his cup and sipped the steaming brew. "After all, she'll be dealing with children when she becomes a teacher. She might just as well get a full dose now. I'm sure the boys won't sit still for long, either."

Michael and Robert were about the same age as the Aderley boys. They'd need careful tending, no doubt.

"I'm sure Timothy will be a big help, too."

"I've made a bit of biscuits and cakes to be taking with ya. They should last a good portion of your trip if ya dole them out careful like. I've prepared a bag for each of ya."

"Seamus was right, Ma'am. You do keep things running smoothly. I'm grateful you'll be staying on here with Seth. He'll be thankful for your help."

"I'm glad to have a place to live until we see our way clear of setting up our own home in town."

"Don't be too quick to decide. You might want to check with Seth. I'm sure he'll be happy to have you stay on as cook and housekeeper as long as you like." Charley raised the cup to his mouth and took a long swallow. "You make a great cup of coffee, Maggie. Your Seamus is a lucky man."

****

A horse galloped up the road as Seth walked across the barnyard toward the house. The horse and rider were hell-bent on getting someplace fast. He turned in time to see Cassandra Strang ride her horse into the yard. She sat tall and rode well, her back straight. Dark auburn hair hung loose and whipped around her face, her drawstring hat atop her head. She drew the horse to a stop in front of him.

"Hello, Seth. Fine afternoon."

Cassandra flung her left leg over the front of her horse and slid down the right side, landing right in front of him. There wasn't much space between them. Cassandra Strang smelled like wildflowers and fresh sunshine. Her brown eyes looked directly into his, she was mere inches shorter than him, and they stood almost eye to eye.

307

"Hello, Miss Strang. Did your father send you? Is there something wrong?"

Cassandra batted her eyelids. An irritating warmth spread through Seth's entire body. He took a deep breath, and then let it out in a slow stream.

"Is something wrong with your eyes?" he asked. "Do you have a piece of dust in them from your ride?"

Cassandra looked displeased. "Why no. I'm fine. I understand you're all moving out to California territory, and I came to say goodbye. I can't say I'm glad, Seth Carmichael. We're just getting to know each other, and now you're up and leaving. And Daddy was so disappointed too. Said you had the makings of a fine farmer."

"It's true the family is leaving," Seth began but didn't have a chance to finish.

"I'm so sorry to hear you're moving on." Cassandra hung her head and played with the reins she still held in her hands. "I suppose then a simple goodbye kiss is in order before you go."

Seth froze. His eyes popped wide. What was Cassandra Strang suggesting?

She lifted her head. If eyes could smile, hers were doing a bang up good job right now. Before he had a chance to tell her he wasn't leaving, she took one step closer and kissed him full on the lips. And didn't let go. Seth found himself responding and placed a hand around her neck, drawing her still closer. The kiss continued until Cassandra was the one who drew back, her face redder than a hen's comb. For once she was lost for words.

Seth let go and stepped back.

"I'm sorry you rode all this way for nothing,

Cassandra. I'm not going anywhere. Pa is taking the others out to California. Timothy and Catherine will be returning the end of August, but I'm staying put. I'm needed here to run the farm."

Cassandra grinned, ear to ear, not looking so disappointed any longer. She plunked her hat back on her head.

"Why, then you'll need some looking after without anyone here. I guess I could stop by every once in a while to see how you're doing. You know, lend a hand."

"That's mighty neighborly of you." Seth didn't bother to tell her Maggie was going to remain behind as a housekeeper and cook.

"Daddy will be pleased to know you're not going anywhere. Fact is, I'd better get back and let him know you'll be at next week's meeting."

As fast as she had ridden into the yard and jumped off her horse, Cassandra climbed back up and rode back down the road like the wind. Her hat flew off her head and her hair flew unrestricted in the wind.

Had she just yelled yippee?

Seth couldn't help but smile as he headed toward the house. Her brazen kiss had knocked him back on his heels. He stepped up onto the front porch and bumped into his father.

"Was that your Anna Louise?" his father asked, a twinkle in his eyes. "Fine spirited woman. I had her pegged all wrong. I think you've met your match there."

Seth swallowed. He'd been caught kissing another woman.

"No." Seth smiled. "No. It was sassy Cassandra

309

Strang."

If the Strangs were aware the family was leaving town, then the Mitchell's must know as well. Why hadn't Anna Louise been the one to ride up to see him? Seth couldn't picture Anna Louise riding a horse with such abandon. He couldn't visualize her hair flying around her head in a small breeze let alone a gust of wind. And the kiss he'd just shared with Cassandra Strang had his toes curling, his heart pounding, and his blood boiling. Unlike the controlled kisses he'd shared with Anna Louise.

Seth recalled his father was still standing there. With a silly grin on his face. He couldn't remember his father ever smiling like that before.

"I don't think life will be dull with her around, Seth. I'd rethink my wifely preference if I were you."

****

The hustle and bustle around San Francisco was a regular bee hive. After being at Marybelle's where she had gotten the rest and care she needed, Emily wasn't quite prepared for all the commotion of the city again. She hadn't looked forward to the long ride back to San Francisco from Marybelle's, but today the wagon ride hadn't been so bad. Today, she rather enjoyed the sights and even the city wasn't so daunting.

They arrived a bit early, so William took them along the bay area where they stopped to enjoy a lunch and walk along the wharf before going to the station to meet her family. William dropped them off at the station and drove his team down the street to conduct lumber business elsewhere.

"Stop fussing, Em. Your green skirt and matching bonnet we picked up look lovely on you. Brings out the glow in your eyes," Marybelle said.

Emily stood on the platform waiting for the train. The sun shone overhead, and a slight breeze teased her skirts against her legs. Marybelle had insisted on the bonnet, said she needed something to keep the sun off her hair.

"I can't wait 'til Charles arrives." Emily turned to Marybelle, her shaking fingers knotted her cotton handkerchief. "Why, Marybelle, you'll have to come back east for a visit. We'd be so glad to have you."

"Lord, Em, I'm too well-grounded right here. Couldn't leave my William and the boys."

"You can come for a much needed holiday yourself. I'm going to miss you when I leave."

"Maybe someday we'll come for a visit. I'll have to mull it over some. I know you must be so excited to see Charley-boy. Why I bet your heart is just a racing inside waiting for him to step off the train. You must be full of joy waiting to greet your family, too. Now don't forget, I didn't say a word, so act surprised when you see your children."

"I will, Marybelle. Oh, I can't wait to see my baby, Sarah. I hope she remembers I'm her momma. Babies grew so fast in such a short amount of time, I'll be heartbroken if she doesn't know me."

"I'm sure she'll remember you're her momma. You just wait and see. Here, here, now don't you cry, Em. Don't want your family to see you in tears, no matter how joyful they are. Can't be having a whole family sobbing as soon as they arrive."

"I can't help it, Marybelle. I can't wait to hold each and every one of them."

"Soon, Em. Soon."

Emily's eyes were glued to the large black engine as it roared into the station. How Charles could stand to work around those huge, dark creatures every day, she didn't know, but she loved him for his strength, his loyalty, and his kindness. She loved him for his steadfast love for her and their children. She couldn't wait to tell him so.

The whistle blew, the train rolled to a stop, the coach doors opened, and the passengers rushed from the cars.

"They'll be here, Em. Stand still before you hurt yourself," Marybelle said, wiping the tear trickling down her own cheek.

Emily danced from foot to foot, wringing her hands together.

"Let's sit down while we wait, Em. You look like you're about to pee your pants. We can't have that, now can we?" Marybelle laughed.

"I can't sit, Marybelle. I've done nothing but sit for two long months. There's not a thing wrong with me now except wanting to see my babies and Charles. I can't thank you enough for offering to let all of us stay at your place while they're here. Oh, Lord, Marybelle, I can't wait to see my family."

Town folk gathered just to marvel at the monster train full of people, produce, and dry goods after the weeks of strikes. The marshal and a few of his men stood close by, making sure no trouble ensued as people flowed from the train.

"I hope they had a safe journey, Marybelle. I wouldn't want them to experience what Mrs. Aderley and I did."

"We would have had news by now, Em. You just

be patient." She patted Emily's shoulder. "They'll be hopping out of that giant contraption before you know it."

The passengers kept coming. Those disembarking looked tired. A man and his wife were the first off, and then several men in long coats and top hats, checking their gold pocket watches as they stepped down onto the platform. They looked to be men of importance. Emily didn't give them another thought.

Next, a couple of young women dressed in full petticoats and silk dresses, a parasol in their hands and even though they looked weary from their travels, they were smiling and talkative as they were helped down from the train. Others followed before Emily spotted her family. Michael and Robert jumped from the train with an energy released from having to sit still during their long ride.

"Robert. Michael. Over here," she called, waving her hanky.

They ran to her side. She bent over, welcoming them with open arms.

"Oh, my boys, I've missed you so much." She kissed them both and held them to her for as long as they would hold still.

"The ride was great. Papa told us everything there is to know about trains," Michael told her.

Robert, not to be held back, jumped in front of his brother.

"We got to sit up front with the engineers in the big locomotive and help shovel coal, too. Papa said it's hard work keeping trains rolling along. But I think it was fun."

"I bet you did," Emily said and smiled down at her

son. He could be a handful. Thankfully, Charles had made sure he'd been kept busy on the long trip.

Catherine, holding her darling Sarah, approached more sedately.

"Oh. Oh, my girls." Emily broke into tears. "You've both grown so," she whispered. She gathered Catherine close, Sarah still in her sister's arms. Sarah squirmed and held on to Catherine as Emily's heart broke into tiny pieces. She'd been afraid Sarah wouldn't remember who she was after such a long separation.

"Now, Sarah," Catherine whispered softly to the baby, whose head was now buried in her neck. "This here is your momma. Remember we said we were coming to be with her, and she was going to want to hold you and love you."

Sarah's chubby face looked over at Emily and broke into a smile. Emily raised her hands to Sarah and waited for her baby to respond. After a moment, Sarah leaned forward, and Emily lifted her into her loving arms. She hugged her darling baby close, covering her with tiny, soft kisses and cooing words. Sarah giggled and squirmed. Emily looked up to find Charles and Timothy standing next to Catherine. Her knees trembled, and her hands shook. Catherine took Sarah out of her arms, and Charles wasted no time wrapping her into his own strong arms. Thank goodness, or she would have fallen right there in front of everyone.

"Emily. My Emily. God, I've missed you," Charles groaned, then finally kissed her. "It's been too long."

"Oh, Charles, I've missed you so. I love you."

"I'm so sorry I sent you away, Em. I'll never send you away from me again. Never. You can count on it."

"It was the right thing to do, Charles. It was the hardest thing leaving my children, but I regained my health. Marybelle's doctor confirmed I don't have consumption after all, but I did need the rest. And now I'm better, I can't wait to get my family back home."

"Thank God you're all right." He leaned his chin on the top of her head, soaking in her essence.

After a moment in his arms, Emily disentangled herself to greet Timothy with a quick hug and peck on the cheek. Even a small show of affection in public was too much for her son to handle. Timothy's cheeks turned a handsome shade of red, and Charles smiled and winked at him.

"It's good to see you, too, Timothy. You're growing into a fine young man," Emily told him. "I've missed you so much and can't wait to hear what you've been up to these last few months."

Timothy's blush deepened, and he stepped back just as Marybelle and William stepped forward.

"What a fine family you have, Em."

"Yes, they are. Let me introduce them all to you and William. This here is Catherine." Emily drew Catherine forward. "She's going to be a teacher. Going to Normal School this fall. We're so proud of her and know she's going to be a great teacher. And this is my precious baby Sarah I've talked so much about."

"Well, ladies, it's great to meet you both." Marybelle tweaked the baby's nose and smiled up at Sarah. "Your ma has talked a blue streak about you, you can be sure. And now who are these fine young gentlemen?"

"Timothy is the shy one, and I understand has been Seth's right hand man on the farm. As you can see he looks like his father. And this is Michael and Robert who can't sit still for a minute. Moving them up to the country has been a blessing for them. They can run around outside to their heart's content."

"Fine looking boys, Em. Charles, you both do yourself proud," Marybelle chuckled. "I just know they'll love living here. Now, you can all stay with us while you settle in and get a foot-hold here in California."

Marybelle rattled on, and Emily almost didn't catch what she said, as usual her cousin talked in riddles.

"Marybelle. Whatever do you mean?" Emily said in dismay, then stopped mid-stride on the way to the wagon where William and Charles stood talking. The baggage was already collected and ready to be loaded onto the wagon.

"We're only staying a week before going back home," Emily said.

"Oh, my gosh, Em. Guess I let the cat out of the bag again. Sorry, you'll have to talk to your husband." Marybelle turned to where the men were waiting for the baggage to finish unloading, a guilty look on her face.

"Charles," Emily called in desperation.

"Looks like my wife just did it again," William said. "Never could keep a secret. I'm surprised she kept this one to herself this long."

"Guess I'd better give Emily the news myself."

"Wait." William grabbed Charley's arm. "I was going to wait to talk to you about this later, but I guess now is as good a time as any. I need someone to run my train operation between the logging camp and the mill. With your expertise I figured you'd be just the man."

"Thanks, William. I do appreciate your offer, but Aderley offered me a job in San Francisco working the Pennsy line office." Charley shook his head.

"Think about it," William encouraged. "Marybelle hasn't been around family in longer than I can remember. I haven't seen her this happy since we settled into our home. Like Belle said, you can stay with us 'til you find something suitable. You'd be able to be with your wife and family every night. I don't have the time I used to, and I'm not getting any younger myself. You'd be in charge of the entire operation."

Charley didn't need much time to mull it over. This was exactly what his family needed. What he needed. His family had been separated long enough.

"It sounds mighty fine to me, William. You've got yourself a deal."

The two men shook on it seconds before Marybelle interrupted them.

"Land sakes, William, you can talk to Charley-boy later. He's got a wife wanting to spend some time with him.

"He's a coming, Belle. Hold on a minute." William turned back to Charley. "You'd better go. I'll distract Belle while you talk to your wife. Emily looks a little stunned. Go ease her mind."

Charley rushed to Emily's side.

"Come, Em." He tucked her arm in his and led her to one of the benches on the platform. "Let's sit down over here away from everyone so we can be alone a minute. I have great news." Despite the commotion going on around them, in a quiet voice Charley told her about Aderley's offer and then William's counter-offer he'd just accepted.

"It's true, Em. We're staying right here. William's job managing the timber rails for him will allow me to be with all of you. We'll have more time to be together. As soon as we can arrange everything, we'll build a house of our own. Early spring. William assures me it's not hard, and there's lots of timber men here to help."

"What about Seth? And Catherine's schooling?"

"Seth has already taken over the farm. He can have it. You know I'm not a farmer, never will be. As for Catherine, arrangements have already been made for her to start school next month. She has a place to say in town, and in the meantime, Seamus and his wife will be living at the farm 'til they can make other arrangements.

"Oh, Charles. That sounds lovely. But I am going to miss Seth and Catherine so much. And my Timothy. How can we leave them all behind?" Tears formed in her eyes, and she dabbed her hanky at the corners. "They're my babies. My family."

"Ah, Em, love. They'd be moving on soon, anyway. They'll be just fine. Seth finally has marriage on his mind and will need the room at the farm."

"Seth? To Anna Louise? I knew he was sweet on her."

"I have my doubts about Anna Louise, my dear." Charley couldn't help the smile that crossed his face. Miss Strang's kiss set Seth back a bit. He certainly had his doubts.

"He met Mr. Strang's daughter, Cassandra, who seems to be smitten with our Seth. Caught them kissing." Charley chuckled. "We'll have to see what develops come Christmas time. We might be heading back east for a wedding come June."

"Oh, a June wedding," Emily sighed. "How lovely." Emily clung to Charley's hands. "Tell me, Charles, what of the Flanagans? Will they be going back to Philadelphia now the strike has been settled?"

"No. They're going to stay right in Candor. Seamus came home with me and has already taken a job on the Delaware, Lackawanna, and Western Railroad in town. And their daughter Madeline is happy on the farm. She's been following our Timothy around, getting a handle on country life."

"It's terribly sad about Marian Aderley and her son," Emily said. "Such a shame. She's a wonderful lady. Those boys were so full of life. It's going to take a long time for them to get over their grief."

"Her husband is with her now, Em. They'll be just fine." Charley reassured her. He drew her into the circle of his arms and rubbed her shoulder. "He's a changed man. Seeing as what the strike did to many a'family, Aderley has learned the hard way just how important family is. Like me, Em. I worried about you out here, having to leave your family. Drove me half crazy knowing how hard it was for you. If anything had happened to you..." He kissed her the way he had wanted to kiss her when first he'd stepped off the train. He'd given her time with the children while he got his own emotions under control. Now all he wanted to do was hold her and never let her go.

The railroad might have temporarily derailed their lives for awhile.

Never again.

Charley drew back, and placing his fingers under her chin, he lifted Emily's face to his. He lowered his head and met her waiting lips.

Words were unnecessary.

Charley's kiss promised a lifetime of togetherness and a renewed love that had been sidetracked for far too long.

A word about the author...

Carol Henry is an author of historic women's fiction (*Ribbons of Steel*), contemporary romance (*Northing Short of a Miracle*), and Destination: Romance—Exotic Romantic Suspense Adventures, (*Amazon Connection*; *Shanghai Connection*).

She is an international traveler and travel writer of exotic locations for major cruise lines' deluxe in-cabin books.

Carol lives with her husband in the beautiful New York State Finger Lakes region where they are surrounded by family and friends.

As a local New York State Historian, Carol has written numerous books and articles on the history of her hometown. And, when time permits, she writes travelogues, human interest, and historic articles for several local newspapers.

You may visit Carol's website at:
http://www.carolhenry.org.